ALIEN SAFARI:
WHITE WATER

Robert Appleton

This book is a work of fiction. Characters, names, places and incidents either are the product of the author's imagination or are used fictitiously, and any resemblance to any actual persons, living or dead, events, or locales is entirely coincidental.

ALIEN SAFARI: WHITE WATER

ISBN-13: 978-1080146840

Printed in the United States of America

First Edition: September, 2019

Published by Mercury Seven Books

SAFARI

WHITE WATER

Chapter One

"If you look across to the starboard bow …"

Captain Jan Corbija rolled her eyes when the majority of her tourist passengers on both decks, maybe two thirds of them, pivoted completely around to face the stern. She had to point them the correct way *yet again*. "You'll see a school of Sabatini corkscrew eels: *spiralus Sabatinum*. Gorgeous, aren't they? With the sun behind us, you get a nice coloring effect there. The arc of their jump, and the way they spiral through the air like that, sheds thousands of tiny water droplets that disperse the light, forming a miniature rainbow each time."

Quite a few oohs, and even a smattering of applause, spurred her on. These might be the most lubberly rock-hoppers she'd piloted all season, but they were a lively bunch, and they seemed to have a genuine appreciation for the aquatic wonders she'd shown them among the West Equatorial Keys, Hesperidia's freshest and most popular Alien Safari tour.

"Notice how they jump high out of the water like that when they sense our approach, when they're ready to flee. It's so they can take an extra-deep breath of air and stay

1

derwater for much longer. Like most creatures on speridia, they have well-honed survival instincts."

The same antsy man clinging to his stupid sou'wester, ho'd already quizzed Jan several times, called out, "How gh *can* they jump?"

"Up to seven meters, I think. But don't worry, they on't come anywhere near the *Alcyone*. We're the Big Bad a the big blue today." One or two chuckles. Not one of r best one-liners of the season; all week, in fact, her trusty it had mutinied at the most inopportune moments. Maybe se was just tired – of talking, of patronizing, of ferrying ch squibs around instead of doing her *real* work here: lazing a research trail in the fields of xenobotany and enozoology, to Jan the two most important subjects in interstellar exploration, and the only pursuits worth her tme on Hesperidia, a spectacular riot of a planet whose abundance of natural life was surpassed only by its bizarre variety. With fifty lifetimes she couldn't hope to complete all the research demanding her attention here. These Safari excursions, then, while fun in a show-the-squibs-what-they're-missing kind of way, were an almost criminal waste of her time, particularly this White Water tour, which, being a sell-out all season long, kept her occupied for two solid months out of every year (a Hesp year lasted 291 days).

But the squibs brought in the clips to fund this whole shebang. *No bucks, no Buck Rogers,* as the old saying went. So this was Jan's seasonal high-dive, her extra-deep breath before the plunge into obscurity, her research work, where no one could bother her, where she and Stopper could study day and night in the field.

Right now he looked as fed up as she was. They'd taken this same sightseeing cruise together more times than she could count, and the poor boy had lost all enthusiasm for seafaring. He lay slumped across one of the aft seat cushions, snoozing in the heat, a trickle of gloopy saliva hanging from his twitching jowl as he dreamt of, well, whatever a genetically engineered canine cutie-pie dreamt of out here. Stopper had been her only real companion on Hesperidia for years. Indeed, he'd been modified from his original Earth species – something like a large Boxer dog – specifically for this atmosphere and this environment. He breathed the planet's toxic air as easily as Jan breathed oxygen, while his engineering had also resulted in marked improvements in his sense of smell, his overall intelligence, and a borderline precognitive ability to sense danger.

He'd saved her life umpteen times, and would rather die than leave her side in a crisis, just as she would gladly give her life to protect him. It was a well-documented but little understood aspect of life on the Hesp that even the most mismatched or adversarial of species cooperated in the face of any threat that jeopardized their established local ecosystem. A kind of instinctive truce occurred between inhabitants, a temporary "switching off" of hostilities, whenever a super predator or an unfamiliar element, like a vehicle or a drought or severe weather, encroached on their ecosystem. Not only that, she'd seen species which otherwise had nothing in common rush to each other's defense in the direst of such times. Strength in numbers, interspecies style!

She and Stopper were perhaps the newest variation on that ancient and beautiful evolutionary symphony woven through millions of generations of life on Hesperidia. They weren't a part of it, but they were playing its tune. And because he could never leave this planet, she would never leave it while he was alive. If the Hesp had taught Jan anything it was that even the most solitary and complicated life-forms couldn't survive alone. Isolation might benefit groups, or ecosystems, but never the individual. Life here was just too competitive for that, too unforgiving. No, to survive here you had to belong to something bigger than yourself, and when a serious threat arose you had to be able to rely on that something or that someone to stand with you against all odds. It could be one of your own kind, it could be a group of creatures you'd never personally had contact with before, living in the same ecosystem; it didn't matter, so long as you were both attuned to the peculiar subtleties transferred down through the genes of your forbears, those hidden patterns and signals learned and reinforced by the toll of a billion deaths, that, when triggered, combined to command your obedience for the sake of mutual survival.

Man's best friend had originated on Earth. And for all Jan knew, Stopper's ancestors had hunted alongside hers on Old Blue. That idea made her smile as she saw his front paws twitch under his nose. The rascal probably *was* dreaming about the hunt, only here on the Hesp, during a foray into the rainforest or, one of his favorites, a trek

4

through the shallow ocean pools dotted among the myriad atolls and wrinkly sandbars that teemed with life around their home in the West Equatorial Keys.

His ears pricked, he lifted his head and looked up at her. Jan waved to him. He yawned, then lashed his gaze to the cabin below her. He jumped down from his seat, barking like mad.

"What is it, boy? What's wrong?"

Jan trusted his fine-tuned instincts implicitly; he only ever barked like this when he sensed a threat or when something was seriously awry. She climbed down from the roof of the bridge. Most of the tourists had their Alien Safari goggles on and were using the interactive field guide to track a flock of *Atla gannetopteryx* flying low over the water. A small group of men, though, was standing in front of the cabin door, barring her way in.

"Our cousin's not feeling well," a tall, broad-shouldered man in a windbreaker told her. He tried to hide a small handheld device up his sleeve, but she noticed its flashing amber glare reflecting off the nano ink of his wrist tat. "She went to lie down inside," the man said. "Hope that's okay."

Before Jan could reply, another man asked her, "Do you mind if we stop the boat while I administer her medication? It shouldn't take long."

"What medication? What's wrong with her?"

"It's a vestibular condition, a side-effect of early fragmentia," the second man explained. "It's triggered whenever her equilibrium is out of whack."

Jan shielded her eyes from the sun, squinting at him. "You mean to tell me you brought someone with delicate equilibrium on a sea voyage called *White Water* and you *didn't* think she'd get seasick? Are you smogged? Who are you?"

"We thought she was in remission. The doctors told us the fragmentia was dormant." The man's steady poker face and bristling confidence reminded her of a Phi officer she'd encountered here on the Hesp a few years back, during that nightmare manhunt involving the Golden Fleece. Just as that officer had told a pack of lies, this man was trying to pull the wool over Jan's eyes.

"Why didn't you mention any of this on the medical disclosure form?" she asked. "We wouldn't have let her anywhere near this cruise."

"Must have been an oversight."

"A pretty big oversight, Bub. What else haven't you disclosed?"

"I don't know what you mean."

The *Alcyone's* engines suddenly cut out. Jan spied someone at the bridge controls inside the wheelhouse cabin. "What the ..." She barged her way passed the two men and yanked the door open. "Oi, you ..."

The sneaky shit darted away from the dashboard when he heard her voice. He didn't appear to have caused any damage that she could see; he'd merely cut the engines.

"Get back here!"

Jan chased him down to the lower deck, where he ran straight to the moon pool – the *wide-open* moon pool – and peered into it. He started a stopwatch. Glanced at Jan. Then he sat cross-legged, lit a joint, and lifted his filtration mask so he could enjoy a few tugs.

The bulkhead behind him, where the two diving suits and underwater breathing apparatus ought to be, was bare. Whoever these people were, they'd taken *all* her submersible gear.

After re-affixing his breather, the man flicked her an insolent wink, as if to say, *Relax, sweetheart, we're in charge now.*

One of the things she'd had to work on as an Alien Safari tour guide was her banter. Engaging dozens of rich tourists for hours, days at a time, required a ready-steady facility for chit-chat. Even when she had nothing to say, she had to find something. It had been tough at first, but lately – and Vaughn had teased her about it no end during his last few visits – she'd found it difficult to shut up once she got going.

At this moment, however, she drew a total blank.

These suck-baits had just violated every rule she had aboard the *Alcyone*, and they'd done it right under her nose! What idiots. What absolute freaking idiots! Diving in daylight out here was suicide even if you *did* know what creatures and plants and ocean currents you were up against. The White Water tour stayed on the surface religiously for a very good reason: human science had barely touched the depths of Hesperidia's oceans. To swim off like this, unsupervised, all the way out here, was one of the dumbest things she'd ever seen.

No, she couldn't restart the engines and leave those people down there, as much as it would serve them right.

But she could – and *would* – get to the bottom of what had to be a premeditated mutiny. Reckless though it was, these bozos knew exactly what they were doing. They had planned this operation carefully. Which begged the question (one of many): what were they looking for down there?

Before she reported them to Vaughn, her Omicron detective boyfriend who was way, way off-world right now, she would try to find out as much as she could about these mystery divers.

"Not satisfied with the tour, I take it?" she said to the smog-head as he peered into the moon pool again.

"Nothing personal, *senorita*."

It had been a while since anyone had alluded to her Latino heritage. Vaughn had always liked it about her – the slight Spanish accent and her fiery Mediterranean looks – but few people nowadays seemed able to pinpoint the origins of such traits. Many colonists, particularly those born in the Outer Colonies, had never visited Earth, knew little of its geography and racial histories. This decentralization of humanity had given rise to new classifications of peoples, as all manner of exotic accents and dialects, not to mention world-specific behavioral traits, had emerged. Separated from Earth, people were diverging in all sorts of ways.

But in this they would never change, not in a billion light-years: people were selfish assholes!

Smog Boy inhaled another mouthful of contraband and then tossed the smoking stub into the water. Jan fished it out and flicked it back at him. In his attempt to dodge it the man toppled backward and lay there, gazing up at the light shimmering on the ceiling, completely blissed out. He hadn't re-affixed his mask properly, so the drug fumes leaked out while the Hesp air leaked in. It didn't take long for him to start coughing.

By this time one of his associates had arrived – the big man in the windbreaker. He scragged Smog Boy to his feet and roughly adjusted his mask. Then he cuffed him upside his head and said, "Next time you light up, I'll cremate you on the spot. Are we clear?"

"Uh, actually, you're a bit, uh, hazy." Smog Boy went to touch his colleague's visor, missed. He pawed at thin air instead. "Why don' you stay still, Bronston? Jeez."

"Right, that's it. Sit your ass in the corner and don't move till they surface!"

"An' you're tellin' *me* not to move." Smog Boy jived his shoulder, spun and stumbled toward the bulkhead. "That's what you call a hippo ... crate—no, hyper ... critter ... something."

"Okay, maybe you can answer my questions." Jan squared up to Bronston, who was about six inches taller than her. White-haired. Fiftyish. A permanent, weary frown wrinkled his sun-kissed brow.

"Not right now." He held her aside with one arm while he checked the reading on his handheld device. Its amber lights had deepened in color, almost to a golden-brown, and the flashes were a lot quicker. The readout display appeared to show coordinates, suggesting some kind of GPS locater. But the planet's satellite net was protected by several layers of Heisenberg-level encryption, almost impossible to break. If he had access codes, who had given them to him?

He fingered his earpiece to open a comm channel. "Milady, this is Bronston, requesting a progress update." No immediate reply. "Milady, please come in."

Several anxious moments of rolling static later came the reply, in a posh English accent, "We're at two-niner-zero feet, still descending – just. The water's thick with plankton or something – almost like soup. It's slowing our descent. Visibility poor but starting to improve …"

A sudden inrush of gas, most likely the helmet's automatic pressure equalizer, hissed over the woman's next few words.

"Say again, Milady. All after 'visibility starting to improve.'"

"I can see slivers of light below, getting clearer. We're almost out of the soup, Scott. Hold on … I think I can see the bottom! Repeat, the sliver of light appears to be some kind of bioluminescent material covering the inside of a trench on the sea bed. It probably stretches for miles – jagged but definitely trending northeast. I think this might be a fault line."

"Are you close to the signal?" asked Bronston, chewing his lip, his visor misting with each nervous breath. He'd called the woman Milady, and she definitely seemed to be in charge; but Jan sensed his anxiety was not dutiful. There was something personal between them, not least because she'd used his first name, Scott, while Smog Boy had referred to him by his surname.

But who were they? What were they looking for down there?

Ten minutes passed. Fifteen. Jan kept close tabs on the time on her wristwatch. EQ3 (3rd Equatorial Daily Time Quadrant, the period of twin shadows, with Hesperidia's glassy moon reflecting full sunlight during the day) was coming to an end. The sun would set shortly, and quickly, leaving only a few Core hours of "moonlight" before the West Equatorial Keys were left in complete darkness for the night. She would ordinarily be heading back to port about now, so she could give the tourists that final magical experience of seeing sunset through the gem-specked rocky archway between The Pitons, the last remnants of an extinct volcano sticking up like twin incisors out of the sea.

This was going to get dicey, she decided. EQ4 was no time to be all the way out here: the most dangerous oceanic predators ventured up from the depths at night. They seemed to lose all their inhibitions, and several had attacked rangers' vessels over the years on the Hesp. Jan herself had never been attacked at sea, at least not in saltwater, but she knew full well the ferocity of Hesperidia's apex predators, having almost been killed twice by *Hesperidus tridenticus*, the Hesperidian hydra. Both times Stopper had thrown himself in harm's way to save her. The last time, they'd *both* succumbed to their wounds and it was a miracle they were still alive. An illicit alien biotech miracle known as the Golden Fleece. She shuddered at the memory of being impaled in the mouth of the hydra, of seeing Stopper crushed beside her. No dose of miraculous healing could

11

erase that awful sensation – that feeling of failure, of utter helplessness.

But the Fleece was not here now. No one knew where it was, except (hopefully) its outlaw custodians, Finnegan and Polotovsky, who, the last she'd heard, had formed a sort of *pro bono* interstellar healing partnership to save the lives of those who didn't have the resources to cure themselves. But they were not here now. And there was very little Jan could do to look after her passengers if something as big and vicious as the hydra came hunting them.

"You morons need to realize you're risking the lives of everyone on board." When they didn't answer, Jan slammed her fist against the bulkhead. "Listen to me! You're not getting it. There's a child up on deck, and it's going to get dark soon. Do you know what *happens here* after dark?"

But Bronston brushed her off with a glance, then asked Milady for another update.

"Copy that, Scott. The trench is bigger than I thought. Corazon has pinpointed the rad signature: it runs roughly southwest along the bottom of the trench. No telling how far it goes."

"Do you think you have time to reach the source?"

"That's a negative. It's really hot down here. The undertow is a bitch; it's getting difficult to stay on coordinates. And I don't want to spend days decompress—" A scraping, crunching noise, rather like a strong tide dragging a storm-swept beach, filled the comm channel. Bronston rushed over to the moon pool and peered in.

"Milady? Is everything all right? What was—"

"We seem to have disturbed … something inside the trench walls. Something brushed past my helmet. Okay, we're out of here. They're really starting to slither. Soon as Corazon gets a rad sample for analysis, we're coming up, Scott."

"Be careful, Milady. Slow ascent. Remember the decompression sequence."

"Copy that."

Even Smog Boy started to feel the tension. He crawled over to the moon pool on his hands and knees in front of Jan. Furious, she kicked her way past him and returned to the deck, where the two men guarding the bridge grudgingly parted to let her through. She was, after all, the only one who knew what the hell she was doing out here *on* the ocean. They at least ceded that much to her. Assholes!

But what to do now? Heading back right away and leaving the divers stranded down there was not an option, as much as she felt like it and as much as they deserved it. Not that the mutineers – yes, mutineers – would let her do that. Captain Jan would just have to pretend like nothing had happened, if only to keep the tourists calm. Make something up, say, a technical glitch, and then speed back to port and unload this whole nightmare off her boat and onto the authorities.

That was it. Provided the divers surfaced unharmed and that was the last of their insubordination, this White Water tour need only be delayed a little. Vaughn and Kraczinski and their Omicron pals could take care of the rest.

She assured the tourists everything was okay and that they would be underway soon. Not everyone was satisfied, however. The man in the stupid sou'wester, who'd grilled her on her scientific tidbits throughout the voyage, now led a mob of disgruntled squibs following her around the foredeck seats.

"I said why are those men barricading the bridge?" The nerd had asked her twice already; this time he hollered it in her ear, spittle running down the inside of his visor.

She halted him with an outstretched hand. "That's far enough, Mr Noxious."

"Nixon," he corrected her. "The name's Nixon."

"My apologies. In answer to your question," she addressed the whole group, about a dozen of them, "those men are helping me resolve a technical issue in the impetus module. I didn't want anyone going below decks until I was sure there was no leak. There isn't."

"But those other men went down with you," someone else pointed out.

"They helped me check the keel binders for leakage," she replied, quite pleased with how fluently she could make this stuff up and how plausible it sounded. "It involved a short underwater dive. But it's all done with now. We're almost ready to resume the tour."

None of them seemed entirely convinced, especially Mr Noxious, who gesticulated to the others with his back to Jan, perhaps trying to keep their protests frothing. But they slowly returned to their seats, grumbling, and Jan left them in order to look in on Stopper. He'd ceased his barking but the poor lad was in distress. He'd peed in front of the scuppers, just like she'd taught him (so it would run through those holes and over the side), but he'd also done it on his seat as well. The skin around his eyes was wrinkled even more than usual. After rearing up to slobber all over her neck and her mask, he sat on his haunches, tail wagging, following her every move with a look of deep concern.

"I'm fine, sweetheart. Really, everything's good."

He knew her moods intimately, and recognized an astounding number of spoken words. His genetically modified intelligence had shaped that knowledge into a sharp, almost human intuition. Indeed, it was better than human, because Stopper, born naturally on Hesperidia of two lab-modified canine parents, possessed instincts and sensorial insights far beyond anything in the human experience.

And she hated seeing him so distressed.

"Aw, come here, you big softy." Hugging him at times like this was important for them both, Jan knew. They might not breathe the same air, but they co-inhabited this world in a way no two creatures ever had: neither was strictly-speaking indigenous, yet both were bound never to leave while the other still lived. "I know you don't really like sailing." Hearing him pant in the heat, right into her ear, made her smile. "It's okay, sweetheart. It'll cool off soon, and you can have an extra-big portion of Rip 'Ems when we get home, I promise."

Home. It suddenly hit her right between the eyes: this was no longer just a prolonged research placement or field assignment; it was much more permanent than that. She made her living here, had helped build her own living quarters on a small island here in the Keys, fed and kept her boy Stopper, and shared her life with Vaughn whenever he stayed here whilst on leave (as often as he could, not often enough). Yep, she lived here in every way a licensed colonist was living his or her dream on any of the thousands of habitable planets inside the 100z border.

Stopper wriggled free and bounded forward along the starboard gangway, where he reared up, front paws on the access gate, and barked into the crowd of spectators. Several of them jumped out of their skins – he did have one helluva bark when he sensed danger – and quickly parted from the line of his gaze.

Jan immediately saw what he was concerned about. But he'd done well to spot it, or sense it, through the crowd like that. The little white-haired girl dressed in a cute pink-and-silver designer survival suit was leaning over the taffrail, too far over, one hand clutching the guy rope and the other reaching for something attached to the anchor. Jan switched on her speaker-com and announced, "Someone please lift that young girl back on deck on the starboard …" She sighed, knowing she would have to point. "On *this* side! There we go. Thank you, sir. I know I said you have to keep a close eye on the sea, but I didn't mean *that* close, young lady. At least not without a bathing suit and Factor Fifty."

Her joke sounded tired, but it drew a few chuckles and seemed to dispel a little of the tension on board. If the captain could still make bad jokes, maybe she was telling the truth about the engine glitch. Speaker-com off.

"Okay, wait here, Stopper-lad. Good boy." She made sure no one was close enough to hear her whisper, "I need to go check on those screw-ups, make sure they don't fizz up when they surface." He cocked his head to one side as if he understood every word she'd said, then promptly dug his muzzle into his butthole to tend to an itch.

Below deck, Bronston and Smog Boy were watching the moon pool too closely to pay her any mind. The mystery divers were about to finish the first stage of their decompression, having spent about five minutes between ten and twenty feet below the surface, and the big man, Bronston, crouched ready to receive the first diver. Jan didn't want to spend a moment longer than necessary stalled out here, so she decided to muck in and help the divers into the decompression chamber.

Bronston nodded his approval, while Smog Boy gave her a cross-eyed *Hey, which one of you is you* look that made her hate him a little more. This might be a dumbass thing his colleagues had just done, but their lives were on the line and he'd smogged out at the crucial time. He deserved every kicking he got, she decided.

A woman surfaced first: rangy, pale-skinned, with dirty blonde hair and cold, gray eyes. Bronston lifted her out and immediately peeled off her pressurized diving suit and her personalized under-suit. Jan noticed the initials IJT embroidered in an elaborate gold-leaf motif on the breast of her under-suit. The woman had no compunction about being naked in front of the others, simply thanked Jan for opening the door to the pressure chamber for her, and stepped inside. Her exquisitely toned body suggested she employed a personal trainer. A top-class boob job, and nano-ink on *both* wrists (highly unusual outside elite corporate circles, as it required special dispensation from ISPA, one's ink being *the* unique personal ID every scanner in the IC or OC read to identify its bearer) were even more telling. Milady was a woman of some influence, though what she was doing here, diving into the unknown, was anyone's guess.

Next up, a man of about thirty-five – buzz cut, quiet, built like a high-g miner. He was courteous to the others' help in undressing him, and looked as though he was about to apologize to Jan when Milady shouted out, told him to hurry up and bring the sample and the analyzer into the chamber with him. Corazon obeyed without a word.

Jan shut the door after them and set the atmospheric pressure and time duration accordingly. They hadn't been down all that long, but they had been fairly deep for a suit dive; one could never be too careful when it came to pressurized diving. Plus, she *was* Captain. The safety of every passenger on board was her responsibility, no matter how moronic they were.

A little over seven nautical miles from Keyhole Key, roughly half that from The Pitons, a dark band of cloud rolled in, its fat, swiping rain attacking the *Alcyone* with drunken blows from the north and east. The erratic wind began to whip up sizeable crests, rendering the ship's fastest propulsion method, its hydroplaning "skim" across the surface, hazardous. Jan had no choice but to lower the hull fully into the water and extend its twin keels for full displacement, to cut her way home through the waves the old-fashioned way.

Time to pass the sick-hoses. Throwing up in one's regular breather was dangerous because it could easily clog the air filters, so a sick-hose, a flexible tube that attached to the wearer's face like one of those ancient Earth gas masks, provided a safe outlet for the upchuck *and* an uninhibited influx of filtered oxygen via separate flanking tubes. Jan had never needed to use one herself, but several of her ranger colleagues on the Hesp, not to mention her boyfriend Vaughn, swore by them whenever they went out in the chop (in Vaughn's case, as infrequently as he possibly could).

Most of her passengers chose to wear them this time. They'd all taken their precautionary seasickness pills, but it was impossible to tell who was susceptible to "ocean motion" until they experienced the violent chop for themselves. Jan mentally patted herself on the back. At least these tourists had heeded her safety advice. It wasn't the first time one of her tours had been hit by bad weather, but it was the first time she'd experienced a mutiny. The combination of the two nagged at her superstitiously while she led Stopper into the wheelhouse to keep him safe.

As she gripped the console's safety bar to steady herself, the *Alcyone* slammed bow-first into the trough of a twenty-foot wave. The impact threw at least four people out of their seats.

Christ! Why weren't they magnoed in? She'd shown them the childishly simple procedure twice now and still they needed to be babysat.

"We'll both be glad when this one's over, huh." She glanced down at Stopper, whose short tail wagged even though he was struggling to stay in one spot on the wet floor. After petting him for his loyalty, she added, "Whatever it was they used to call the dog-watch, it's all yours," then she kissed him through the glass of her visor and ventured out on deck to make sure everyone's magno-buckle was secured.

All around the vessel, white water raged.

Of the four idiots flapping around loose on deck like tuna fish, three belonged to the gang of mutineers. They'd taken it upon themselves to clip their belts to the port-side davits, so they could maintain their position guarding the cabin, on foot, but neither belt clips nor davit anchors were designed for that; the violent motion had wrenched the two apart and flung the men through the air. They'd crashed into other passengers, including one who'd momentarily unclipped himself to readjust his harness. In the tangle, *he'd* somehow lost his breather overboard, so Jan had to scramble to the storage locker to get him an emergency replacement.

What a freaking mess!

There were injuries but nothing serious. After securing everyone in their original seats, and trying her best to disarm the mutineers (for their own safety, for chrissakes) – alas, they stubbornly clung to their weapons – a weary Jan made her way below deck to check on Bronston and the others.

All this to-ing and fro-ing was making her a little dizzy.

At least the jerks below had more sense. Bronston and Smog Boy had harnessed themselves onto the bulkhead gainsays – smart. Even the two divers, still in the barometric chamber, had figured out how to use the gimbal rigs to stay suspended and more or less impervious to the ship's violent motions. Theirs would be the most comfortable journey of all, pearls in a pressurized oyster.

"I hope it was worth it," she said to Bronston. "Whatever you grid-licks are after, it'd better be worth more than the lives of all my passengers, 'cause if it's not …" She wanted to threaten him, wanted it so badly it was like acid biting her throat, but Vaughn had taught her not to provoke, or be provoked by, untested opponents. She was on her own out here. Omicron law enforcement was hours, days away. Far better to stay out of the mutineers' way and call for help later than challenge them here, give them a reason to get rough.

Next time, she promised herself, *I'm going to be armed to the teeth*.

"Just get us back in one piece, Doc," he replied, "and you won't have to see us again. I promise."

"You're leaving Hesperidia for good?"

He didn't answer.

"I said are you leaving—"

21

"I heard what you said. Maybe you should be more concerned about piloting your ship. Last time I checked canines aren't exactly rated sailors."

"No, but he's worth any ten of *you* squid-shits!"

"Hurry along now, *senorita*. Wouldn't want the tourists to get mutinous."

Incensed, Jan snatched a can of waterproof resin from the holder above Bronston and sprayed the contents onto his visor. He immediately wiped it with his hand, but it left a wishy-washy white coating that couldn't be removed without a special turpentine solution. His vision was now so poor he missed her wrist completely when he tried to grab it. "Get this crap off me!"

"When we get back," she replied, "I'll think about it."

Smog Boy snorted a laugh as he waved at the obscured face of his colleague.

"Not a smart move, Doc," said Bronston. "You've no idea who we are, what we're capable of."

"As for the last part, I'd say not a whole helluva lot until we get back to port. Now *stay where you are,* all of you. I don't want to have to come down here again, okay?"

"Whatever you say, Juanita." Bronston gripped the bulkhead rail as the *Alcyone* lurched to port. This time the jolt vibrated up through the ship's hull, as though something had struck it. It happened again, this time from the stern, tipping Jan forward, forcing her to shuffle her footing. Then a third impact, this one much more violent, smashed the vessel from what felt like the starboard aft side. It spun the *Alcyone* around several degrees in the water before *lifting* its back end partially out of the ocean. Only hooking her arm around the bulkhead rail prevented Jan from being hurled into a stack of O2 canisters, each of which weighed twice as much as she did.

"Doc, what *is* that?" yelled Bronston. "Those aren't waves hitting us."

"I—I don't ..." She wondered at first whether they'd sailed into uncharted rocky shallows, but the *Alcyone's* autopilot's sonar mapping would have steered them well clear of any such obstacles. No, this was something mobile, hitting them on the move. Something underwater but sentient. It had to be. Attacking them from all sides ...

Her xenozoologist brain burst to life, questing at a lightning clip – thousands, tens of thousands of species she'd looked at or read about here on the Hesp. Many she'd discovered herself. But in all her years of study, marine biology was, if she were honest, the one she'd shied away from, and for good reason. Yet the hydra was a *freshwater* predator. No known saltwater variety existed. This had to be something equally big and quite powerful, but what?

She suddenly remembered the divers.

The trench.

The slithering-to-life walls of the trench. What had Milady and her companion disturbed down there? What had they awoken in the deep? What the hell had tracked them all this way under the storm?

Stopper went ballistic on the bridge. He leapt around and barked and growled, slobbering saliva through bared teeth like she hadn't seen since that day in the crater lagoon, moments before their last deadly encounter with the hydra.

But this was a different beast altogether, one she hadn't come across before. All around the *Alcyone,* pairs of dark, undulating shapes, like the wings of giant rays, rose above the surface and almost touched together at their apex before thrashing back down with horrendous whip-cracking force, covering the ship with white water. Others thrashed against the sides, while some were clearly performing this same aggressive maneuver upside down against the vessel's hull. They were able to generate phenomenal force: just before impact, the flexible wing-tips actually broke the sound barrier. Gun-claps preceded deeper, hurtful cracks as the already storm-tossed surface was assaulted by the newest species of sea creature to make itself known to human science. Despite her concerns as Captain, Jan couldn't suppress a quiet thrill as she switched the vessel's omnispheric camera system on (not quite three-sixty, as at least four of the external viewing ports had been smashed) to record the spectacular discovery.

Her passengers' screams barely registered through the roaring wind and the thunderous broadsides unleashed by the fury of alien nature. But she'd endured worse, far worse on Hesperidia. The pissed-off giant rays could batter the *Alcyone* all they wanted, but unless they had some way of reaching onto the deck over the reinforced gunwales, Jan felt reasonably confident no one's life was in imminent danger. This was a territorial show of force, she decided, not a predatory ambush. But just in case, she set the vessel's ultimate protective measure to standby, warming up the reserve cells required to power it.

The photonic ribbing, when activated, formed an impenetrable dome of energy over the upper deck. It would repel everything – rain, wind, waves, sea creatures – but it would also suborn every joule of power the *Alcyone* had in its mains. No impulse, no mapping, no cabin air filtration, no comms in or out. The vessel would be dead in the water, beam-on and therefore vulnerable to these capsizing waves, but at least everyone on board would be alive as long as their breathers and the reserve store of O2 tanks lasted. Meanwhile, SOS buoys would broadcast their coordinates and last pre-rib status report to the nearest EMS rock-hoppers.

But that was only as a last resort. The ship was still making decent progress toward home port and away from the fault-line trench where the giant rays probably called home. Jan whistled tunelessly as she braced herself at the helm. Fifteen and twenty-foot waves continued to pile in her path, luckily none of them breaking. But each time the *Alcyone* crested one, its bow dipped steeply and slammed into the foot of the next, drenching the deck and her terrified passengers.

This wasn't how she'd imagined this day going *at all*.

After about a quarter hour of grim concentration, during which her thoughts barely escaped the punishing rhythm of the storm, Jan spied the first comma of molten dusk through the black cloud. Soon others began to punctuate the gloom. By the time the rays ceased their dogged chase, the shimmering viscous bars of the setting sun had spread across the western horizon. The heat in the light was palpable. It was as though someone had fired up a blow-torch and was melting away the storm.

Jan's stomach lurched and she lost her grip on the handles of the console. A massive punch from outside tipped the vessel up to about sixty degrees on its port side. She flew into the cabin door, her right shoulder taking most of the impact as it smashed into the panel sensor. The door whooshed open. Pain splintered right through her. Shock dampened out everything else. Again, her stomach lurched, but the opposite way this time. The *Alcyone* splashed back down, spilling her across the wet cabin floor and into the pilot's seat. It wrecked her shoulder a second time. The pain flared and then receded, washing waves of relief through her sore, quivering body.

Her guess: the first impact had dislocated her shoulder, the second had jerked it back into place. Jan coughed, struggled to her feet using her good arm. She couldn't *see* any more giant rays around the vessel, but that last blow had to have been from underneath, from something much bigger or much more pissed off.

Passengers … all here, all look fine.

Engines … still running.

Storm … starting to settle.

She slumped onto her seat, head resting on her arms crossed on the dash, and promised herself this was the last White Water safari tour of her season. *Science!* She was here for *science!* This was in no way or shape even remotely scientific. Soon as she got home, she'd sleep for a week, bathe for another week, then she'd take Stopper out on one of their favorite specimen-collecting expeditions across the shallow sandbars, where he could …

Stopper?

She glanced around the cabin, saw that he wasn't there. "Stopper?"

The cabin door was still open. She rushed outside, searched every inch of the quarterdeck, then ran around to the foredeck. The gates were closed, but he *could* climb over if he really wanted, if he thought it was worth disobeying Jan for. But what? Everyone was still magnoed in. There wasn't a single empty … *Oh, hell.*

A middle-aged woman was on her knees and sobbing as she clung to the taffrail. The sea had settled a little (though its rolls were still dangerous), and a few nearby passengers left their seats to see what was wrong. Jan rushed to join them, but in the back of her mind she'd already guessed what had happened. She was already scanning the open sea, her heart dying a little each time she glimpsed a fleck of orange and had to move on. The sunset reflecting off the choppy surface was the same color as the life-belts.

"It's my niece," the woman pleaded. "I-I couldn't stop her from … She dropped her lucky bangle and had to fetch it. She *always* has to fetch it. She never does as she's told. It wasn't my fault. I swear … I swear it wasn't my fault. Please tell me you can get her back. Please, you have to find her. You have to find Dorcas!"

One of the men held her while she sobbed.

"The girl in the pink suit," someone else said. "I didn't *see* her go over. Did you?"

No one affirmed.

Similarly, when Jan questioned them, not a single passenger had seen Stopper jump overboard either. But she knew, knew all too well, that his awareness and his instincts were sharper than all theirs put together.

He was a protector of human life. It was in his genes.

But the currents he'd have to fight against to bring her back to port were very strong, even for him. The girl could stay afloat indefinitely; he could not. It was likely she'd seen her best friend for the last time, that he would die doing what he was born to do. That this was the end of their dream.

No! She had to blank out that thought. Somehow. To steel herself, for Stopper and the little girl in the pink suit. Clenching her fists as she gripped the bulwark, she recalled the countless dangerous situations she and Stopper had survived together. He was smarter and tougher than anyone else knew. Only she knew … he would never give up. And neither would Jan.

The Hesp had taught them that.

Chapter Two

The frozen body swung through empty space at the end of a long tether cable. With nothing to slow its momentum, it arced around the spinning tunnel slightly quicker than the structure's own rotation. The cable began to wrap around the tunnel's outer shell.

A violent yank on the end of the line sent the corpse spinning off into a kind of crazy mannequin dance. That would make it harder for the shooters to hit. And that, in turn, would up the sporting factor. Several projectiles missed by a meter or more. Then one miner got lucky with his first shot – a bolt from his maghammer winged the frozen body, shattering its left arm. Cheers erupted throughout the packed tunnel.

Vaughn sighed, backed away from the lynch mob. They'd won this round. They'd had their pound of flesh. Interrupting them now would achieve nothing except start a riot. He opened the secure comm channel to his team instead. "This is Vaughn. Stay at your posts. Rankin is dead. Repeat, they've killed Rankin and they've overrun Section One-Three-One; we don't have time to contain it. Does anyone have eyes on the primary?"

An undercurrent of distant, angry voices, but no response from his agents. Maybe they couldn't hear him. The moon bridge workers were one more incendiary rumor away from tearing the whole place apart. After the first terrorist explosion had hit, severing three of five em couplings on a vital load-bearing section of the bridge, the evacuation alarm had only been triggered in a handful of corporate and VIP sections. Probably not as callous as it sounded – the millions of miles of wiring had not all been installed yet. But for the underpaid employees, and the tens of thousands of ex-workers stranded here with no prospects after years of difficult null-g construction, it was all the excuse they needed to rise up and vent their fury.

But Vaughn had a bigger problem: the primary bomber was still at large. His accomplice, a legitimate union worker named Rankin, had not disguised himself well enough. Security images of the two terrorists, taken moments before the bombing, had since been circulated right across the moon bridge. An understandable move on the part of Gilpraxian security. But it had made the whole situation a nightmare for Vaughn and his team of agents because every man-Jack from the planet to its moon now saw himself as an avenger.

Apprehending the bomber now was like trying to isolate a spark inside a bonfire.

"Agent Melekhin?" he asked over the secure channel.

"Nothing here. All sorts of rumors, mostly just noise."

"Where are you?"

"Section one-five-zero. Security's sealed us in like you wanted."

"Good," said Vaughn. "No way he's got that far yet, not with all this traffic. Stonewall everyone at one-four-nine if you can. Don't let him get close enough to throw an explosive your way."

"Copy that. But what happened to Rankin?"

"They glassed him. He's in smithereens about now."

"Animals!"

"Whatever happens, we can't let them get our primary. We need him *alive*. My hunch is he's inked-in at a high level somewhere in the Sheiker ranks. Whoever smuggled those explosives in past Gilpraxian security beat a Heisenberg net. That's supposed to be impossible. So the Sheikers might know something we don't about our own failsafe measures. I don't need to tell you guys what that could mean for the war."

"No, sir," they both replied at once.

"Okay. Hold your posts. I'll work my way back to you at one-ten, Sondergaard."

"Copy that, Vaughn. Stay frosty, um …" Probably not the most apropos word to use while a man was being glassed outside. "… I mean watch your six," he said.

"You too." Vaughn suddenly remembered how inexperienced the young Dane was – not yet six months out of his Omicron mentorship. Deadly, then, but unused to seeing himself that way, the way most civilians saw Omicron agents, as surgical instruments: necessary, even life-saving, but not something they wanted to be reminded of between operations. Well, Sondergaard had better get used to it if he wanted to last in this game. The effusive praise and adoration after a successful assignment, followed by the long periods of isolation, the averted gazes, the cold shoulders and unanswered personal calls.

If he didn't have Jan in his life, Vaughn couldn't imagine being able to do this job much longer. These bursts of adrenaline he craved – hunting perps until he had them cornered – really took their toll. Not physically but spiritually. On his own self-image as a lawman. Christ, you weren't supposed to *enjoy* tracking killers and sadists, sifting through the human wreckage they left behind, dragging them magno-cuffed (and bruised and beaten if necessary) into a holding cell ready for transfer to their ultimate punishment.

No, you weren't supposed to enjoy it, but at the end of the day that was what made him great at it. One of the best in the Bureau. And it was what made him certain he would stop this bomber. Because when you carried the Omicron badge, being right got you killed if you didn't have an edge. A way through. Some guys injected to sharpen their senses. Others got off on the celebrity aspect of it, of being a known and feared lawman. But Vaughn was as much a natural hunter as any of Jan's predators on Hesperidia. He was quite simply at his best, most efficient, most dangerous when he had the scent of his prey.

While the people cheered, they weren't moving about. He was able to scan and rule out dozens, hundreds as he made his way back, section by section, toward Sondergaard.

One glimpse was all it took. Experience, intuition, a perception sharpened by years in the field and honed by a hunter's channeled hate. The bomber's disguise might be able to fool this angry lynch mob, but Vaughn had had a good look at him on the security footage and also on the fake electronic ID he'd been wearing.

Two images. Two different disguises. But Vaughn could mentally cross-reference them. And the terrorist had been in a hurry. There was only so much prosthetic work he could have done in such a short space of time. So his disguise would have to be minimal, or close to the one he'd used at the time of the bombing, or if it was more ambitious it would be sloppy.

Dozens more, dozens discounted. He had to manhandle several in order to get a better look at them. Most were male, adult, under sixty. This gargantuan project had employed most of the null-g construction crews from both the Inner and Outer Colonies. Joining Planet Gilpraxia to its static moon was by far the most ambitious engineering feat ever achieved by mankind. It had taken the combined resources of eleven planetary systems fourteen years to finish the bridge, a full six years over schedule. But since its completion, those workers had been stuck in a quandary. Most construction had stalled elsewhere across the colonies on account of the war effort and the imminent Sheiker-Finagler invasion. So the only paid work available to them was in the lunar mines, or the hospitality and retail areas inside the moon bridge they'd helped build – those job opportunities were quickly drying up – or by signing up for military service. Which was why so many had elected to stay here, subsisting on their meagre union benefits, until something better came along.

It probably wouldn't. Not for a long time.

"Vaughn, this is Sondergaard. I've got a battalion chief from engineering here with me. He says there's been a local airlock override between one-eighteen and one-nineteen."

"Not destructive?"

"No. I'm going to patch him through. It sounds like this might be for us."

"Copy that. Go ahead."

After a few spits of static, "Detective, this is Chief O'Rourke. I've just got off the horn with Planetside Central. Their system logged an unscheduled ore-side airlock breach a few minutes ago."

"Unscheduled, not unauthorized?"

"Yes and no. The ink belonged to a David Rankin, who works here. Or at least he did. Detective Sondergaard just told me he's dead."

Vaughn whipped his duster off, slung it away. Magnoed up the collar of his bodysuit and started to run. "I'm on my way. Fill me in on the structure of these sections, Chief. When you say ore-side, that's underneath us, right? Those pipes where they send the mineral ore through?"

"That's correct. But underneath is a relative term, Detective. The whole section spins to create artificial gravity, so there's really no up or down."

"Chief—"

"But I get what you mean," O'Rourke continued. "Okay, I've got the structural blueprints here. The airlock access between one-eighteen and one-nineteen is for maintenance only. That's the smallest type. Anything bigger than a single thruster rig wouldn't fit through."

"How much damage could an explosive do to those ore conveyer pipes?"

"I'm not sure what you mean?"

"If he set off an explosive on one of those pipes – let's say the same blast force as the previous one – how much damage are we looking at?"

"Mm. I'd have to say not as much as the last one. It would destroy the pipes in those sections and definitely rip a hole through the sections' outer shell. But all ore transport was shut down the moment the first explosion hit. Any damage he could inflict from inside a section could be repaired without too much trouble. And those aren't critical couplings, even if he set off an explosion between the sections. They're not load-bearing joints. The em stabilizers would kick in, preserving the bridge's integrity."

"Okay." Vaughn upped his pace, had to barge his way through a group of elderly men arguing in front of the hatchway between sections. One of them grabbed him by the collar, tried to yank him back. A high-g miner from the looks of him, stronger than his silver hair suggested. Vaughn didn't mess around. He chopped at the old-timer's neck, right on the pressure point at the base of his skull, felling him instantly. Not fatal but he might be out for a while. The others stepped back when Vaughn palmed his holster.

"Chief, where's the nearest load-bearing section to the breach?"

"Uh, let me see. He's at one-nineteen, so that would be … ah, yes … that would be one-two-seven."

Vaughn noted the section he was currently running through: 122. So, the bastard was clearly heading in the opposite direction, back toward the scene of his *first* blast at 107. "Are there any critical couplings between one-two-two and one-oh-seven?" he asked.

"No."

"Then that's his play. Sondergaard?"

"Here, boss."

"He's going to try and get by you but from *outside*. He's heading back to finish the job he started."

"*Jesus*. That's ballsy."

"We lose one more of those em couplings, we could lose the whole bridge. The two halves would fly apart like a broken necklace. I don't know if they've got enough tug ships in the whole quadrant to reverse that."

"Copy that. You want me to jaunt?" Sondergaard sounded way more excited than he should be at the prospect. Any kind of EVA was risky, but facing a potentially suicidal bomber on the spinning outer shell of a damaged moon bridge … Vaughn wished he had this kid's enthusiasm.

"I want you to jaunt. But no heroics! Once you're outside, plant yourself ore-side at the next forward section coupling. That's between one-eleven and one-twelve. Stay low. Don't give him a clear shot, in case he's armed. Use the teeth of the coupling casings for cover. I'll pursue him from this side, make sure he knows I'm here. When he's trapped between us, I'll try to talk him down. If not, I'm gonna have a little surprise for him. Let me know when you're in position."

"Copy that, Vaughn. He ain't getting past me, that's for damn sure."

"Watch yourself, brother. My gut's telling me this is one of their top killers we're dealing with. Is O'Rourke still with you?"

"Yes. You want me to patch—"

"No. Just have him move everyone forward of one-fifteen, as quick as he can."

"Copy that. He's already doing it."

"Good." In Vaughn's hip holster, a sonic shock-gun, Mach 30 max. yield. No good for the vacuum of space, where sound waves didn't exist. In his utility baldric, a pair of collapsible wrist-mounted cisors, perfect for close or medium range attacks but the beams were so narrow you were lucky if you hit anything over a stone's throw away. Which left his 'germs'. Ordinarily used to scan and record a crime scene using multiple wavelengths of light and radiation, they hovered, circled, touched down in whatever sequence you programmed them. But Vaughn also knew how to control them manually, up to five at a time. His old mentor, Saul DeSanto, had made him practice the tricky maneuvers over and over until Vaughn was performing them in his sleep. Surprise was key in any standoff. The ability to wrongfoot your opponent. And five bug-sized little bastards packed with enough explosive force to blow a man's head apart like a watermelon were the digipedia definition of *didn't see this comin' now, did ya.*

He showed his bare wrist to the hatch security pad at 119, inking himself in. Slid down the access ladder to the ore-side shaft. The lighting down here was a lot darker, reminded him of brackish water. There were several pipes. The largest transported mined ulcifium ore from the moon directly to its planet, Gilpraxia, and was over twenty-eight thousand miles long. Pneumatic pods filled with the precious metal shot through the pipe at frightening speeds.

A second pipe, almost as large, transported empty pods and supply pods the other way, back to the moon. A clutch of smaller pipes circulated water from the recyclers and air from the greenhouse sections. It was a mind-boggling operation, and hadn't exactly gotten off to a smooth start last year, with union strikes and logistic snafus galore, but the builders had done the math. With the amount of ulcifium inside the moon – right down to its core – and the monopoly price they could charge for it, the moon bridge would save them trillions of credits in transport costs over a period of decades, maybe even centuries.

Vaughn climbed into one of the EVA suits pegged near the airlock's inner hatch. It reeked of rubber and dried sweat inside, almost made him retch. The helmet was no more inviting; someone had thrown up in it at some point, and the smell still lingered.

To hell with this.

He delved into a pouch on his baldric, fished out a stick of gum. Let the minty chocolate taste infuse his mouth and nostrils before he affixed the pukey helmet. At least it would be bearable now.

He noticed a bizarre-looking apparatus left in the middle of the walkway just before the hatchway to 118. It was copper-colored, green around the edges and octagonal in shape. Almost a sphere but not quite. It stood on the points of its edges, and was less than half the size of the hatchway. It had been split in the middle. The two halves gaped, but Vaughn couldn't see inside. Other than a mess of melted wires jiving like a tuft of hair in the aircon stream, he had no clue what was inside the thing. The brackish light only added to the mystery.

He called it in, told Melekhin to send a security team to check it out. In case it was another bomb of some kind, they needed to evacuate 118 and 119 asap.

Outside, the ore-side solar strips running for miles in either direction lit his way just fine whenever the tunnel spun him into shadow. No need to waste extra juice in order to power his suit lights. Null-g had never been his favorite milieu, but the warm orange glow made him feel strangely at home. Ditto the heavy rhythm of his magno-boots on the hard surface.

He double-checked the fuel level in his thruster rig. Over 97 percent. At least these suck-bait workers passed muster on safety, if not hygiene. As soon as he got his bearings, he'd have to thrust ahead, staying as low as he could, to gain some ground on the bomber.

In the meantime, he trudged on, focusing on the planet and the slight snaking curves in the insanely long, flexible bridge. An ocean bed of stars wheeled by as his section spun and spun. He tried to blank out that sensation, to orient himself *inside* the spin instead, on solid things, unchanging things. They were the planet, the surface he was on, and his Omicron training. Nothing more certain than that, the incorruptible legacy he'd forged.

He suddenly thought of Jan, the only woman in the galaxy he couldn't wait to return to. And her crazy, wondrous planet, the only place in the galaxy he returned to with any kind of frequency. It was fast becoming a home away from home for him – the other being his private Bureau shuttle, the *Pitch Hopper,* which Jan described as his "man cave with wings."

Vaughn had used up most of his annual leave, but in another month or so he'd have a couple of weeks to spend. With Jan. With Stopper. Light-years away from the human scum of the colonies.

"Vaughn, this is Sondergaard. I'm in position. Our primary's on his way – I can see him but not clearly. It looks like he's got something with him."

"How big?"

"Not sure. Pretty big. He's trailing it behind him through space on a tether. Looks like a damn balloon, the way it's drifting like that. But it has sharp edges. Not quite a sphere. Any of this making sense?"

Vaughn un-magnoed his boots, thrust diagonally forward at 10km/h in sync with the sections' rotation. "I'm on my way. Whatever it is, I think he's left one back inside 119."

"You think it's a bomb?"

"Unknown. Just don't let him get anywhere near you."

"Copy that."

"How are you holding up?" asked Vaughn.

"Like a geriatric porn star in a threesome. You?"

"This your first jaunt on the job, Sondergaard?"

"Yes, sir. I aim to milk it, too. As long as it takes to bag this bastard."

"Don't worry about that. Just hold your position. We've got the upper hand. Remember that."

"Copy that, Vaughn. Ass cheeks clenched and holding firm."

Vaughn snorted a chuckle, shook his head. The kid was a typical new grad, right down to the borderline insolent tone. But Vaughn trusted it, trusted this young Dane. Anyone who got the Omicron nod had to be a tough little sonofabitch, and plenty smart where it counted. Vaughn had had to sharpen his act on a daily basis for two whole years before his mentor had deigned to even acknowledge that he had a name and wasn't just simply "kid".

"Be right there." Moments after Vaughn upped his velocity to 20km/h, he caught sight of his quarry. Just under three sections ahead. Clomping along on the ore-side exterior, his bizarre octagonal luggage floating above him on a barely visible cable. But Vaughn also noticed the man was carrying a backpack loosely over his O2 tank. It bulged. Probably not his packed lunch unless he'd opted for a seriously high-energy diet. The kiloton kind.

A section away, Vaughn deaccelerated, killed his momentum. Magnoed his boots once again so he could stalk his prey on an even footing. He scanned the couplings ahead, counted the sections. The previous blast had torn 107 wide open, had rent its reinforced, rad-shielded panels outward like tinfoil petals. Luckily there hadn't been many people in there at the time. Just one personnel carrier riding the maglev – five workers on board. 107, like all the load-bearing sections, was a non-stop passage for commuters and anyone without security clearance.

How the hell had the bomber gained access to the moon bridge in the first place, let alone bypassed a critical security point? His accomplice, Rankin, had either been a lot more creative than his pay grade suggested – Band A3 was something like a greenhouse air & water technician – or there was more going on here than met the eye. Something they'd all missed.

Three things Vaughn knew for sure about the bomber. One, he hadn't passed through the security gates at either end of the bridge, planet-side or moon-side, or at any of the access docking checkpoints. Two, he'd flashed fake ID ink at least twice in order to gain access to off-limit areas: first to go ore-side in 107 and plant the explosive, then to breach the airlock at 119. But Planetside Central had flagged both those unscheduled activities. Why hadn't they flagged him before that, however he'd gotten onto the moon bridge? The guy couldn't have just materialized out of thin freaking air. And three, this was a one-way trip for him. Several squadrons of the Gilpraxian fleet, as well as a dedicated satellite net, were monitoring local space to make sure nothing bigger than a cornflake got to within fifty thousand klicks of this enterprise. No way the bomber could escape from here, and he must know that.

It made a second explosion a near-certainty. Vaughn had half a mind to pull himself and Sondergaard out to a safe distance using their thruster rigs, and let the fleet pepper this asshole where he stood. Sure, they'd destroy a section, but they'd keep their critical couplings, and therefore the bridge's overall integrity, intact.

No. There had to be another way to neutralize him, to bring him in alive. But what?

The bomber stopped and glanced behind him, right at Vaughn. He seemed unusually short, five feet if he was lucky. Sunlight reflected off his visor, hiding his face. A chill brushed up and down Vaughn's spine, signaling the start of the endgame. So it was on. Vaughn halted, crouched low. To keep his opponent guessing but also to unleash the five little germs at his feet.

"Watch him, Vaughn. He's got a hand behind his back."

The terrorist slid his backpack off. Not good.

"Copy that," said Vaughn. "Has he seen you?"

"You bet your ass. Right before he clocked you. But he didn't seem surprised. You think he's been expecting us?"

"Probably. He must have thought it was worth the risk for him to finish what he started. Maybe he thought we'd be slower to respond."

"Well, hell – how many times can a guy shit in his own cup before he stops calling it coffee?"

Vaughn shook that nonsense out of his mind. Instead, he activated the remote guidance pad on his forearm. From a distance anyone would think he was simply typing a message, but that was the beauty of it. The little germs hovered a fraction of an inch off the surface, practically invisible, waiting for his instructions.

"I'm going to hail him on all radio frequencies," Vaughn told his colleague. "See if he's willing to talk."

"Copy that, sir. But I hope you've got other moves as well, 'cause I don't like the way he's reeling that object in."

Damn. Sondergaard might talk crap but he had a good eye. Vaughn hadn't noticed the octagonal thingamajig lowering at all. But it was. Subtly, just like Vaughn's own chess move.

"You want me to take him out?" asked the young Dane, almost breathless. "Y' know, *before* he punches the dark? This blast might be a lot bigger than the last one."

"Not yet. We wait."

"But sir!"

"Stand down, Sondergaard. I'm hailing him now." Vaughn keyed his Omicron ID into the suit's wrist module, bringing up his customized interface. He selected 'All Frequency Comms', then recorded his message for the transmuter to broadcast on as many radio bandwidths as possible. "This is Agent Ferrix Vaughn of the Omicron Bureau. Whoever you are on the outside of Section One-Twelve, I'm ordering you to put that bag down and step away from it *right now.* You have ten seconds to respond."

No immediate reply, but Vaughn felt confident the man had received the message. Their suits and helmets were identical, probably already attuned to the same comm channel. He moved his germs in wide arcs around the bomber, discreetly flanking him. But the man kept fiddling with the contents of his rucksack. If it *was* an explosive device in there, maybe Sondergaard was right and they should take this asshole out now.

Vaughn repeated his message, adding at the end, "… before we open fire. This is your last warning."

The man stood and stepped away from his rucksack, arms aloft. But it was not an act of surrender. No, he was reaching for the octagonal object, pulling it down to him.

Vaughn pursed his lips, gave a big sigh through his nostrils. "Okay, Sondergaard, take aim. This prick's off the reservation. The second he tries to open that thing, let him have it."

"Copy that. I've got him."

Barely visible even as they crossed the solar light strip, the tiny germs inched toward their prey. Vaughn now stood tall, one eye on the bomber, the other on the five colored blips converging on his forearm display.

The man set the copper object down, then turned to face Sondergaard. He kept on turning until he'd done a three-sixty and was in his original position. He wagged a finger at Vaughn, as though he was onto the Omicron's tactics.

Crap. Had he seen the germs? Vaughn couldn't tell, but he did see the man's face for the first time. It was oily blue, shiny; he had to have coated it with something. He had a hook nose and a finely trimmed beard. He didn't appear older than forty, but the blue paint made that more of a guess. A steely focus kept the man's eyes wide and his features frozen. If he was rattled by this confrontation, he sure wasn't showing it.

"What are we waiting for, boss? He's clearly not turning himself in."

"We don't know that. We have to wait till he makes his move."

The young Dane grunted his frustration. "Standing by."

Vaughn decided to halt his attack. Surprise was everything, and he wasn't sure he had it anymore. If the bomber saw the germs closing in, it might provoke him into doing something he might otherwise not have done.

This was getting trickier by the second.

"Vaughn, he's going for the object. Do I have a greenlight?"

"Negative. Not yet."

"What the hell are you *waiting for?*"

"Shut it. Don't interrupt again." Vaughn clenched his fists, spat silent expletives onto his visor. He'd forgotten how much he *hated* these team operations. Alone, he was a licensed hunter, a predator. In charge of a team, he was constantly adjusting inferior men. He'd give the insolent little shit an earful when all this was over, but right now he had to be careful.

We need this lead, he reminded himself. If at all possible, they had to collar this guy, interrogate the hell out of him. If he hadn't blown himself up by now, under all this pressure, maybe he had no intention of doing it.

Vaughn reopened the all-frequency broadcast, knew he had to choose his next words carefully. Too hostile or too soft and this would all be for nothing. "This is Agent Vaughn. We've got—"

The guy plucked up the octagonal object, bent his knees and launched himself off the bridge into space. Vaughn took a step forward, glaring after him. It was a completely unexpected move, and he hated that he couldn't figure it out. Without a thruster rig the man would just drift into the clutches of the Gilpraxian fleet or the satellite net. Or if he was going to blow himself up using the octagonal device, why do it out there in space when his job was to inflict as much damage as possible on the moon bridge?

"*Now* can I take him out?" Sondergaard's tone was now flat-out disrespectful, but Vaughn had bigger fish to fry.

"No, you can stay where you are. And before you ask, we're not thrusting out after him. It's too dangerous."

"So we leave him for the fleet to pick up? Isn't that a cop-out, sir?"

"We're not leaving him to anyone. Not yet. I want to see what he does."

More grumbling from the young Dane. Vaughn ignored it. Instead, he sent his germs after the bomber. They shot out, self-correcting their trajectories to encircle their target as they would any other crime scene.

"Whoever you are drifting out into space, think about what you're doing," he broadcast across all frequencies. "The local fleet won't try to retrieve you while you're carrying that device. They'll destroy you and it with you. Your only chance is to throw it away and let us come get you. I can guarantee you a fair trial, but only if you're in Omicron custody. This is your last chance. Surrender now or you will be dead in a few minutes. It's up to you."

The germs hovered around the bomber, feeding their images back to Vaughn's display. What they showed made no sense. Not only had he opened the octagonal object, he was detaching his own *helmet*. In minus 270 Celsius, zero-g space. Insane.

A clear view of his face showed it icing up. Mouth and eyes closed, the man was nonetheless acting fast. Having pushed his helmet away, he now peeled out of his pressure suit as well, revealing a silver insulating body suit and head cap underneath. The oily blue coating on his face and neck suddenly made a lot more sense. It was protection against the cold, and might buy him a few more seconds before he glassed out here.

Vaughn could only watch in astonishment as the man balled himself as tightly as he could in order to climb *inside* the hollow object. The two halves snapped shut after him. Moments later, alternating currents of blue electricity crackled between all the points of the octagonal shape. It shimmied. The live feeds garbled for a moment on

Vaughn's display. When they returned, the object was dark again, dark, still and lifeless.

"So that's what that thing was – a popsicle maker," said Sondergaard. "Just imagine the brain freeze *that* guy's feeling."

"But why?"

"Beats me. First he wants to light himself up, then he glasses himself. Me, I'll take a double Arinto, straight up. Melekhin's buying."

"I don't get why … after going to all this trouble, coming out here like this …"

"A serious case of blue-balls, that's for dang sure."

"Just keep watching that rucksack," Vaughn reminded the rookie.

The germs were still sending their live feeds. The copper coffin spun slowly. Vaughn took a deep breath, relaxed his face – he'd been frowning for a while now and his brow was beginning to ache. He maneuvered the germs right up to the object, flew one against a sensor pad the man had touched to unlock it before he'd climbed in.

The two halves of the octagonal coffin flung apart, knocking his drones away. But they quickly resumed their reconnaissance and circled the object again, sending him several different points of view.

"Impossible!" he said aloud.

"What is?" asked Sondergaard.

"It's empty. He's not *in* there."

"Huh? You mean he vaporized himself? That thing's an incinerator, not a fridge?"

"Looks that way." He sent the germs in for a closer look, had one fly inside the empty halves. Extraordinary. There was literally *nothing* in there. No ash, no smears or blemishes of any kind on the myriad reflective surfaces inside. "Okay, you're not gonna believe this," said Vaughn. "We need stellar forensics here asap."

"Why? We saw him go in, didn't see him come out. What more is there? He's toast."

"Just trust me on this, brother. Right after bomb disposal, it's gonna have to be stellar forensics. We're not equipped to solve this one on our own."

"Then let me try."

"What?"

"Command says someone from Herculean L-Twelve is hailing you," explained Sondergaard. "Apparently it's urgent. Your missus lives there, right? L-Twelve?"

Vaughn's pulse began to jackhammer. "She's a ranger, runs a safari tour. What's the message?"

"Don't know, sir. You should go check it out. I can take over from here."

"You're sure? I'm telling you, you're not gonna like what you find."

"Stop it. You're scaring me," joked the young Dane. "Say, Melekhin won't mind if I take point on this, will he?"

"I doubt it. It's not his first rodeo, and you're not his first dipshit with delusions of grandeur."

"That going to be the title of your report?"

"Depends."

"On what?"

"On whether or not you prove me wrong from here on."

"Sir, I want this one. It's got my name on it."

Vaughn slowly shook his head, wondered if he'd ever been that ambitious, that sure of himself before he'd done anything worth a damn. He recalled his five germs. "It's all yours, kid. For now."

"Thank you, sir. I won't let you down."

But Vaughn's thoughts were already dozens of light-years away, on a protected planetary Eden with all the dangers his nightmares could conjure, and all the dreams his heart desired. Jan was hailing him from the Hesp? It was urgent? Then nothing else in the galaxy mattered.

Chapter Three

Staying out at sea this long into the night with a ship full of tourists could very well cost Jan her license, she reckoned. Mr Noxious and his gutless gaggle had screamed as much at her for hours now. Some were still sobbing into their misty breathers, swearing to sue her and the tour company for every credit they had. Well, technically they might be right. She *should* have headed for port as soon as the search had hit sunset. This *was* a gamble in the dark, a blind, maybe even futile effort.

But Stopper and the little girl were out here somewhere. Adrift at night in a hostile alien ocean. Jesus. If Noxious and the gaggle were that frightened, how the hell did they think little *Dorcas* felt? Protocol or not, it was insane to even think about heading back in while she and Stopper were lost and there was still a chance, however small, they might be found.

"You can piss and moan all you want," she yelled to a hysterical plump woman who was getting more and more colorful with her insults. "I'm not leaving them out here. If it was your daughter, you'd be manning the searchlights with the others. So shut your cake-hole and do something constructive. That goes for all of you."

"And what if those things come back?" a man argued.

"She's already told you, that was a territorial thing." Bronston, one of the ringleaders of the earlier mutiny, had become surprisingly vocal in her defense since he'd learned of the little girl's disappearance. "We've sailed a long way west of there, and we haven't seen those creatures for hours, have we?"

"No, but you're putting all our lives at risk without our permission. That's called kidnapping where I come from."

"And the girl's life?" replied Bronston. "You're willing to just abandon her? Bear in mind the longer she's out here, the less chance she has of surviving."

Noxious adjusted his over-sized sou'wester for the umpteenth time as he scurried to the head of the gaggle. "*You've* got room to talk, mister," aimed at Bronston. "It was you that stalled the engines. You and your men. I don't know how you did it or why but something happened back there, something Jan isn't telling us. All I know is you're at the back of it. This is all *your* fault."

He and his posse exchanged glares with Bronston's men. Bronston turned to Jan, rolled his eyes as if to say, *Are these dorks for real?* But she didn't reciprocate, didn't acknowledge him at all. So what if he was taking her side now? The truth was he had mutinied. He really was to blame for all this. Noxious was right about that much. And until she had her beloved Stopper back at her side – and the girl safely aboard – he occupied slot no. 1 on her seaborne shit-list.

Noxious could have slot 2.

The yellow beams from the *Alcyone's* six mounted searchlights, a pair at the bow, a pair aft and two amidships, slid across the rolling black creases of the western ocean with more skill than she'd imagined these squibs were capable of. It wasn't quite a fifty-fifty split on board: the gutless gaggle outnumbered Jan's supporters; but it was good to know there were a number of brave people here too, enough to ensure her command. They figured, like she did, that anyone on the *Alcyone* had time – time and high odds of seeing tomorrow. Dorcas and Stopper did not. As long as their O2 reserves lasted, it was their duty to keep looking.

"Sonofabitch!" Jan hammered her fist on the dashboard in frustration. Another sighting, another false alarm. Seaweed this time. Lichen last time. A half-eaten fish carcass before that. She rolled her sore shoulder to limber it up, then lifted her breather in order to rub her tired eyes.

It was roughly three-and-a-half hours into the search. Or was it four-and-a- half? She'd lost track. Scanning an endless dark surface that heaved and sloshed and seemed to be taunting her with its coy hints and red herrings: Jan had grown pricklier by the minute. Her omni-goggles searched for heat signatures across the water, a much more fecund way to find survivors at night than waving tiny pools of light over nothingness. But she hadn't seen anything constant. Anything that stood up to scrutiny. The occasional creature would breach, only to submerge quickly when she shouted its bearing and a pair of searchlights hit the thing right in its eyes (or other sensitive spots).

And with each false alarm, her own situation, let alone Stopper's and the girl's, was becoming more tenuous. About three quarters of the passengers were against her now. Those who'd sided with Jan on moral grounds earlier were starting to doubt her wisdom, maybe even her sanity. Even one or two of Bronston's goons had voiced dissent and received a not-so-private tongue-lashing from him below deck.

Come on, Stopper lad, I know you're looking for me too. I know you'll never leave the girl. But you've got to keep swimming, keep watching for the lights. Just like when we used to fly out in the vicar, late on – I'd always leave its lights on, wouldn't I, so we could find our way back if we got lost? Come on, boy. Come to me. Come to the lights.

Bilali, one of the rangers from up north, hailed her over the *Alcyone's* radio. At almost the same moment, he dipped the wing lights of his hover cruiser a few hundred feet above, signaling he was going to help with the search.

"I got your message, Jan. Sorry it had to Stopper, but I think if anyone's going to see the girl safely to rescue, it's him. Over."

"Appreciate that, Bilali." She checked to make sure no one was close enough to hear her. "I just don't know these ocean currents well enough. I'm freaking guessing out here, man. And these squibs, they're ready to toss me overboard. It's getting—"

"What?" he interrupted. "You're still carrying passengers?"

"Yeah. So?"

"How many?"

"All of 'em ... minus the little girl."

"*Jan!* You need to take them back."

She tightened her grip on the throttle lever. "Not you too! That's all I've been hearing."

"Do you know how many laws you're breaking, keeping them out overnight *after you've been attacked!*"

"Aww, boo-hoo. So they got soaked a little. I'm not giving up on the search while there's still oxygen on board. I don't care what anyone says. I'm captain of this vessel, not the goddamn cowardly rulebook." She suddenly pictured Stopper sitting beside her, gazing up, head cocked slightly to one side, wearing a half bemused, half treat-starved, fully adoring expression she just wanted to wrap her arms around and kiss. "You know what? *Screw you,* Bilali. You find the little girl 'cause you have to. It's your job. Me, I'll find him because I'd rather die than leave him out here on his own. Over and out!"

"Okay, but you said *him,* not *her.* I know what Stopper means to you, Jan. We all do. But think about what you're doing. All those frightened people on board are frightened for a good reason. They're—"

She cut the connection. Didn't respond to his omnipod call either. Any more whiney talk and *she* might have to start throwing people overboard. Of all the gutless, ass-covering, selfish yellow grid-licking sons of bitches.

"This is my safari tour," she reminded herself out loud. "I say when it's over, not that chickenshit Bilali. He doesn't like it, he can kiss my—"

Several excited voices yelled to her from the prow. In her haste to reach the hatchway Jan slipped on the slick decking, landed painfully on her carbon fiber hip and elbow on her right side. There, at eye level, she spied a rash of scratch marks low down on the bulkhead behind the hatchway. Persistent, mischievous scratching. It stung her in places she'd forgotten she could be hurt. Her darling Stopper had spent so much time on board the *Alcyone* with her, even though he hated sailing. He'd been so patient over the years, snoozing on deck in the shade near the davits, until his patience would run out and he'd let her know by how much, in no uncertain terms, with that piercing howl or that bark that made the tourists jump out of their seats, or that endless, rapid scratching that drove Jan to despair.

For the first time, the reality of it dawned on her, opened a well in the pit of her being. *I might never see him again.*

"Jan! Jan, come quick! You need to see this!"

She got to her feet, made her way across the crowded foredeck to the bow. The mood of her passengers was difficult to gauge: some chewed their lips, some craned their necks to see over those in front, while others stared, stony-faced, out to sea.

"What is it? What have you found?" Jan asked the woman who'd shouted to her so excitedly; but that same woman was now in tears. Her fellow tourists were consoling her.

"Heads up, guys. Make way." Bronston swung one of her hooking poles in over the heads of the prow hogs. Seawater streamed onto them and peppered the deck. "Wish I had better news," he told Jan. "Really I do."

He lowered the lifejacket to her, let her be the first to inspect it.

Jesus. It was shredded. Something had bitten a hole right down the middle, lengthwise, had torn it almost in two. The halves hung limp from her hands like wet, pink-and-silver skin sloughed from some deflated thing. Most of the buoyant material inside had been ripped out. Only the shoulder panels remained, enough for it to float. No blood, but why would there be? Blood only stained when it dried. This had been in the water for a while, maybe dragged down to the depths while the unimaginable had happened …

"I guess this means we're heading back," a man said from somewhere to her right. The words lit her like a fuse, scorched her inside out while she held proof of the little girl's death in her hands.

She heard a crack. Then the tourists parted, backed away from one of their number who now lay flat-out on the deck. It was Mr Noxious. He didn't move.

Standing over him, Bronston scanned the faces of the other passengers, massaging his knuckles, almost daring them to goad him further.

Jan felt a swell of admiration. He'd done what she should have done, what she *would* have done if only he hadn't stolen the opportunity from her. Then it hit. This wasn't just anger burning inside her, it was vengeance. In that moment she knew, unequivocally, that she'd lost her boy.

Stopper was gone.

He'd left her to protect a helpless little girl. And neither of them was coming back.

She ran back inside the cabin, crouched in the corner near Stopper's scratch marks, and shut her eyes tight in order to fight the panic welling inside. These shallow, rapid breaths would starve her of oxygen if she wasn't careful. She could hyperventilate, and then she'd be in real trouble. The squibs would have the excuse they needed to take command, to head back to port.

She couldn't allow that. Not yet. Couldn't allow fear to break her promise to him, her brave, sweet boy, when he needed her most.

No. It was not time to give in, to even *think* like that. If there was even a tiny chance he was still out here looking for her, she would keep on searching to the bitter end, and *no one* would get between her and that promise.

No one.

Chapter Four

"Hey, come on in, bud. Thanks for swinging by." In Pavel 'Crash' Kraczinski's huge, bandaged right hand, an open bottle of rare coconut Arinto liqueur. In his left, an insect swatter. The way he tried to squeeze and contort himself around several piles of supply crates in order to reach and exterminate said bug was not the most reassuring sight in the annals of Omicron law enforcement. It suggested he was unaware of a) the expensive bottle in his hand; b) how insane it was to turn an entire room upside down to find an insect; and c) how gross he looked – he'd packed on at least four stones of pure fat since Vaughn had last seen him, without upsizing his wardrobe to keep up. The result was sad and pathetic. Flab poured out of his old uniform, which dripped with sweat. If it weren't for his trimmed beard hiding a serious blubber-neck, he'd be almost unrecognizable.

"Everything okay?" asked Vaughn, trying hard to see how it could be.

"Hell no! This little bastard's been creeping around here for days, shitting in the sugar. Wait till I get my hands on him. He's had his last sugar rush, that's for *damn* sure. *There!*

There he is." *Thwack!* "Gah. Stay still. Stay where I can get at you, you little—"

Vaughn cleared his throat. "Listen, I can always come back later, brother. You seem plenty busy as it is."

"What? Aw, no, no. I can pick this up later." The big guy attempted to suck in his gut in order to squeeze his way back between the crate towers. Failed miserably. He panted and wheezed and scraped his skin on the rough edges several times. But he didn't spill a drop of Arinto. Not one. It was like some demented vaudeville act that would have the kids howling with laughter, just as they might expect him to hit a large woman's backside with the swatter at any moment.

"Rough day, huh?" asked Vaughn, offering to shake hands.

Kraczinski dropped the swatter, switched the bottle to his left hand and used his right to shake Vaughn's. A firm, sincere grip as usual. "It's good to see you, pal. I mean that. Even if … well …"

"Well what?"

"Well, it's just that whenever you pass this way, my switchboard lights up like a hooker at a lotto winners' after-party."

Vaughn quirked an eyebrow. "So you've had news?"

"You could say that. From up above *and* down below. HQ's been breathing down my neck all day, quoting jurisdictional babble at me like I'm some wet-nose fresh out of the coop. This thing on the Hesp, it's a pretty big deal."

"What thing on the Hesp?" Vaughn snatched the bottle from Kraczinski's fist before the big guy could down another swig. "First tell me what the big deal is, then we'll empty this together. Okay?"

Kraczinski took a step forward, pursed his lips, thought for a moment, then licked them instead. His fifty-proof breath overpowered any hint of coconuts. "Nah, you can have that one." He glanced at two of the three access hatches to make sure no one was around. Crooking a finger at Vaughn, he said, "Come with me, pal. We'll finish this up somewhere more … private." That seemed to amuse him as he led Vaughn to the third door and inked them both through.

It was Kraczinski's personal rec room (or "man-cave", as Jan would describe it). He owned a hacienda on one of the new prospect moons nearby, quite a nice set-up for a lawman, but Vaughn reckoned the big guy didn't spend much time down there. Kraczinski collected ex-wives like a self-harmer collected scars, and they all hated his guts. He'd go through the same routine over and over. Get himself in decent shape, stop drinking, find a target-rich bar or party somewhere and sweep some poor pioneer girl off her feet with his surpassing charm. Then he'd marry her, promise her excitement and a life surpassingly charmed. As soon as the novelty wore off, however, he'd turn back to the eating and the booze and his Omicron duties with that zeal only a born addict could understand. So she'd ask what had happened to all that excitement and charm, and he'd tell her to stop complaining and find a hobby or a cause and do something constructive, you know, like he did day in and day out for the greater good. Only that was bullshit and they both knew it, and before long she'd see that his surpassing charm had been surpassed by his other, more enduring, attributes: the kind that repeatedly tore down whatever he tried to build outside his career.

After all that, he'd be an easy man to hate, Vaughn reckoned. Utterly self-absorbed. A borderline narcissistic personality disorder. On the home front he was a wrecking ball that had such highs and lows it was small wonder he'd recently gone through his eighth divorce. He'd received his nickname, 'Crash', at the academy all those years ago. It was short for 'Crash 'n' Burn', a reference to the endless short and sharp relationships he'd had with local girls.

But there was no ignoring the fact that Kraczinski, one of the most flawed men in the Bureau, had integrity when it mattered as a *lawman*. Sure, he bent the rules around the edges, typified by the crate of illegal Arinto bottles badly hidden here under a jacket behind his sofa. But he had your back and would defend it to the death whenever you needed it. DeSanto had seen that in him during mentoring. The old man had hated most of his other traits, but that one was the keystone in the Omicron legacy. With it, you could make a real difference. Without it, the badge was only a decoration.

"Nasty business over on Gilpraxia." The big guy heaved a sigh as he sank into the sofa. "How's the new fish doing? Summerlee, is it?"

"Sondergaard. He's just like we were, only more so."

"A real shit-for-brains, huh."

"Can't help it at that age. But he has solid instincts. Soon as he learns caution, he'll be a decent agent."

"Yeah, if he lives that long."

"Amen to that, brother." Vaughn thought about taking a sup, decided against it. He wanted to be as sharp as possible when he heard what Kraczinski had to tell him. "So what's the news from the Hesp? Has Jan been in touch?"

The big guy popped open another bottle, lapped up the fizz that spilled out. "Um, yeah. Jan. Bad news, I'm afraid. They found the little girl's lifejacket. It was all torn up. Sounds pretty final. For the dog, too. Apparently, those ocean currents can be wicked strong. I feel really bad for her, bud. The other rangers are bad-mouthing her, saying it was her fault, that she kept the squibs out there too long, well after dark. And the squibs are giving her hell for it too. Me, I want to know what *really* happened out there. You know I've always liked Jan. She's worth a planet full of those rich, pampered assholes. No way she'd put anyone at risk without a damn good reason." There he took a hearty swig, didn't seem to mind that illegal liqueur was dripping onto his bare belly, each drop worth the price of a full shot of regular booze.

"But we're gonna have to be real careful how we handle it," he went on. "HQ is sending down a primo scouting crew. Some heavy-hitters from R and D. Highest clearance. And she just happens to be in the way – her safari tour, that region where she works, it's real close to where they're touching down."

"What are you saying? What does it have to do with Jan?" Vaughn couldn't help but recall the last time someone with "highest clearance" had visited the Hesp. His old mentor, DeSanto, had brought a Phi posse with him on an illegal manhunt that had turned all sorts of sideways on them. On Vaughn, too, and Jan. He'd sworn after that that he'd never let anyone from ISPA use their clout to bypass Hesp security. No matter how high their clearance. Not without an okay from Core Congress.

"Nothing to do with Jan, bud. At least nothing direct. She's just in the wrong place at the wrong time. HQ isn't telling me much except I've not to interfere. You know how it is, what they're like when someone from on high sits his full moon on a classified op."

"Yeah, they don't want us sniffing around. They've trained us too well for that." Vaughn massaged his tired neck muscles. The moon bridge case had left him weary, unfulfilled. "What kind of bona fides do they have?"

"A writ straight from some Congress sub-committee. Airtight credentials. I checked. They definitely have permission to touch down. And the sat net can't watch them while they're down there, either. It's only watching spaceward. They've rigged it that way."

"Great. So we can't even carry on the search for Stopper and the girl via satellite? This is getting better by the minute. Tell me some good news." Vaughn rubbed his eyes with the heels of his hands. "Is Jan safely ashore?"

"Unknown."

"What? Why?"

"She's not responding to my hails. And she won't talk to the other rangers either."

"Any idea why?"

"'Cause the whole planet's against her right now, bud. And you know how she likes to do things her way."

Vaughn smiled to himself. The more people told her she was wrong, the more convinced she was that she must be right. That much he did know. And if the whole planet was against her, she'd be the most stubborn creature on Hesperidia right now.

Little did she know what was heading her way. The trouble she could get into if she kept up her prickly indignant routine with the wrong people. She was already in a heap of trouble as it was from the sounds of it.

"Watch your six down there, bud." Kraczinski saluted him with a tilted bottle. He stared at the end of it before he took his next drink, just held it in mid-air. He seemed to be contemplating his life in there, in that sparkling contraband, as he added, "She's going to need you. She's going to need a straight shooter down there with her. So do me a favor: be your old self, don't take any crap. And if you need me … well, you know …" He slapped his belly, jiggled the folds of flab.

"I know, brother. I know. Me too."

"Glad you're around, Vaughn."

Vaughn got to his feet. "Save some for me, okay?"

"Yeah. Not a chance."

"Then do something for me," said Vaughn. "Punch me up one of those back-channel links. You know, a Kraczinski special. I need to stay in touch with you and Sondergaard out here, but I can't have anyone listening in. If they've rigged the sat net, they're probably controlling all signals to and from the planet."

"Is that Agent Vaughn I hear, asking a colleague to set up an illegal hack of a satellite net? I'm shocked. Whatever is the galaxy coming to?" He threw Vaughn a wink.

Vaughn flicked him a salute in return. "Take it easy, brother."

"I'll take it any way I can get it."

"No kidding," Vaughn muttered to himself on his way out.

Chapter Five

The *Alcyone's* foredeck was a grim tableau. Most of the passengers were in their seats, facing forward, neither speaking to each other nor openly protesting any more. Not openly, at any rate. The sobbing had (mostly) ceased, the hateful stares aimed at Jan and Bronston were now few and far between. But it was a kind of silent protest, their sitting there all obedient like that. It held the promise of vengeance, either the explosive and imminent kind, when she and Bronston weren't paying attention, or the slow-burn litigious kind, through which they would thoroughly destroy her and this whole safari enterprise with their outside influence once they returned to civvy life. The rich could afford to wait to get even. The rich could afford anything.

But Jan could not afford to wait. She kept her gaze glued on the multiple camera-fed images on her screen; between them they offered more than the complete visible spectrum, backed up by a constant cycle of detailed pattern recognition scans looking for anything solid breaking the water's surface around the ship. Occasionally she would glance up to deflect a hostile look from one of her patrons, but she never backed down. Never looked away first. It steeled her every time, but she could also feel the pressure building on board, one reprimanding glare at a time, against her.

It felt like the eye of a storm.

Someone rapped on the open hatch to her cabin. Someone who had to have gotten past Bronston, who was still there outside, arms folded, leaning against the wheelhouse, guarding her. In truth he was the only reason the mob hadn't rushed her before now. Since he'd decked Mr Noxious, no one had confronted him, and that was just fine with Jan.

"Who is it?" she replied.

A calm, pretty face peered around the hatch door. "Jan, sorry for disturbing you. If you've got a minute, there's something I'd like to—"

"I don't. And we've got nothing to say to each other. Not until we set foot on dry land."

Milady blinked a few times, then sprouted a pensive pout, nodding a little as she stepped inside, unbidden. "You've every right to be sore – that's awful, what happened to that young girl – and your dog, of course – I feel really bad about that – but I'm here to help. I *can* help."

"Like you helped provoke those giant rays? Like you helped lead them right to us? Like you've helped this whole time from decompression?" Jan leaped to her feet. "*Get out before I throw you out!*"

Milady stepped back, made a gesture of surrender with her right hand. With her left she tried to wipe away streaks of moisture from her visor, forgot that it was condensation on the inside caused by the change in temperature from the decompression chamber to the upper deck. "I can send out a real search party," she said, "if you'll just listen to what I have to say."

"What do you mean? What search party? It's just us."

"Hmm … not exactly. There's a large-scale search and retrieval operation about to get underway on Hesperidia. It's setting up as we speak, not all that far from where we set sail."

Jan's anger had peaked and troughed endlessly through the night like the swells of this unforgiving sea. She had neither the energy nor the mercy to relinquish her stiff grip on the impossible situation she was in.

"*You're* not here to search for the girl, or for Stopper. Why are you here? What are you looking for?"

"I'll explain everything when we reach shore, I promise." Milady's perfect poise and posture, not to mention the note of sincerity in her well-enunciated accent that otherwise dripped privilege, left Jan feeling a little unsure of herself. Vaguely inadequate. Extremely tired. This woman was coming at her fresh and powerful and with a promise of a life-line. Not only would Jan get to continue her search, this woman's colleagues – retrieval professionals – would *help* her? A large-scale search party ready to find Stopper and bring him back to her?

"What's the catch?" she asked.

"No catch," the woman assured her. "The sooner you get us back to port, the sooner you can start a real search."

"You promise?"

Milady smiled, crossed her heart. "If they're still out there, we'll find them."

"We'd better."

The woman gave a gentle nod, then went outside, placed a reassuring hand on Bronston's shoulder. He didn't respond at first. But as she walked away, he caressed her shapely hip with his fingers. Jan thought she saw the woman shiver a little. Curious. Were they having an affair? Or just flirting?

Where was *her* man? Vaughn might be halfway across the galaxy right now, fighting crime, but she'd give him hell to pay if he left her alone in this nightmare much longer. Bronston had done her a solid, but he was no longer her protector, he was Milady's.

Gripping the wheel, she shook her head at the bitter twists and turns of the previous night. And the ordeal wasn't over yet. No. For hours she'd fought tenaciously against the idea of heading to shore; now, gunning the throttle, she flipped the fight toward it.

The gradual swell of chatter on deck ahead seemed to signify a collective sigh of relief, anticipating an end to this not-exactly-ripped-from-the-brochure tour. Meanwhile, Jan ignored the inky black clouds gathering in her rear-view monitors.

* * *

A light drizzle swept over the upended gazebo and its awning bearing the company logo – *Alien Safari*, now in tatters – as the bedraggled group disembarked onto the short, wooden jetty. The beach was a tiger-striped beige color – dark where the storm's rain had soaked in, lighter where spindrift had recently blown across it and had gathered to form shallow, distended dunes. The cool "doctor's wind" had almost died out, leaving the entire area, usually a tropical alien seafront paradise, as humid and as shriveled as Jan had ever known it.

Her sturdy port HQ still stood a stone's throw from the water's edge, but it was in bad shape. The storm had flung an *aguarbor* tree through its reinforced lookout window. Most of its perimeter fencing had either disappeared completely or was a twisted, mangled mess. Its ten-meter vertical observation tower now measured about eight meters horizontally, lying some distance up the beach. Rocks and seaweed and all manner of crustaceans now populated the front and the east side of the building.

It almost made Jan retch, seeing all her hard work and pedantic planning reduced to a ramshackle beach hut overnight. And for the first time on Hesperidia, Stopper wasn't here to distract her, to cheer her up when things got on top of her. A horrible emptiness spread over all she surveyed, made worse by the fact that it was here, on *terra firma*, that she'd lived with him for so long. Out at sea, there had been a tinge of unreality, a temporary waterproofing over what had happened. They didn't belong out there. They belonged here. But now that she looked around, hoping to glimpse him or hear his bark, it hit home. It hit hard.

She heaved a ragged sigh and let it deflate until her lungs cried out.

"Where do we go now?" a young black woman asked, tugging at Jan's sleeve. She sounded hoarse, looked tired enough to curl up and sleep right there on the sand. Her boyfriend stood a few paces behind her with his back to Jan.

"In there." Jan pointed at the HQ, then raised her voice so the others could hear. "There's food and refreshments inside. Get refills for your breathers as well. The shuttles should be here soon. Those booked on another safari tour, we'll get you where you need to go. Those leaving the Hesp, make sure you gather all your personal items from the lockers inside as soon as possible. I'll be heading back out shortly, and I don't know how long I'll be. This place might be unmanned for some time. So my advice is don't leave anything behind."

"Who do we speak to about lodging an official complaint?" someone else asked.

"Anyone but me," she snapped.

"Who's you direct superior?"

"God."

"Can we stay to help out?" An elderly Japanese man, arm-in-arm with his tiny wife, stepped out from the group. Jan recognized them as having supported her at some stage during the night. "My wife Ichi was a hydrographer for ISPA when she was younger. She doesn't speak English, but I can translate. We would like to help with the search."

Jan glanced at the others, who mostly avoided eye contact with her, then marched over to shake hands with her two aged allies. "Thank you for the offer. That means a lot. I can't tell you how much that means. You might be better off getting some rest, though. It's been a long night." *And you're not exactly spring chickens,* she wanted to add.

"Your dog is big and strong," the man replied. "He could keep the girl afloat without her life-jacket. The only question is: for how long?"

"But it's been *hours*," someone added. "In rough seas, with no shoreline in sight, he wouldn't even know which way to go. The odds of him making it on his own, let alone with a girl to keep afloat, are practically nil. Sorry to have to say it, but when that shredded life-jacket turned up, that's when I couldn't support the search any longer. It's over."

Jan ignored the cretin, spoke to the Japanese couple instead: "I don't know much about hydrography, but we have all sorts of versatile instruments and charts and scanners in the storeroom upstairs. Ask your wife to take a look. If she finds something she thinks might help us map the sea currents, by all means, you're welcome to come with. I'd be honored. Meantime, I'm going to grab a few extra supplies."

The couple bowed. So did Jan.

Meanwhile, tourists began filing into the building ahead of them. Jan dashed up the steep sand dunes at its rear to get a clearer view of the surrounding inland area. She scanned the wet, sand-ribboned veldt for miles around. There was no sign of any search operation. The coastline, too, appeared uninhabited in either direction for as far as the eye could see.

She ran back down and accosted Milady from behind. "So where's this support you promised, Princess?"

"On its way, I guess."

"You *guess?*"

The woman threw Jan's hand away. "Listen, you'll have to take it up with them. They're here somewhere." She glanced skyward, slowly shaking her head, and with a wry smile muttered, "You'll have to be quicker than that, sis."

"Who?" Jan stepped in front of the woman, blocking her way to the HQ. "Either you tell me what's going on here or …"

"Or what, Tammy Tour Guide? You'll throw a pamphlet at me?"

Jan gritted her teeth and leaned into her opponent. Their visors pressed together. "I'll throw more than that, you bony little bitch. You promised me a search party. Where is it?"

"On its way. I promise." Milady brushed something off Jan's shoulder with her fingertips. "You'd better have something to bargain with, though, Juanita. My sister doesn't do charity. She was born jealous and spends her every waking minute getting even. She despises me and can't fathom why I don't hate her back. What can I say? We're … complicated. But if I was you, I'd get your business head on. If you've ever dealt with a CEO before, you'll know they like to be able to see through you at all times. So ask her for help, then tell her what you can do for her in return."

"Like what? You won't even tell me why the two of you are here."

"We're here to retrieve something we lost."

"Such as?"

"Such as the answer to that question is worth more than you can possibly imagine."

Again, Jan barred the woman's advance, this time pressing her outstretched palm to Milady's sternum. "Wait! You haven't answered my question."

The woman shot out an impatient sigh. "Which one? And make it quick. I've a rendezvous of my own to keep."

"I don't get it." Jan dredged her tired mind for a glimmer, an edge, came up empty. "You sneak in here on a tour boat, risk your life by diving unprotected, putting us all at risk, while your sister's bringing a *salvage* crew? Who are you? And how has she got permission to bring anything on to my planet?"

"Your planet, is it?" Milady flicked an amused wink. Then she glimpsed Bronston's approach – he towered over Jan from behind, was probably getting ready to manhandle her for laying a hand on his boss. But she shook her head at him instead, and gently lowered Jan's hand.

"For what it's worth, I'm impressed," added Milady. "The world *and* its custodian, if that's what you are. I underestimated both. But you'd be wise not to interfere further in our business. Search for your castaways, but leave this retrieval operation to us. My sister doesn't know I'm here. The longer that's the case, the smoother things will go for all of us. She doesn't have friends in high places, but she

76

spends in high places, which amounts to the same thing in politics and in commerce. So if I were you, I'd omit any mention of me and my men. And for your own good, because you've impressed me, believe me when I say this is *not* your planet, not while she's on it. As deeply attached as you might be to everything here, it means nothing to my sister. Absolutely nothing. Only what we came here to find matters to her. And that makes her a worse enemy than you can possibly imagine. So, like I said, do yourself a favor and don't get in her way."

Jan narrowed her eyes at her eloquent opponent. "And you?"

"Me? I aim to find it first. So don't get in my way either."

Jan didn't reply, merely looked Milady up and down as she brushed past, sizing her up for their inevitable next encounter. She'd never liked ultimatums. And she'd always hated sneaks.

This might not be my planet, she thought, *but it's sure as hell my home. And no one else is gonna destroy even one piece of it. Not while I'm here.*

She waved to the Japanese couple as they signaled to her from the upper balcony of the HQ. The woman held an object aloft, an instrument of some kind she'd found. They both appeared excited by the discovery, so Jan rushed in after them, buoyed a little by the prospect of any scientific advantage. On her way in she brushed past Milady and deftly lifted an item from a pouch on her belt. No one seemed to notice.

It was a tracking device identical to the one Bronston had held during his boss's dive. Exactly what it pinpointed she didn't know. Precisely what she planned to do with those coordinates she hadn't yet decided. But it was a piece of the puzzle. A potential bargaining chip. And once she found Stopper and the girl, she was going to need every advantage in order to solve the mystery of this highly illegal incursion.

All I need now is my Omicron badge, she mused. *Vaughn, you're gonna be out of a job if you don't hurry your ass up.*

Chapter Six

The dark, scrawled shoreline tilts this way and that as he constantly has to adjust his stroke and his position. To keep the girl's limp arm in place over his shoulders. To nudge himself up against her, into the sounds of her coughs and sputters that terrify and reassure him every time. To stay above water so he can keep her above water.

Nothing else matters.

Not the pain in his back leg that bites like a thorny vine wrapped tightly around it. Not the series of vicious attacks from below he's had to fight off throughout the night. He has no strength left, and neither does the girl; the rhythm of her kicking is erratic, labored; her tired arm shakes with the cold. If he doesn't get her to land soon, she will not be able to stay above water, even with his help.

Nothing else matters.

Not even Jan. The only memories he has of being without her are some of his worst: becoming separated from her while out on safari; or waiting at home, fretting, while she goes off on her own to do a "No Stopper" job; or the worst one of all, when the giant serpent with three heads snatched her up in its mouth and he knew that if he didn't jump in after her that he'd never be with her again.

Nothing fills him with pride like knowing she approves of him, or of something he's done for her. Nothing else makes him so happy. Without Jan, he is alone. He is incomplete. The further he drifts away from her, the more alien his world becomes.

Strangely, now, only the girl matters. Ever since he saw her fall into the sea, the urge to keep her above water and get her to safety has consumed him. Not the pain or the threats from below or his unbearable tiredness or even being away from Jan has swerved him from this one unshakable goal. Those fears bubble away inside him like the hot, yucky geyser pools Jan sometimes takes samples from with her little glass toys. He is not allowed to touch them. He must not go near them. As with all he feels that is powerful, he must obey that which he does not understand. In protecting the girl, he is somehow protecting Jan. He would rather die than fail her.

His heavy blinks catch the first flitters of sunlight over the choppy surface. It dazzles him but also spurs him on. He knows that the dark scrawls of the shoreline will soon give up their secrets, so he will know more about what lies in store. The girl tries to say something, swallows another mouthful of water instead. Her mask isn't supposed to let in water like that, but one of those fights with the sea creatures must have dislodged it. She coughs louder than ever into his ear as she tries to empty the mask and reaffix it in one breath. Panics. He wrestles her to keep his position, that sweet spot under the crook of her arm where he can nestle against her tiny, shuddery body. They've tried everything along the way: her riding him, him riding her, him dragging her by the scruff of her suit when she tried to swim against the strong current, him chasing her when she sped off after the first attack, even her holding onto his tail. But this has been the only mutually comfortable position: both of them working together, touching but each still swimming in his own right. Though she is much weaker than Jan. And she is growing weaker all the time.

The current and the wind carry them toward land. All he can smell is the salt of the sea and the girl's scent. All he can see is a long, bumpy beach with no trees and no signs of life. All he can feel is tired. Tired and determined. Determined to carry her onto the dry sand. Sand like the sand of his favorite place in the whole world. Jan's sand. Where the two of them live, in a place she calls "the Keys" and he's marked every inch of.

His paws scrape tufts of something webby and soft. Then they dig into the shallow sand until he can stand with his nose just out of the water. He snorts a proud, defiant breath. It wakes the girl up but only for a moment. She rises to her knees, then flops sideways onto him as he heaves them both ashore, instinct the only thing powering him, each step an ordeal after a full night of swimming into the dark, endless unknown.

She slides off him, goes under. He bites down on her collar and drags her up above the rolling surf and doesn't dare let go until he has her well clear of the reach of the breaking waves. The rumble and fizz of sea upon sand are familiar sounds. He doesn't know where he is but it's not unlike his playground in the Keys.

He sets the girl down on the dry, wrinkled sand and collapses down beside her, his heavy eyelids shrinking a vaguely lost, vaguely protective gaze fixed on the endless sea between him and Jan.

* * *

Two decades' worth of expensive schooling and college and an ISPA doctorate and one of the most impressive field research posts anywhere in the colonies, and Jan felt like she knew nothing. Less than nothing. The sheaf of colorful charts Ichi Nakamori was sifting through on the desk in front of her might as well have shown globular clusters from the far side of the universe, or Kandinsky paintings, for all the sense Jan could make of them. Yes, they were labelled as areas of the west equatorial ocean, but despite having navigated her way around it for a couple of years now, she recognized almost none of it from the charts.

Luckily, Ichi knew exactly what she was looking for, her husband assured Jan. "These are the sea temperatures at various depths – I do not know the English translation of the exact scientific word," he said, then listened to a bit more of his wife's explanation in rapid-fire Japanese. "She's looking for time-lapse image sequences of the sea and the atmosphere, taken by satellite. It would be a lot easier if we had access to the satellite net in real-time," he added, "but she is fairly certain she can map the currents using the information in these charts."

Jan nodded. "Tell her I'm sorry about the satellite net. I really don't know what's happened there. My access normally gives me a live feed to anywhere on the surface, but it won't let me in. What instruments will she need?"

The man – Matsuya was his name – translated the question for his wife. As per her reply: "These two devices she retrieved from your cupboard. I believe one is an omnipod with a specialized motion-sensitive mapping overlay. The other is an adaptor for the CPU on your ship's bridge. She can use them to find out the precise speed and direction of each sea and atmospheric current we encounter. Cross-referencing that information with the CPU's own vector data and Beaufort measurements from last night, she should be able to roughly approximate the voyage taken by Dorcas and Stopper."

"How roughly?"

Ichi shrugged at her husband, then rolled up the charts with impressive dexterity. The two of them exchanged heated words, after which she slapped the charts against his chest and gestured that he was lucky she didn't stick them some place less convenient.

"So we're ready?" Jan asked.

After nervously straightening the creases in the roll of charts, Matsuya offered Jan a sheepish smile. "We are ready."

"Okay. You two go ahead, make yourselves comfortable on board. I've a couple more things I need to do first, then I'll be right there, I promise."

He bowed in reply. His wife copied him, utterly sincere. They were going to make an interesting crew, Jan reckoned. But she had to know more about the mysterious retrieval operation set to get underway, well, sometime soon, somewhere close by, if Milady was even telling the truth.

Uplinking with the sat net was a no-go, so she couldn't message Vaughn or Kraczinski. But the radio comms still worked, albeit with a crackly reception. She switched to Bilali's frequency and made contact.

"Yes, I *know* the tour schedule's gone all to cock," she said. "Can't be helped. We are where we are. Let's get on with it." She drummed her fingers along the metallic radio console and rolled her eyes at his sanctimonious lecture. "Uh-huh. Paragraph nineteen, sub-section three, is it? Well I guess you learn something every day. Oh, really? Brother, does it sound like I give a flying—" The roar of hover thrusters overhead interrupted her. She glanced out through the window. "Good timing," she said. "You can take them off my hands and I can get back to doing what I *should* be doing. Yeah, paragraph eleven, sub-section eight: when lives are at stake, ignore any and all candy-ass advice and steer clear of all cretins named Bilali. No, I know you don't get why I'm talking to you this way. You just ferry them out of here. Leave the rest to me."

Jan heaved an impatient sigh. He was getting ready to soapbox again, and she needed to cast off. "Listen, any assistance you and the other rangers can give with the search would be appreciated. Put the word out, by all means. No, I can't. The sat net is locking me out, so you'll have to do it. Oh, and one last thing: what do you know about a salvage or retrieval operation? Uh-huh. One of the squibs said there's some heavy-duty equip— Really? Omega-level clearance. Several klicks south. Yeah, yeah, I know the bay. It's ideal for a landing. And that's definitely where they'll be? Right, well, I guess we'll see what happens, won't we? Oh, and if you happen to see Vaughn, tell him to come find me. I'm going to get my boy. Over and out."

* * *

His dream is a good one, a familiar one. He bounds over the waves on the beach outside their home in the Keys to fetch a spongy seaweed bulb Jan throws for him again and again. Each time he drops it at her feet and shakes himself dry, she beams at him, hits him with that loving gaze, and says his two favorite words in the whole world: *good boy*. It's bliss. He's in bliss. There's nowhere else he'd rather be and no one else he wants to be with.

Then his eyes blink open.

The surf crashes a ball's throw away. The edge of the sea has moved while he's slept, like it does outside his home. But nothing else is the same. He can't smell Jan or their home or any of the spots where he's marked his territory.

The little girl's arm rests over his neck. She's snoring but not as loudly as Jan sometimes does. The sounds are softer, wheezier. He slips out from under her. She stirs but doesn't wake. In the throes of a full-body wake-up stretch, he winces. A jolt of pain shoots up from his hind leg, reminding him of the coiled creature that's been there through most of the night and all the while he's slept. It attached itself during his fight with the fourth and final beast from the depths, the one that thrashed around beneath him, the one with mandibles and that skin-like cape that propelled it through the water and those long, long proboscises that tried to wrangle the girl away from him. If he hadn't chewed his way through one of those proboscises, he might not have won the fight because the beast was a lot bigger than him and seemed to be figuring him out, its feelers on the edges of that skin-like cape pulling and prodding him this way and that.

He'd chewed his way out of that nightmare, but the smaller coiled creature had fastened around his leg while he was pulling the girl to safety. Biting it was tricky for two reasons: he hated dipping his head underwater and that was the only way he could reach it, by stopping swimming; and when he did sink his teeth into it, the thing only squeezed harder. It hadn't really hurt at the time, just tightened and tightened until he'd felt pins and needles. Another had attached to the girl's ankle. It had made her panic and cry, but there was no blood, so he figured it was better to just leave them there and concentrate on swimming instead.

They haven't drawn blood in all this time.

But now that he's had a good, clear look at the things, they trigger a memory. An old, sneaky fear starts to gnaw at him. He's seen them before, though these are much bigger than the ones he remembers. It was during an expedition with Jan, back when they used to live in their previous home, far inland. Jan had flown them to a remote marshy forest to collect tiny creatures with her glass toys. After dipping her hand into a stagnant pool she'd given a yelp and had tripped over a tree root, pale with sweat. Several small, worm-like creatures had coiled themselves around her fingers. They were milky white with red, distended veins. They looked and smelled disgusting. Stopper had snarled and barked for all his worth but it hadn't gotten rid of the things. Jan had even tried to burn them off with one of her hot-tipped toys. No good.

But one thing she tried *did* work.

He'll know it by its scent. One of millions of scents he's stored in his olfactory memory – easily the most sophisticated and accurate record of Hesperidia belonging to a creature not indigenous to it. If he can locate that scent anywhere near here then he might be able to remove the coiled parasites before they do any real damage. But he'll probably need the girl's help. His own claws and teeth might not be enough.

First, he limps up the beach and scrambles to the summit of the highest sand dune, where he lifts his nose to catch the warm, offshore breeze and all the subtleties it contains. A craggy ridgeline protrudes from the sand and winds low into some kind of crater up ahead. There are signs of vegetation, and a miasma of organic smells wends his way on the wavering air currents. There's heat coming from the crater. Its haze liquifies the horizon beyond. But he can't discern the scent he's after. He doesn't give up, though. Not yet. It was a long time ago when he last smelled this particular plant, and there are more plants on Hesperidia than there are faraway islands in the night sky.

A punch of a gust delivers the hint of a memory – of *that* memory, if he's not mistaken. And he's rarely mistaken. No toy in Jan's expensive toybox is better than him at divining the whereabouts and particulars of life on the Hesp.

The plant he needs is somewhere inside that warm crater. It isn't very far, but going there alone to fetch it means leaving the girl on her own, out of his sight, unprotected. That he cannot do. No, she'll have to come with him. Until he can find his way home, wherever he goes she'll have to come with him. He limps back to her and, just like he does with Jan when she's being lazy and not getting up to feed him, licks the little girl's face all over. Mostly he gets her mask, but contact with her ears and neck seems to do the trick. She groans, coughs ever so delicately. Runs her tongue over flaky lips. Then she curls up into a ball, shivering.

Get up, he barks at her. *You need to get up now.*

"W-where are we?" she asks. Her voice is so weak it sinks into the sound of surf fizzing across the powdery white sand.

He barks his command. She shifts position once more, this time winces out loud and grabs her ankle. The creature visibly tightens its grip. Frozen for a moment, wide-eyed, the girl can't believe she's forgotten about the thing attached to her any more than she can believe what it looks like now that she can actually *see* it.

Her scream pierces the cocoon of her mask. It hurts Stopper's ears. Before it's finished, she's on her feet and hobbling away as fast as she can move. Skinny arms flailing to help her balance. Up the beach toward the dunes. Right where he wants her to go. Her pink-and-silver suit reflects the sun, dazzling him. He limps after her, barking like crazy. He can't help it. This whole outing, ever since the bad people sneaked below deck, has been a crazy-making series of challenges. If he could scream, he'd do it loud enough for Jan to hear him. Wherever she is.

"I *can't* get up. I can't go another step! Don't you see? I can't *move*. It's squeezing me. Mommy, it's — it's — it's squeezing. Help me get it off, Mommy."

The girl's impossible. Her cries and sobs sting him deep inside. They make him feel like he's failing her, that he's somehow failing Jan by not keeping this helpless little girl out of danger. But she won't do what he wants her to, what she *needs* to do. Nothing works. Barking. Growling. Nuzzling up to her. Prodding her. Even biting the arm of her suit to drag her up hasn't worked. She's stubborn. Helpless. Inconsolable. In a word, she's impossible.

So he resorts to the only other tactic he can think of. It's something Jan does to him whenever he's being stubborn, refusing to come when she blows her yellow whistle or calls after him. Dawdling to buy himself more playtime or to stay outdoors that bit longer, it's one of his favorite things. It's a game he and Jan play. Sometimes it makes her laugh when he starts rolling around or hiding. Other times she gets cross at him, and he has to gauge the tone of her voice to make sure she isn't outright angry, that she's still giving him a little slack. He thrives on knowing her moods, on reading them well. Mostly she lets him get away with that extra playtime. But if he pushes it too far, she knows exactly how to scare him into obedience – by leaving him. It's that simple. Once she's out of sight or close to it, he comes running. He can't help it. Even if she's only pretending to leave him – sometimes she'll wait behind a tree or land her ship just over the next rise – he can't take that chance. He can't handle even the idea of her leaving him.

That was the hardest part of last night. Knowing that the strong movement of the sea and the direction of the wind were combining to take him away from her, and her away from him, and that there was nothing he could do about it while the girl was with him. If he was alone, he might have been able to get back to Jan. But him and the girl together, no chance.

He gives the stubborn girl a single sharp bark and then hobbles away toward the crater. She's already half way to it, curled up on a thin layer of sand over rough, volcanic rock. She screams after him but he doesn't look round. He pricks his ears to pick up every sound she makes, but he daren't look round. Not yet. This is what Jan does to make *him* obey and it works every time. He has to be cruel to be kind. Make the girl think she's going to be all alone in this place she's never been before. Only then will she be ready to help herself. Only then will he be able to help her.

He stops on the rim of the crater, just before he's out of sight, and barks again. She's on her knees watching him, still sobbing. *Come on, impossible girl. What are you waiting for?* he barks. *Being alone is not good. You have to follow me sooner or later.*

She flops down again, crying louder than ever. He bounds around on three legs, frustration whirling him into despair. If this doesn't work he might never get the parasite off his leg and neither will she. And they'll never make it home, limping about like this.

He makes a decision, to pick his way down the rocky slope until he's out of sight of the girl. There he waits, stiff, afraid. He can sense her fear, too, and that affects him strangely because he knows he's causing it. He's making her feel alone because that's the only way she'll follow him. That it works is no great insight; it's always worked on him. But he can feel Jan working through him, guiding his instincts and his experience and all those lessons they've learned together as a survival unit out in the wild. She's somehow telling him what *she* would do if she were here now. That's the best way to keep the girl alive, he feels. To become for her what Jan has always been for him. The girl cannot survive on her own, so she must do his bidding.

He suddenly feels a surge of pride. That *attaboy* approval he's craved from Jan all his life courses through him now. It's his best and dearest affirmation that he's done something right. The girl lurches over the rim of the crater, baring her teeth with determination. She hisses and winces her way over the sharp rocks, but she's no longer sobbing. The urgency and the effort have changed her. Angered her. She's angry at him for leaving her. "Don't you *dare* do that again," she scolds him.

If Jan had said that to him, in that tone, he'd have moped around with his tail between his legs until she relented. But oddly, his tail wags faster than ever. The girl is on her feet and moving in the direction he wants and is no longer feeling sorry for herself. Things are going well. It's worth her being angry with him as long as it gets them both home.

He repeats the tactic, luring her further into the crater. She reiterates her displeasure, this time with a few familiar curse words he's heard Jan and Vaughn use when they've been really cross. Bad words because they're only ever used for cursing.

"I said *stop!* I can't keep going," she groans, plonking her backside down on a tuft of spongy weeds. "It's squeezing really tight. I'm getting pins and needles."

He rubs against her, licks her ear.

"*Eeuww!* That's really gross."

He does it again, slobbering all over her. The girl pushes him away, laughing, holds him at arm's length. Stopper could easily overpower her but he likes this interaction, he likes that she's engaging with him.

"I'm sorry I yelled at you," she says, hugging him. "It's just scary when you run off like that. Promise me you won't run off like that again. It's really scary being out here on my own. We are *soooo* lost. I'm not even kidding. And we really, really need to stay together. I think leaving the beach is bad idea. What do you think?"

He wriggles out of her embrace and immediately runs ahead until he's out of sight again. Old, wrinkly trees and leathery vines hang off the sides of the crater wall. Some kind of yellow sap oozes from the tree bark and drips down to the ground in long, elastic globs. Over time, the fallen sap has formed wax-like stalagmites, some as high as the roof of Stopper's and Jan's beach house. Colonies of insects inhabit them; the creatures use their tiny pincers to constantly reshape grooves in the wax to channel the newly fallen sap into different chambers of the hollow interior.

He's seen creatures like them before, but none this clever. No doubt Jan would want to visit them with her glass toys and bring a few back to her lab and obsess over them while Stopper waited impatiently for *his* turn for a little attention. Not that he begrudges her that alone time with her toys and her specimens and – okay, he does – can't stand it in fact. She's often in her lab for hours, sometimes days at a time, only visiting him at mealtimes and just before bed. If he didn't have the run of the compound it would be the cruelest kind of torture – her ignoring him in favor of creatures and plants so uninteresting, so unplayful that he could cock his leg up over one and barely even know it's there. Yes, it gets old fast, that fascination of hers with all the little things of the wild.

The girl gives the insect colonies a wide berth, so wide that she veers away from his tracks and into dangerous territory. The prevailing breeze alerts him to the threat. He dashes over to her and gives her sleeve a yank. It catches her off balance and, not wanting to put much weight on her constricted leg, she topples over, lands in a dusty heap. She whips him an angry look. But she misses seeing the danger behind her: a very different kind of whip, a vine so thin and strong it slices out through the air and retracts into the safety of its thorny coil before he realizes he's seen it. Stopper and Jan were stung several times during their first encounter with these plants. The whipping vines injected tiny, hooked barbs into the skin that didn't hurt at first but created a devilish itch. The more he licked the wound, the more it itched. It damn near drove him mad until Jan rubbed some kind of ointment on it and gave him an injection to make him sleep. When he woke up after, she put a plastic cone over his head which stopped him from reaching the wound. It had still itched in a hot, throbby way, but that eventually wore off, and a few days later he was cone-free and itch-free and had a working fear of yet another hostile life-form.

Luckily its whip missed the girl. But when she tries to get up, her sore leg gives way. She tumbles toward danger *head first*. He barks and makes ready to leap in to protect her, but the vine whips out before he can get there. It smacks against her visor. She scurries backward, terrified. She hides behind Stopper, breathing fast and loud. He doesn't dare attack the plant. It's actually hiding inside a bush with brown, droopy leaves that appear almost dead. He'll remember that, and so will the girl, he hopes. If she's as smart as she needs to be, she's just learned her second survival lesson.

The further they descend into the crater the warmer it gets, the thicker the vegetation grows. In his experience there aren't many plants that attack as viciously as the whipping vines, but he's never been here before. He picks a path as close to bare rock as he can find, but every surface is becoming mossier, more slippery. Elusive trickles of water tease him. If he were alone he might venture to find them, but the most important thing right now is to find the key to removing their live shackles. It's not far. The breeze blowing up from the heart of the crater is a big help. It draws, with scents, an invisible road map of everything he's likely to encounter in a given direction.

"I'm telling you, this is, like, totally the wrong way." The girl grumbles but she doesn't protest strongly. That spurs him on. And the farther they go, the closer to him she stays. That means he no longer has to resort to running ahead out of sight. No, whenever she stops to sulk or to feel sorry for herself, he just tugs her sleeve.

"Okay, okay. I'm coming!" She gives a long, fed-up sigh and dawdles by fiddling with her hair at the back. It irritates him because they're so close to their goal. He rears up on his back legs, risking the pain of constriction, and paws her hands away from her hair.

"Ouch! God, when did *you* get so bossy?"

He sets off again, glancing back every few seconds to make sure she's coming.

"You're like a doggy version of a Sergeant Major," she says. "Like in those old war movies." Nursing the back of her hand where his claw accidentally grazed her, she adds, "You know what? I think I'm gonna call you Sarge from now on. You really are bossy enough, Bossy Boots. You can be Sarge. Yeah. And that makes me a private, I think. Private something. What do they use – last names? Private Tiernan. *Eeuw, no!* I don't like that. I would *never* answer to that. My full name, Sarge, if you really must know, is Dorcas Molly Tiernan – Molly is my mom's name as well – but all my teachers call me Dorcas, so I guess you can too." She takes a pause. "Uh-huh. I've decided, Sarge, I don't like the whole *private* thing. I'm going to be just Dorcas. I think we can get along okay with that, don't you?"

He wants to focus completely on the source of the scent up ahead – so close now he can practically taste it – but he's growing fond of her voice. It isn't adorable like Jan's, but it sounds playful, silly. He finds himself listening to each and every silly word.

"Sarge, if this is a shortcut home, I'll take back every bad thing I said about you. But I really think we'd be better off waiting on the beach."

The faint smell of the sea grows stronger with every step. But the beach lies behind them. If there's seawater up ahead, is this an island they're on? If so, how big is it? Are there other islands nearby, a chain of them perhaps, like those around his and Jan's home in the Keys? He wants to know more, *needs* to know more.

Some of the most pungent local smells he's found outside of the eastern equatorial rainforest abide right here, all around him in a misty grotto the size of Jan's shuttle garage. A variety of colorful flowers he's never come across before give off an even greater variety of scents. Some are foul. Some are inviting. Others combine to resemble the smells of dangerous animals. He can tell the difference, but maybe other intruders can't. It's a deterrent he's found elsewhere, a kind of scented camouflage. If he had more time he'd sniff around this grotto to his heart's content. Jan would love it too.

Following his nose brings him straight to the origin of the singular scent he's tracked since the sand dunes. It's an unremarkable plant in every other way. A white, grooved stem that stands stiffly upright, with generous violet fronds that slowly – very slowly – tickle the stem in a winding, caressing motion, an action that produces the very particular scent he was able to discern from so far away.

There are two problems, however. The plants are not on the ground. They grow in the silty hollows of a tree with silvery bark. The hollows of this tree are cavities running half the length of its thickest branches. Only one of the plants is within Stopper's reach, and even that one just barely. He would have to climb for the rest, but he cannot climb trees. Neither could his mom or dad. It is one of the many things humans can do that he can't.

So he scrambles up and tears a jawful of fronds from the lowest plant. Wasting no time, he takes them to the girl and begins to rub the bulbous ends of the fronds against the skin of the creature coiled around her leg.

The girl pulls away but he persists. She tries to run, so he bowls her over and lies across the backs of her legs to immobilize her. He continues applying the mysterious substance. He doesn't know how it works, only that it worked for Jan. Ignoring her cries of pain is one of the hardest things he's ever done, but it's either this or they both don't make it home. He can't reach the other plants. She can't climb the tree to get them unless he removes this parasite.

Jan would call him a "clever boy" for this. She often does when his instincts drive him to do things he's never done before. Anticipating her "clever boy" reaction is one of the main reasons why he tries to muck in and help her so much. It yields him the best treats. He thrives on that approval. It pushes him to see around obstacles and situations in new ways, and his actions sometimes – not always – leave her gaping at him, love filling her adoring eyes. He can't explain how he can suddenly see past obstacles when before he couldn't, but it has a lot to do with Jan, he knows. In the words themselves: "clever boy." In the way she speaks them. And most importantly in the way he anticipates them.

Shortly after he's finished rubbing the frond heads to squelchy nubs against the parasite's skin, there's movement. A shudder at first, followed by a jiggle. The distended veins start to pulse, then to quiver. Stopper stands upright, panting. Backs away a little. The girl lies still, pale and shaking in horror. The creature stiffens. He wonders if he's done something wrong, if Jan did something he didn't see. Panting and slavering, he drops the headless fronds from his mouth. Catches the girl's terrified sidewise glance. Then, with a slither and a snap the creature flies off her leg. It disappears into the undergrowth in the opposite direction of the silver-barked tree and the plants with violet fronds.

The girl gapes at him for a moment. It isn't Jan's approving, utterly adoring gaze, but he's feeling that same anticipation of her reaction just the same. Instead, she scrambles to her feet and runs behind him, where she crouches, hiding. There's no sign of her parasite. They both watch the undergrowth in silence. Then something happens that makes the whole ordeal worthwhile. She slides her little arms around his neck and, nestling her head against his, whispers, "Is it gone?" When he's done licking her ear, she adds: "Okay, okay, I knew you were sweet, and I know you're bossy, but I had no idea you were so *smart*. Sarge? How clever *are* you?"

He wriggles free of her embrace and limps back to the tree. Gazing up at the fronds, he starts to bark.

"Ah, so that's it. You need me to go up there and get some more for your horrible thingy?"

He looks at her, tail wagging, then reaffixes his stare on the fronds.

"Cat claws, dog paws. You can't climb, can you. You're a clever boy but I guess you can't do everything yourself." She gives him another hug. "Okay, time me, Sarge."

Gone is her limp. Her lollygagging is a memory. She's not very agile – Jan can bound around with a lot more spring – but the little girl manages to twist and haul herself up between at least four tangled branches. There she crawls out on her hands and knees along a precarious limb, to where the plants are most numerous. She wobbles a little, has to steady herself when she tries to tear out a fistful of fronds. It takes her three more tries with her legs astride the branch for better balance.

The way her face lights up when she reaches the ground and runs toward him is like something from a dream. He's so happy she's safe, so happy that she's so happy, he lets loose a giddy bark of pleasure. If he could speak the words he would, but a bark is the best he can do.

Clever boy, he tells her as she does for him what he did for her.

"You and me, Sarge, we're a unit now," she tells him, rubbing the frond heads on his parasite's skin like crazy. "Our mission is to find a way home, okay?"

Chapter Seven

Despite having gone almost two days and nights without sleep, Jan marched up the sandy verge with a spring in her step. She glanced over her shoulder down toward the sheltered inlet where she'd left the Nakamoris aboard the *Alcyone*. Their voyage had not been a long one. Ichi had done a remarkable job of gathering data using her instruments and fluid charts and the *Alcyone's* own readings taken during the previous night's search. Once she'd determined the likely direction the storm and the ocean currents had whisked Stopper and Dorcas – the coordinates at which the girl's life-jacket had been fished out certainly tallied – they'd all decided it was useless to continue the search by boat. Given the strength of the currents and the time they'd been adrift, if the two castaways had reached land at all it would almost certainly be in that vast, mostly unexplored archipelago far to the southwest. Time was now the crucial factor; if she was alive, the girl had a few days' worth of oxygen at most; once the compressed reserves in her breather were exhausted, the intake filter would automatically kick in, attempting to separate the sparse oxygen content from the otherwise poisonous Hesperidian air. The only realistic chance Jan had of spotting them before that filter finally gave out was from the air. And the more craft she could employ, the greater her odds of success.

Rhombus Cove lay beyond the next rise. Like most of the geographical features of this region, it had a name so boring and obvious it could have been thought up by the dumbest flying computer exploring the planet on its own. Which was precisely the case – though the Mk. 48 'Eagle Scout' had been cutting edge at the time, well over a decade ago, an A.I. aerial mapper whose relatives had done much of the initial gaming and naming on dozens of worlds. One of these days, Jan mused, she'd have to provide the maps of Hesperidia with some real color, some real personality. Rhombus Cove sounded like it belonged in the least interesting board game ever devised by the saddest high school math club reject of his generation, during detention. And she'd been *in* the math club – and detention, more often than any other girl in her year, if memory served. Random flashbacks of blazing rows with her teachers, her parents, fights with classmates, with her brothers, with kids from the neighboring settlements: combined, they painted a fairly monstrous picture of that always-angry girl who'd never felt like she belonged. Colonial life could be bleak. Community cohesion hung by a thread. It was easy to slip into irrelevance in those backwater settlements. Too easy. For any girl longing for a life of independence, of rock-hopping, it wasn't fight or flight; it was fight *for* flight. That shuttle off-world was not cheap. Either you were born with the knack for clip-spinning, that entrepreneurial gene, or you worked your little hiney off at school and fought tooth and nail to get noticed by the regional Scholarship Board.

Jan had worked, fought, loved, played, and died hard ever since. She'd never have gotten this far otherwise. And those same attributes were driving her now as she scrabbled up the steep verge onto the mossy summit overlooking Rhombus Cove.

"You've got to be kidding."

She crouched on the cliff edge, gathering her breath, and muttered every swear word in her considerable arsenal. Invented a few new ones. Why hadn't anyone warned her? The enormity of it, the sheer megalomaniacal brazenness of the operation unfolding below, was hard to swallow. Milady had led her to believe the salvage was some sort of family affair, one sister sneaking in to get the jump on the other, maybe landing a couple of boats and submersibles apiece for an underwater search and retrieval of a lost heirloom. Or something.

Instead, it was an industrial scale invasion! Hundreds of state-of-the-art craft of all shapes and sizes, designed for air, sea, or land, or any combination thereof, gathered into clusters across the huge shale beach. Medium-sized shuttles constantly took off and came in to land via a large cleft opening in the cliff wall, which became a dusty valley winding far inland to the southeast; access was fairly easy and private. The biggest transport shuttles had to have landed either somewhere up-valley or offshore, because several of the amphibious craft here were far too big for any birds of sufficient heft to have made a safe beach landing. Indeed, wheeled amphibious vessels were still grinding out their very own shale trails as they arrived via the valley opening.

Jan wasted no time in picking her way down the craggy cliff face. It wasn't as difficult as it looked from above, and she soon found herself grinding tiny rocks underfoot as she marched toward what appeared to be the command trailer near the rear of the beach. She clocked the satellite dish on top, as well as the officious-looking types milling about outside with their expensive comm tech and spiffy head rigs and breathers.

With the vehicles and vessels arranging themselves into like groups all around her, it felt as though the war had come to Hesperidia, and that she was so out of her depth in this military theater that perhaps she'd missed some catastrophic news from elsewhere in the galaxy; maybe this was the last untouched planet, the final haven for humanity. All these crazy thoughts and more assaulted her as she strode through countless judging stares, past more hardware than she'd ever seen assembled in one place. At the end of this, anything less than an Omega Fleet Admiral or Wing Marshal and she'd be disappointed.

"And you are?" an insistent male voice caught her from the side. Jan halted, chose the shortest guy in a group of several over-dressed squibs poring over a flexi document one of them was holding. They all gawped at her in unison, but in her experience a man's height and his authority tended to have an inverse correlation – the shorter the man, the bigger his ambition. Something to do with over-compensating.

"Who's in charge?" she asked Shorty.

"I am." he replied, looking over her casual attire. "Which one are you again?"

"Doctor Jan Corbija, resident xenozoo—"

"Yes," he interrupted. "One of the caretakers. I thought we made it clear that you're not to interfere with operational personnel."

"Oh? I mustn't have got that memo."

"We're a little busy, Miss …"

"Corbija. Doctor."

He pressed a button on the temple of his breather, which flicked the dark tint from his visor for a few moments, long enough for Jan to get a good look at his face – youngish, maybe late twenties, with pale, shiny skin, almost porcelain-like as the sun hit it, and a breezy, high-school jock confidence that didn't impress her in the least. Her college days had been full of boys like him. Boys who knew, and had always known, that their futures were paved with the bright sheen of privilege. They'd never really had to fight for a single thing they'd gotten.

"The name rings a bell," he said. "Mine's Haneke." One of his colleagues immediately signaled to an underling across the beach.

"So the buck stops with you?" Jan asked Haneke.

She could feel him weighing her up from behind his darkened glass, figuring out the most expeditious way to remove her from his neat and polished little sphere of influence. No way was he in charge, then. If he was, he wouldn't have hesitated to flash his title in her face. So he had to be careful not to make waves here. His career prospects might be on the line. If he didn't have the authority to get rid of her, she had the upper hand. And he'd asked: Which one are you? Which suggested some of her colleagues were involved in this project, only they'd kept it from her. Not her favorite deduction of the day.

"The resident personnel are supposed to report to Epsom," he told her. "You should head on over—"

"Is Epsom in charge of this operation?"

"He's the liaison for resident personnel. A good man. He'll answer all your questions." Haneke pointed her to a large trailer being dragged into position by one of the multi-tasking amphibious vehicles.

Jan plucked a small husk of dried seaweed off her shoulder. A breeze had got up. It was blowing bits of flotsam inshore; several clung to Haneke's posse. "If it's all the same to you, I want to speak to the person in charge," she said. "It's important. Can you point her out?"

"How did you know it was a woman?" one of them asked.

Jan shrugged. "Just a hunch. Hickey here seems reluctant to tell me who's holding his pink-slip. Either he's under orders not to give out that name – unlikely, seeing as everyone can see everyone at this picnic – or he doesn't want to admit his balls are a purse-snap away from being the property of a lady."

"Uh-huh. Mouthy little piece, aren't you." Not one of Haneke's most cutting retorts, she wagered.

Jan sighed. "Just point her out. I've told you it's important, and urgent."

"Like I said, there's – *ah!* No need. Here they are now." He turned to one of his colleagues who was jabbering into a private comm channel, and flicked him a knowing wink. To Jan: "Epsom's the bald gent out in front. He'll sort you out. The others I believe you already know." The note of spiteful sarcasm in Haneke's voice shrank him even further in her estimation.

Meanwhile, the line-up of her colleagues following Epsom like so many obedient goslings waddling up the beach didn't exactly improve her mood. Her immediate thought: why hadn't she been included? For something this big, this important, in *her* back yard, surely they should want to at least give her the heads up. Her second thought: they knew her well enough by now to know she'd never fall in line and submit to anyone else's authority on the Hesp. She'd never personally claimed any kind of leadership, but they'd often joked that when it came to this planet, there was God and then there was Jan, and not necessarily in that order.

Two out of the seven rangers waved. She couldn't quite tell who was who until they got a bit closer; they all wore matching green-and-gold *Alien Safari* vests and those godawful standard issue khaki shorts that writhed up into your butthole at the least physical exertion. Ken Oswambe, the geologist (and notorious polygamist) was there, and

Shirley Albright, one of the elderly botanists ISPA had sent in to synthesize antibiotic serums derived from the high-altitude orchids in the far north. They were both a long way from their usual haunts. But they were also the best in the business in their respective fields; hiring them as advisors was a smart move, Jan had to admit, as much as it stuck in her craw to see colleagues she admired herded around and referred to as "caretakers".

Pavel Karkova, the scruffy Russian naturalist, refused to look her in the eye. And rightly so – in going along with this, he'd proved himself a complete hypocrite. After all that big talk about leaving money and authority behind for a mould-breaking career with alien nature, he'd taken his paycheck *and* his orders along with the rest of them. Natty Randall, too, the little turncoat, had dropped her precious (and hugely important) study of winged insect migration across the Avalon mountains in the east, in order to feather her retirement nest a little. No wonder she looked so sheepish.

And the others? Well, if there was a silver lining here it was that at least they hadn't *all* been bought. In total, there were a couple dozen top-ranking scientific personnel on Hesperidia now, and Epsom only had seven in tow.

Jan snapped off a sarcastic salute in their direction. One of them actually saluted back – Shirley Albright, who'd waved the first time around as well, clearly seeing the fun side of all this.

Epsom, bronzed, solid-built, bald as a golden egg, kept his "caretakers" back as he approached Jan, extending his hand to her. She gave him the benefit of the doubt and shook it. His grip was weaker than hers, not a great sign.

"So, Honky here tells me you're the man to see," she said.

"It's *Haneke,*" the little man corrected her. "Try to remember it, Missy."

She snorted a laugh, jabbed her thumb in his direction. "He just called me Missy. That's wild. Where was I? Oh yes. Epsom, is it?"

"Pleased to meet you, Doctor Corbija." At least the man's warm smile seemed more genuine than Haneke's. "I understand you need some help with a missing person?"

"Two missing. If you could spare a handful of fliers and pilots for a day or so, our odds of finding them would increase a hundredfold. And my colleagues, too, if they could help with the search, that would be fantastic. It's really quite urgent. The girl only has another thirty-six hours' oxygen at most."

"I'm sorry to hear it."

"Three fliers are all it would take. Or as many as you can spare. Obviously, the more the merrier."

As one side of his mouth hiked up, it gave off an odd clicking sound. "Here's the thing …"

"Don't tell me that. Tell me you'll help. You're the only chance I've got." She whipped a stinging glance at her colleagues. "Or should I go straight to them, ask them what they think?"

"They've signed contracts, I'm afraid. As have all the other personnel here. Without a direct say-so from Miz De

Brock, they're all obligated to do exactly what they've been hired to do."

Jan rudely mimicked his empty talk with her fingers wagging onto her thumb. She did it right in his face. "You're not in charge. You're just a politician. Why am I talking to you?"

He shifted his weight, nodded contemptibly at her a few times. "Ralph Epsom, official committee delegate, Core Congress. One word from me and you'll be watering daisies on a nursery school porch for the rest of your so-called career. Just so you know who you're insulting."

"Keep talking, Baldy." She repeated her chatty hand gesture. "One word from me and you'll have Omicron's best agent digging so far into your shit you'll suffer night terrors for every dicey thing you've done since Third Grade, including jerking off to Ariel the Little Mermaid in your mom's brassiere. Just so you know who *you're* insulting." She took a step toward him. "Put me in touch with the woman in charge and stop acting like you're in any way calling the shots here, Core Congress."

"Has anyone ever told you you have a big mouth?"

"Uh-huh." Jan sighed, glanced around the beach trying to locate the elusive Miz De Brock. She strode about and raised her voice to a shout: "I'm looking for the woman in charge! Miz De Brock, where are you? This is a matter of life or death. I need your help. Just a few minutes of your precious time. Miz De Brock, where are you?"

"Stop that!" Epsom told her, mindful of the scores of personnel who'd flat-out stopped what they were supposed to be doing and were staring instead. "Stay right where you are." After stiffening his posture and pursing his lips, he gestured to Haneke and then stormed off, shooing the other rangers away with him. About a minute later, Haneke tapped his e-pen on the side of his headset to get Jan's attention, then pointed it at the shoreline. "The woman with the short red hair. White suit. You tell her what's so urgent, maybe she'll let you meet Miz De Brock. But I wouldn't bet on it, *caretaker*." He sniffed a chuckle, then returned to his confab with his underlings, most of whom towered over him.

Jan marched down to the water's edge, where a stocky redhead with a bob cut and a physique more suited to cage-fighting than a personal assistant stopped her short of the reaching surf. The woman's wrinkled brow said she frowned for a living. But she also had an open, honest face, someone who knew how to be reasonable.

"Miss Corbija?"

Jan accepted the woman's handshake, as firm as her physique had suggested. "Hi. I was told I could have a word with the person in charge. It's an urgent matter."

"Okay. If you give me the heads-up, maybe I can help. Miz De Brock is extremely busy right now."

"Mm. I've been through this twice already, but okay. If you're authorized to loan me a few of your fliers and pilots, then maybe we don't need to disturb her."

The woman slowly, pensively creased her brow into a mother of a scowl. It made her look twenty years older.

"Are you serious? Loan from *us?* Do you know who Miz De Brock is, who she's brought with her?"

"I know precisely shit about any of you, lady, and I don't much care. I'm just here to save two lives – my boy's, and the little girl who was swept away with him last night. I need help searching for them."

"Swept away? In that storm?" The woman un-balled her fists onto her hips, cupping her waist. "I'm sorry to hear it."

"Thanks. Can I have the fliers?"

"Well, it's just that we've—"

"It's a simple enough question," said Jan.

"No. It really isn't." The woman's affable personality had a steel undershirt, Jan realized. She was likely ex-law enforcement or ex-military, but well-adjusted enough to have calibrated both sides of her character – the civil and the uncivil – to become an ideal bodyguard for the elusive VIP, Miz De Brock.

"I'm running out of time," Jan reminded her. "Whatever prize you people are here for, it can't be more urgent than mine."

The woman looked Jan up and down a few times. "You know, you're nothing like your colleagues. Browbeating a Core congressman like that takes a special kind of woman. Are you sure we can't hire you? After you've done what you need to do, that is."

"Save it, whoever you are. I'm just here for the fliers."

"Kincaid," the woman said. "The name's Kincaid. I doubt Miz De Brock would be willing to spare more than a couple of single fliers, but I tell you what: you've impressed me. Bulldozing your way past Jim Haneke *and* Congressman Epsom like that is no mean feat. So I'll put in a good word for you. Miz De Brock will have the final word, though. What she says goes, and right now she's as single-minded as I've ever known her. But good luck. Follow the surf in that direction." She motioned south along the shoreline. "You can't miss her."

"Thanks, Kincaid. You should know, you're not much like your colleagues either."

The big woman gave the slightest of bows, then marched off up the beach, clicking her fingers and pointing at two crewmen who'd sneaked off duty to build a rather rubbish sandcastle in the wet sand – shale was not good for building sandcastles.

Less than a minute's walk parallel to the surf brought Jan within sight of the elusive Miz De Brock at last. Having long since come to expect the unexpected on Hesperidia, she felt sure she'd seen pretty much everything this planet could throw at her. That was perhaps why a solitary leather armchair perched on the edge of the sea struck her as so surreal. Banal human comfort in the throes of wild alien nature. The woman sitting on it appeared so restful, so ruminative, the rhythm of the surf all around her was so soporific, it could easily be a daydream.

The woman had long, flowing white hair, like her sister, Milady, but there the similarities seemed to end. Miz De Brock, while a few years younger than her sister, wore her age much more heavily. There was a gloominess about her, an almost gothic grayness in her aura, as though Milady had inherited all the vitality and this younger sibling had thus far sulked her way through life. It was a striking contrast, even in this first impression. It left Jan unsure of how to handle her.

"Kincaid tells me I should listen to what you have to say." The closer Jan got, the more distant the woman's voice seemed, as though there was an invisible fog surrounding her, marooning her in a time and place from long ago. A sad childhood spent in a garden of dashed dreams. "The operation won't begin proper until tomorrow," she added. "Right now we're marshalling the fleet, finalizing things. It's going a lot smoother than I thought. Those men you were rude to are actually doing splendid work. I'd hate to see it all unravel because we're missing vital air support."

"With all due respect, we have different definitions of the word *vital*." The gradual weariness Jan had felt earlier that morning returned with a vengeance, bleeding into her calf muscles. She crouched beside the armchair, then sat on the sand, crossing her legs. "No one will tell me why you're all here, what you're looking for," she said, "but I know one thing: it isn't to save lives."

"Maybe not today. But soon, if we're successful, who knows."

Miz De Brock peered down at Jan once or twice from the corner of her eye. The rest of the time she gazed dead ahead, almost in a trance, out to sea. The effect was calming and chilly at the same time.

"What do you mean?" asked Jan. "What is it you've come all this way to find?"

"A life's work, Doctor, lost to us a long time ago. It's here, somewhere in the western ocean of your world. In this vicinity. I'm certain of it." Her responses were like cold flakes falling from some pesky pick chipping at her icy solitude. Reality was a distraction. Only her dream mattered. Her holy grail. Whatever the damn thing was.

Jan knew she'd have to try another tack. These bozos had brought everything including the kitchen sink with them, but common sense seemed to be the one thing in short supply.

"How about we do a trade?" Jan suggested.

"Excuse me?"

"Your help in exchange for mine. We're both searching for things we've lost. If you loan me the fliers and spotters I need, I'll give you the coordinates you need to start your search."

Now she had the woman's undivided attention. There would be no more flakes from now on, only avalanches. Pitting sister against sister in a family treasure hunt might be the only way to get what she, Jan, wanted right now.

"What coordinates? Who have you been speaking to?"

"A third party. She gave me explicit instructions to keep her presence and identity a secret from you. Unfortunately for her, I don't take orders from anyone, least of all someone who commits mutiny against me *and* is in large part responsible for everything bad that's happened since."

"*Imogen!*"

"Well, everyone seems to call her Milady."

"Typical. She always did love to show off her title – paid for by her first husband, I should add. Where is she?"

Jan shrugged. "I stole the GPS tracker with her first dive coordinates. You might want to start there. But I'd send remote vehicles if I were you. The creatures down there are big trouble."

Miz De Brock sat up straight, raked her hair back behind her ears, and gave off a dirty laugh of disbelief. "She actually had the crash coordinates all along! And here was me about to dredge an entire ocean if I had to. Tell me everything, Doctor Corbija. Everything she did, everything she said. There's no limit to how generous I can be if someone is useful to me."

Jan replied with a reserved nod. Meanwhile, her heart lit fireworks in anticipation of the greeting Stopper would give her, and vice versa, when they finally found each other. It wasn't a question of if, it was a question of when. To hell with probabilities. She *would* find him and the girl. Picking Milady's pocket might just be the smartest thing she'd ever done.

"Well, it happened something like this …" she began.

* * *

The afternoon had grown very gusty while they'd talked. Now, as Jan neared the top of the cliff on her way back to the *Alcyone*, reassured that by sun-up tomorrow she'd have a small fleet of fliers with which to conduct a thorough search of the southwest island chain, jabs of cold wind kept hitting her side-on, threatening her balance. She began to time her little clambers past the dangerous sections, hewing as close to the sheltered spots as possible. These tended to be populated by *elcipuli* and *valsirius Brevigum*, tough, firm-rooted, heather-like plants that she clung to umpteen times near the summit.

No sooner did she stumble onto the peak, exhausted, than a dazzling flash from the tall grass forced her to cover her visor. It had to be the sun reflecting off something, but what? She tromped through the swaying stalks, not wanting to leave any human litter behind. It was one of her pet hates on the Hesp, one she'd pestered her colleagues with for years. Most of them were as careful as she was, but it was the non-scientific visitors that tended to be cavalier when it came to their footprints. The younger tourists were the worst, and she'd had to embolden the font for the paragraph on littering in the official Alien Safari handbook.

A figure leapt up and darted out of the grass not five strides in front of her. Shuffling back, she lost her footing. Twisted her ankle in a divot. A splinter of pain shot up her leg, but she knew right away it wasn't serious. The number of sprains she'd suffered in the field over the years had told her when it was time to worry. She got up, limped after the fleeing man. He was nimble, despite carrying some kind of audio-visual recording rig over his shoulder. He had on a Gore-Tex jersey, blue jeans, and the exact same hiking boots she wore – Mons Endeavour, the old-fashioned lace-up variety.

"Just stop!" she called after him. "There's nowhere to go. Why are you even running?"

On his way down the steep, windswept slope, he stopped to glance back. Jan thought she'd seen him before but she was too tired to place him. Confident she could run off her ankle knock, she flung herself after him down the sandy decline. Her momentum got the best of her and she found herself airborne in all the wrong ways. One undignified faceplant later, she brushed herself off, reaffixed her breather, and took off after him with renewed poise, practically surfing her way down the sand.

He didn't stop running, even at the bottom where the sand gave way to a dicey rock shelf which the crashing waves had slowly eroded from below, leaving the surface pocked, rugged. Spray spumed up out of several holes in the rock, geyser-like but cold, showering the entire shelf, making it slippery.

She pulled her face at the thought of sliding about and bruising her ass all the way through *that*. But it was too late. Her mind was stuck in forward gear. She had to know who'd been spying on her, or if not her then the whole De Brock invasion.

Luckily, she didn't fall, only slithered. The shelf tapered to a slender finger of rock that stretched out a fair distance over the heaving water, only a few feet above sea level. It was sheltered from the wind on either side by a hidden gorge, sheer cliffs that towered almost to the height of the peak she'd just summited. The gorge also snaked northward, which probably explained why Jan hadn't seen this inlet before. From a vessel cruising the coastline it would not be visible.

She followed the man past the end of the promontory onto an even narrower shelf that skirted the right-hand cliff wall. This one climbed twenty or so feet above the water, at which point the only light was from directly above, the sliver of daylight tracing the course of the gorge.

Jan switched on the twin torches either side of her breather. Damp little grottos appeared in hollows in the cliff opposite, coated with curious white molds and sponges. Were they self-contained ecosystems? Everywhere was dank and eerie. The constant under-rumble of breakers outside and the echo-pops of moisture dripping into rock pools all around reminded her of the caving adventures she'd had as a girl, most of them forbidden. She'd always wanted to be an explorer, she remembered, and now she was living the dream in a way few humans had *ever* done. A rush of giddiness hitched her breath. For a fleeting moment she felt glad to be alive, thankful to be making up the rules as she went.

Yes, more than anyone's, this was *her* planet. She knew its dangers, its excitements, its secrets. She'd shared in so many of them. And no one was going to outwit her on Hesperidia. No one.

A nib of daylight in the rock ahead flared as she followed the winding ledge. The gorge opened onto an almost perfectly sheltered cove, bathed in sunlight but protected from the full force of the sea winds and the breakers by sheer cliffs all around. A single curved channel at the far side of the cove resumed the course of the gorge and fed directly to the ocean beyond, but, again, the gap was so well camouflaged by the shape of the cliffs it was almost invisible to the untrained eye. All in all, a splendid hideaway.

Her quarry had already reached his flier before she set foot on the powdery white sand. She was about to kick into a sprint to get there before he took off when the shadow of a cloud swooned over the beach, removing the blinding edge from the sun's reflection. She glimpsed the *Alien Safari* logo on the side of the man's craft – a clean-looking stork, one of the surface to orbit taxis that doubled as personal fliers for the rangers qualified to fly them. But which ranger had she been chasing? Who had taken it upon himself to spy on the De Brock operation?

Whoever it was, he wasn't working alone! A small group of six – no, eight people exited the stork and started toward her. One of them wore the dorky official ranger's uniform. Jan recognized his lanky, awkward urban gait right away. Bilali was a lab rat only playing at field science. While most of the other rangers liked to rough it on occasion in the wild, spending the night in a tent – taking the proper precautions, of course – Bilali was always back inside his safe little compound before bedtime. And where most scientists felt that overwhelming urge to explore this fascinating world at every opportunity, off the beaten path, Bilali stuck religiously to the rulebook, to his clockwork routines and familiar haunts. He was a nice enough guy, all told, but he was from an altogether different breed from Jan and those like her – the adventurers, the settlers, shaping new frontiers with their dreams and their fingernails. To someone like Bilali, biodomes were paradise. That control. That safety. Places where scientists could literally play God. But out here in the alien wilds, he was a frightened bunny rabbit; he clung to regulations and procedures because they were the only things that made him feel safe.

"What happened to *you?*" she shouted. "Engines die on you or something?"

He strode to the head of the group, threw his arms apart and shrugged. But why didn't he reply? And why had he flown tourists in this direction anyway? The other safari tours were all east of White Water.

"What gives?" No sooner had Jan asked the question than she saw the slim, gym-toned figure in the expensive custom survival suit. *Milady.* Together with all her mutineers. Bronston, towering over the others, brought up the rear. He was chatting with the man Jan had chased from the summit.

Suddenly it all made sense.

"Monthly stipend not enough for you, Bilali, you snake?" She lashed them all with an accusing glance.

"It's all good," he replied. "No harm done. The customers are all where they need to be."

"Not all," she reminded him.

Again, the empty shrug. "Hey, I've sent word to the other rangers to help you with the search," he said. "The rest is up to them. Who knows, maybe they're busy?"

"Uh-huh. Busy whoring themselves to the highest bidder. How does it feel, *brother?*"

"You make it sound like we're committing a crime."

Her turn to shrug. "I take it you're not going to help?"

Bilali shifted his weight, turned to Milady, who replied for him: "Word has it you've got all the help you need, Juanita. I see you took my advice. My sister drove a hard bargain, no?"

"The name's Jan. And let's just say she was a lot more cooperative than you were, *Imogen.*"

After silencing her men's protests – how dare anyone talk down to their beloved titled employer – Milady began to laugh, a loud belly laugh that both amused Jan and made her want to dry retch.

"Yeah. Let's see if you're still laughing when little sis snatches the prize right from under you." Jan stood her ground while the group of men encircled her. "So how much did Sneaky Pete there overhear? More than howdy-do, I take it?"

Milady's laugh tailed to a girly tinkle. She slowly shook her head as she approached Jan. "You shouldn't have stolen that tracker, and you really shouldn't have given it to Edith. It's forced me to up the ante. You won't like what that means, Juanita. None of you will."

"Threaten me one more time and they'll need more than a tracker to find what's left of you."

"Aha. There's that savage side again." Milady sidled up to her, rubbed the backs of her fingers against Jan's shoulder blade. "You really do belong here, don't you. I'm thinking permanently." She sidestepped to avoid Jan's aggressive grab. "Savage but slow. If you were half the woman you pretend to be you'd have made sure every last ranger on this planet had helped with the search last night. Every last one. Instead, you let that dumb mutt drift out of reach when you could have—"

The woman was flying backward into two of her men before Jan realized how quickly her fury had acted. The uppercut to the chin had not felt that hard to Jan, but it had *sounded* savage. Double-tap savage. It had caught Milady's chest on its way up to smashing the underside of her breather. She just hadn't anticipated that lightning blow – expected it, yes, but not at that speed. The woman's momentum bowled over both men who tried to catch her. She clutched at her sternum with one hand, struggling to breathe. Her other hand clawed at the cracks in her Plexiglass visor. Eyes as big as boiled eggs glared out, unseeing. She sucked in hurtful, choking breaths, coughed out whatever her lungs didn't like. But where was she most hurt? For chrissakes, had something *broken* inside? The crunch still echoed through the hot, close airways of Jan's own breather. It throbbed in her knuckles …

Her artificial knuckles! God. She'd forgotten all about the cybernetic surgery she'd had to reconstruct most of her right side after the first hydra attack. It had made her stronger than she'd ever cared to find out. The nerve repairs had made her quicker, too, at least on that side. No wonder Milady hadn't seen the uppercut coming. No wonder it had done so much damage.

"What the hell have you done?" yelled Sneaky Pete, the man she'd chased only a few minutes ago. She now recognized his face from the deck of the *Alcyone*. Smog Boy was here, too. They all rushed to Milady's aid. Only Bilali hesitated. He flashed Jan a wounded look, as accusatory as hers had been toward him a moment ago.

"What are you waiting for? Go get her a spare breather. *Now,* Benson!" Bronston's bark made its target, Smog Boy, jump up. He lost his balance and ended up crabbing back through the sand until he could regain his footing. "You! Bilali!" Bronston was getting ready to lose it. "Fetch your first aid kit or I'll break you in half."

Shaking, Bilali kicked into a knock-kneed jog.

Jan stood her ground, knowing she couldn't escape without being caught. They were circling her again now, four of them. The last man, Bronston, cradled Milady in his arms like she was his dying wife. Exactly who *was* she to these people?

"Listen, guys. This has all got way out of hand. I didn't mean to hit her so hard, I swear." Back-stepping only brought her nearer to the two men circling behind. Their shadows flanked her. "This is between your boss and me. I figure she'd want to fight her own battles. When she's better, she can always come find me, take a poke at me, whatever it takes. *This* – this isn't what she'd want."

"You know nothing," one of them snarled.

Before she could reply two of them rushed her from behind. Jan swung her augmented right arm as fast as she could, hoping to catch someone off-guard. But they were onto her secret. They ducked in unison. Lunged apart. One of them grabbed her right shoulder and hung on for dear life as she tried to fling him off. The bastard put all his weight flush against her shoulder joint. Even her extra strength counted for nothing; without room to swing she had no leverage.

The second man locked her left arm up behind her back. Exquisite pain shot through her. Despite kicking and squirming and spitting onto her visor, Jan could do nothing to break free. She was immobilized.

The other two ran in. Incensed, she reared up and nailed one with a kick to the neck. It wasn't her augmented right leg, though. That might have put him out of commission. Instead, he staggered a few steps before launching himself at her like a rabid Borgos dragon. His hateful scream terrified her, left her fearing this might be as far as she was meant to get – this day, this beach. His vicious kick found her exposed midriff. The pain was blunt and sharp at the same time, shocking her vitals. It knocked her sick. He kicked her again, this time in the ribs. Icy hot forks scraped the bones around her side and then stabbed deep, deep into her breaths.

Jan's vision misted. She couldn't see who it was who ripped her mask off, but it seemed as though it was from behind. A cool world of natural air rushed in like a sweetly toxic CPR breath. If she were of Hesperidia, it would be giving her life right now. But she was an alien here. This atmosphere that supported the billions of organisms she'd spent years caring for and protecting, would kill her in seconds. With arms she could barely move, she scrambled to locate her mask.

"I told you what would happen in you laid another finger on her." Without the echo chamber of her breather, Bronston's words sounded distant, unnatural. His was the voice of Death. "You're full of surprises, Juanita. In that, at least, you're nothing if not consistent. But where we're going, they're the wrong kind of surprises. And you're just the wrong kind of consistent." He yanked her head back by a fistful of hair. "I'd say it's nothing personal, but I'd be lying." The vague shimmering line of his outstretched arm led her to a figure as formless as running ink in the sand ahead. "You've hurt Milady, so I hurt you!"

Jan shut her eyes and coughed diamond splinters that jiggled around in ranks in her mind's eye. Bronston squeezed her mouth open while somebody else slugged her in the gut. She swallowed what had to be a fatal dose of her beloved planet's air and found she couldn't expel any of it, not even to cough. It was as though her sore abdominal muscles were tightening reef knots around her lungs, the whole shrunken mass of her vitals dying to explode but unable to, like a lit fuse fighting strong currents to ignite a powder magazine underwater.

I'm sorry, Stopper. I'm sorry, boy. I couldn't keep my promise.

Somewhere close she heard a crack. The hiss of thrown sand hitting metal. There were raised voices all vying for volume. The ground seemed to fall out from under her. For a moment she 'was airborne, and the whole planet seemed to flip on its head. The next thing she knew she was inside the echo chamber again. Inside but not sealed in. Being kicked and trampled was nothing now because her arms were free and she was able to cling to her breather with every quark of strength her body had in reserve. They would have to kill her and snap her rigor-mortised fingers before she'd relinquish this grip.

Breathing still hurt, her vision was still misty, her ribs and abs and pretty much every inch of her was sore, but Jan regained the wherewithal to affix her breather properly, to seal herself in. The next several gulps of oxygen were her most precious since birth. Meanwhile, the threats and the flying sand and the heavy blows and cries of pain no longer hurtled around her. They were off to one side. She got to her knees, nursing sore ribs. Blinked the tears from her eyes.

Two men were on the ground, motionless, while four more engaged in deadly combat. Bronston was one; she knew him from his height. Another was Sneaky Pete, whom she'd pursued from the cliff top. The sonofabitch who'd kicked her in the stomach first was there, too, fending off a barrage of blows. But she couldn't quite tell who was delivering them. He was agile as a *fellfiger*, and solidly built – she knew that much. Not dressed like a ranger, nor a tourist, nor even one of Miz De Brock's goons. Whoever this was who'd come to her aid, he was a) one ballsy hombre, b) handy in the various multidisciplined arts of how to kick unholy ass, and c) nothing short of her guardian angel, having dropped out of the sky in the nick of time like this.

She considered that for a moment. *My guardian angel.* And the truth washed over her like a warm shower shared with a lover at the end of a long and trying day.

"Vaughn!" she tried to shout, but her lungs blew out rasping heat instead. Forced her to cough. The coughs stopped at her ribs.

He turned and saw her, but had to block a haymaker from Bronston, who'd taken advantage of his distraction. With a deft counteracting move Vaughn got inside the big man's reach and locked him in close. He then swiveled him off balance for a powerful hip toss. Bronston hit the ground hard, but not hard enough. Vaughn finished him with a karate blow to the base of his neck.

Jan struggled to her feet to help him, but she was too weak to move fast. Sneaky Pete, in attempting to blindside Vaughn, also queered his last colleague's pitch by stepping in front of his attack. The two collided. Sneaky Pete untangled himself first but it was too late. Ever decisive, Vaughn swept the man's legs from under him, then when he was down, kicked his mask off and bloodied him with a stomp to the nose. The final attacker threw himself at Vaughn in desperation. By virtue of sheer weight and momentum, and of the awkward angle at which he hit, he landed a painful blow to Vaughn's shoulder. Jan could tell it had really stung her man, maybe even as bad as a dislocation. Vaughn yelled with fury (though with Ferrix Vaughn the line between pain and fury tended to be blurry), and launched a vicious kick at the man's kneecap. He put all his weight into it, so that it folded the man's leg back sixty degrees the wrong way. Such a prolonged wail of distress she hadn't heard outside the empty nest of a female hornbill.

Somewhere near the water's edge, Bilali and Smog Boy nursed Milady. They'd dragged her well clear of the fighting and had covered her with a survival blanket from the first aid kit.

From the looks of it, Vaughn hadn't killed any of the mutineers. But they were all down for the count. *All five of them,* Smog Boy notwithstanding. In bad shape, too, a few of them. Bilali's mandatory medical training would have to suffice, because neither Jan nor her guardian angel would lift a finger to help them, she knew.

My guardian angel.

He limped over to her, holding his left arm stiffly at his side. She limped to meet him, holding her dagger-sharp ribs.

"Tell me, is there anyone in this galaxy you *haven't* managed to piss off during the last forty-eight hours?" He shook his head as he spoke, but there was that ironic glint in his eye, that wry curl of the edges of his lips that said: *No matter how much trouble you get us into, you always make me glad to see you.*

"Tell me, is there ever a rendezvous in this galaxy you're actually on time for?"

"This," he replied. "If I hadn't been, you'd be sea food by now."

"Vaughn?"

"Hm?"

"I'm really tired."

"I can't say I'm surprised."

They didn't dare hug one another. Fear of literally falling to pieces tended to have that effect. But they clasped hands and kept them clasped, all the way to Vaughn's ship, the *Pitch Hopper*. As it turned out, he'd left it in a nearby cove, mere meters away from the *Alcyone*.

Chapter Eight

In the quiet moments, when Dorcas rests to gather her breath or empty the sand and grit from her boots, watching her occasionally fills him with wonder. She and Jan are so alike in so many ways: the way they huff and puff when things aren't going their way; how they twine locks of their hair around their fingers when they're thinking; the slow but steady way they run, as if they're carefully measuring every stride; the same loud, confounding bursts of happiness that Jan and Vaughn sometimes refer to as "laughing", but that don't correspond to anything Stopper or his parents could do, and that he's never sure how to react to; the same bright eyes; a similar hunch of the shoulders whilst moving; the same slender, wiry frame that's tougher than it looks; and a similarly – if individual – non-threatening female scent. She's a smaller, less confident version of his beloved mistress.

But there are many secrets in the ways she differs from Jan. As Dorcas sits cross-legged on the damp moss, staring at a babbling blue waterfall, quieter than he's known her since the beach, a few of those secrets nag at him like the wayward trickles that tickle the rock behind the falling stream.

She came down from the sky. Most of the human visitors he and Jan encounter seem to come down from the sky. Those sky ships tend to be bigger than Jan's sea ship, a lot bigger than the striped ship she flies the two of them around in when there are no human visitors. But where do those sky ships come from? Where do they go when the visitors leave?

He looks up but can only see the sky as slits and dots between the choking foliage. A lip of gray rock overhangs the slick wall of this new crater – a crater inside the larger crater – hiding the sun. But it doesn't stop him wondering. When night falls, those slits and dots of sky will be replaced by pinpricks of glowing light in the blackness. Lots and lots of them. Are those where the sky ships fly to? Are they islands like the Keys where he and Jan live, with lights that come on at night? Does Vaughn visit those islands when he leaves? Which one does Dorcas live on?

The idea puzzles and excites him in that *attaboy* way Jan would understand … if only she were here and he could make the same sounds she makes …

He sits on his haunches, looks away from Dorcas for a moment as a memory of his parents hits – slashes and dots of memory, smells of love and fear, that overwhelming feeling of belonging. He misses them, but though he remembers inklings of them every day, countless times a day, this is the first time in a long time he's been able to see them so clearly in his mind's eye, as if they were there, gazing back at him from inside the shadow of the overhang.

It leaves him wondering something he's never wondered before: why aren't there more like him on the Hesp? When his parents were killed, he was the last of his kind. But why? There are more than one of every other creature he's encountered here. And no other creature's scent is even remotely like his parents'. He can't help thinking of those islands in the sky. The sky ships. Are there others like him up there on the islands, where the human visitors come from? Is that where all humans come from – where *Jan* came from?

The idea puzzles and frightens him, so he trots over to Dorcas and gives her a nudge, reminding her she can't rest here all day. They really need to move on. The light will be fading soon, and with it his chances of outwitting any predators that thrive at night. Seeing in the dark is not one of his strengths. In fact, Jan, with her silly-looking goggles, is usually much better than him at finding her way around when the sun goes down. But Dorcas doesn't have those goggles.

"Aye, aye, Sarge." She snaps a salute at the waterfall, then groans as she gets up. "How are you not tired? I feel like I've been walking *forever*." Her attempt to cuddle him would ordinarily be very welcome, but he recoils. Something is awry. He can sense it all around them, like the prickly air before a storm. Stopper backs away from her, doesn't let her touch him.

Cascades of slick, orange-brown weed drape over the lip of the inner crater behind them, smothering the branches of trees and pooling about the boles. As well as giving off an unpleasant odor, they hide the space behind the trees, offering good cover for any sneaky creature. The drape-weeds line the path they've taken for a long way now. But this is the first time he's sensed … whatever this is he's sensing.

"What is it, Sarge? What is it, boy?"

Whatever the new creature is, it's downwind of them. It has the advantage. Luckily there isn't much of a breeze; it isn't constant either. During those lulls his smell sense quests and his fear bristles. The danger inches closer, though not close enough – yet – for him to try to deter it with his bark. Unable to gauge its size or ferocity, he retreats. Tugs Dorcas to follow him. She swallows hard and obeys. They take off downhill, picking their route around the copses of weeping trees, on a spongy surface so slippery the girl struggles to keep her footing. The way winds gradually into the depths of the crater, tier after tier of vaguely spiraling rock saturated with water and freshness and the seeds of life. It grows so warm he starts to pant. Dorcas has to keep wiping the mist from her visor. Her skin is almost as wet as when he first pulled her out of the sea.

Meanwhile, somewhere on their trail, always behind, ever hidden, the unknown creature bides its time, tracking them into a place Stopper cannot predict, cannot trust. He has no choice. Instinct is his only guide now. It told him to come this way and it still does. It is his first and last and best weapon, honed by forces he knows not, on worlds he's never dreamed of, over millions of generations of survivors of which he will probably be the last.

He is a woman's best friend. The first canine ever born on Hesperidia. This is his home, the only home he's ever known, and it's never liked him much. Funny, that – if it weren't for Jan, he wouldn't like it much either. But the thought of being with her again is the promise of so much joy that the quicker he runs, the more he aches inside with love for the place they call home. For the scent of the sea is growing stronger. He can hear crashing waves far ahead.

"Sarge, stop moving so quick! *Don't you know I can't see where I'm going?*" The sharp edge in her voice gives way to a long, ragged puff of frustration. Even though he's let her hold on to his tail for guidance, she struggles with her footing on the wet moss. It's stifling hot, almost choking. He can see only phantom outlines of the shape of the cave and the obstacles in their path: rocks, knotted roots coated with a kind of mucus, pools of hot, sometimes scalding water. It's hell down here. But there's that near-constant summons wafting into his nostrils, beckoning him on, ever on through the gloom.

"Just slow down a bit, will you, just so I can – *ugh!* – see what I mean? That nearly broke my ankle. You're going to kill me if we don't slow down."

He can hear the displeasure in her voice but he can't tell what she wants, and he can't make any more concessions for her. The creature is still following them. Exactly how close it is he can't be sure, nor can he stop to check. But it's there, always there, spurring him on as much as the scent of seawater does, maybe even more so. He's parched now and can't stop licking his lips, tonguing the moisture that drips down his face. He fantasizes about Jan pouring him a bowl full of cool water or yummy goat's milk. And he could easily scoff ten full bags of Rip 'Ems in one go.

Just as the steam in the cave grows thickest, blinding him completely as it billows up from vents in the rock floor, he hears cascading water. Not just the moisture running down the walls of the cave or the steady streams falling from the points of stalactites; no, there's much more: a waterfall, maybe several waterfalls.

"It's burning," she says, and starts hissing her breaths through gritted teeth. Jan never does that, but he can sense that determined vibe the two of them share when things get tough. The little girl has grown strong – stronger than he could ever have guessed when he was barking at her pitiful antics on the beach. "I don't like saying this, but I think we need to go faster," she adds. "Come on, Sarge. I mean it. We're seriously going to get cooked if we stay here!"

Though he has no notion of what she is telling him, Stopper is of the same mind. The gurgling hot pools are only small but they dot the cave floor with increasing regularity; thick columns of steam swirl and about-face under punches of through-draught to form a choking fog that stews the two of them as they soldier on. He's beginning to think he's picked the right direction but the wrong passage to it; many is the time he's pinpointed Jan's position in some strange locale and charged unheeding toward her, only to run into trouble – one of Hesperidia's countless nasty natural surprises – before he's got there. Over time he's become quite shrewd at picking the safest paths, but he's also aware that sometimes there is no such thing as an altogether safe path. He doesn't really want to go on through this heat, but neither does he want to face the creature tracking them, not with the girl so vulnerable like this.

They jog until the pads on the underside of his paws are wrinkled and raw; he keeps slipping on the slick, scalding surfaces and cuts himself on the sharper rocks. Dorcas, too, has a torrid time staying upright. She's battered and bruised all over. She sobs in frustration. But the impenetrable fog frays as they trudge on. It thins to a wisp and is tinged with a pale blueish light. Stopper catches his reflection in the spread of moonlight on a puddle where he stops, panting for dear life. His tongue hangs lower than he's ever known it hang. He's soaked through as though he's just been swimming with Jan in their lagoon. He shakes himself off for the umpteenth time since entering the sweaty hell. Then he tests the puddle water, finds it tepid, and drinks until his insides tingle with delight.

The girl slides her mask off and drinks beside him, but has to put it back on again when she coughs.

"Is this the other side?" she says in a voice so weak and trembly it doesn't sound like Dorcas. She crawls through the puddle on her hands and knees and finds a raised, relatively dry rock ledge to curl up on. Still coughing.

Until they're free from danger, however, Stopper can only think in binary terms: the creature's following them, they have to keep moving. He bites at her sleeves and growls until she gets up, half-asleep. She tries to say something but her words slur into a sudden, startling *eep*. More painful-sounding hiccups follow. By the time she manages to quell them – by holding her breath and then exhaling slowly, just like Jan does – a glittering, winding carpet of night sky rolls forever above.

They're out of the cave!

Below, after a short trot over moonlit rock, he finds a bottomless black ravine. He can smell the sea in there but he can't hear it, almost as if it's been emptied recently. The breeze that's guided him off and on since the dunes is still here; its ingredients excite the same instincts, the same sense of purpose. Across the ravine is where he needs to go. In that direction lies the origin of a particular combination of trace scents that he can barely, barely discern. It's telling him home is far away. He doesn't care. He will find a way to reach the islands in the sky if that's where Jan is.

"Where does it even end?" The light shuffling steps, so different from her clumsy, frenzied strides through the hell-cave, distracts him for a split-second, but his attention shoots away. The shadows against the rock face behind him are not as vacant as they appear. A puddle's glassy surface has been broken, and not by the breeze. His hair bristles.

His shoulder muscles tighten. His upper lip recedes, quivering, showing teeth.

"Uh – I didn't see—"

And neither does Stopper, not until the girl's scream penetrates his guard and he wheels. It all happens so quickly, it's like one of those blindsiding breakers that curls over him just off the beach in the Keys. Dorcas's boots scuff the edge of the rock and fall from under her. The creature's large, pallid form dashes across the flat rock. It's bigger than him but not unlike him. Much leaner, rangier, with one big eye that covers most of its face, a mouth he can't see giving off raspy, guttural breaths, and a strange, hairless growth on the back of its neck. Stopper bolts to cut it off. He's also aware of the girl's precarious scrabbling. Whichever he chooses is a risk. She's almost over but not quite – fighting to hold on with crooked fingers.

He whips a ferocious snarl at the creature before they collide, just before he rears up. It checks its charge, stutters low to a halt in a last-ditch attempt to avoid him. This late submission incites him, sparks an angry desperate flash of dominance that takes him over. He sinks his teeth into the creature and drives it writhing and growling into the cold rock. It does its best to fight him off but he has no time for a contest. He must strike this warning so deep into its being than it will cower at even the memory of him.

From the throes of this fierce pummeling the creature manages to squirm away and retreat. Stopper relents just enough to let it escape. He immediately darts to save Dorcas, but he can't see her pale little hands or her wet hair catching the moonbeams. He doesn't need to recheck his bearings. This *is* where she was and now she isn't there. The notion that she's fallen into the bottomless ravine goes against every impulse that's spurred him on since the deck of Jan's ship. His dominance a moment ago peels back, exposing raw naked loneliness.

He barks so loudly it echoes through the canyon.

"Sarge!"

Ears pricked, eyes bulging, he peers over the edge.

"Sarge! Ah, there you are. You know, I think I've just been really lucky. Like, *really* lucky. If it weren't for this ledge, I might have, you know …"

He barks again, but this time he's jumping around, pawing at the edge like it's a distressing puzzle he can't solve. He's so relieved she's alive, but she's somewhere he can't reach.

"Is that thing gone?" she calls up. "It came out of nowhere. That's when I jumped back and lost my—Hey up! You'd better wait there, Sarge. There's a higher ledge a bit further on, just there. I think I might be able to climb onto it."

Watching her risk her life one feeble hand-hold at a time is agony. But she's doing her part to help him keep her alive. That's something. And it suddenly hits him: how hungry he is, how much that last fight has drained him. They need rest, but they also need to eat.

He glances around the desolate canyon, licking his lips.

Chapter Nine

Of the many types of search and rescue he'd undertaken in his career, this one, the aerial kind over water, endless, aimless water, sapped Vaughn's energy almost supernaturally. It wasn't that he was tired – he'd snatched over six hours' kip on and off since leaving Gilpraxia – but something in the lazy rolling rhythms of the sea kept tugging his gaze into neutral. Horrible really, because he loved Stopper, and not just for the big galoot's complete devotion to Jan; Vaughn had grown genuinely fond of him, enjoyed taking him for walks while Jan was busy with her lab work. He'd never had a pet of his own, or any children for that matter, so the bond had become important to him, unique. More than that, he just couldn't imagine Jan without Stopper. Or Hesperidia without the two of them together.

"Where are we?" he asked her, running the cooler tap and cupping a handful of water that he splashed onto his face. It sharpened him a little. He did it again. "Jan? Everything okay back there?"

"Huh?"

He heard a ping from the navigation console, swiveled to catch the flashing amber light on the display beside her vantage pod in the rear, where she was rapt in a high magnification search of the coastline. "Come on, Nature

Girl, stay with me." He banked a sharp left one-eighty to put them back inside the search grid they were supposed to be sweeping, based on the Japanese hydrographer's parameters. "I'm heading for the next island, south-south-west. Where does that put us?"

"Um, let me see … one of the Crescent Forty-Three islands, the remnants of an ancient supervolcano." Somehow, that verve in her voice refused to wane. Jan hadn't had a wink of sleep in going on three days now. He'd advised her to grab at least a couple of hours' kip, to recharge a little — what if she missed a vital visual clue through being overtired – but she'd just scoffed and pointed out the million visual clues she'd *certainly* miss if her eyes were shut. "That puts us at fifty-nine percent of Ichi's total search area," she added.

"Anything from the other fliers?"

"Nothing yet. But it's still early days. The winds were demonic that night, like you wouldn't believe. It could have blown them much, much further."

Vaughn sensed she was exaggerating, that she was deep in denial, but even so he wanted her like this, in full-on stubborn mode. Hell, Stopper and the little girl needed her like this. She'd pretty much managed an entire world singlehandedly for years precisely because she didn't surrender to Fate. She knew better than to put her life in the hands of something so insipid. "Okay," he replied. "Keep me updated."

The words struck him as cold and formal as soon as he'd uttered them; they left him acutely aware of the isolated rut he'd been in since the last time he'd spent time with her, months ago now. She was literally the only person in the galaxy he looked forward to confiding in, whom he knew genuinely liked to listen to his secret, off-the-record views on life as a rootless lawman in the stars. Alfreda, his official counsellor assigned by the Bureau, was never less than professional and insightful and nurturing and all that, but he'd skipped their last several sessions for one very good reason: she couldn't give Vaughn what he needed most, that messy, vital human connection a guy like him had to have. For in his own way, he knew, he was as reconditioned a version of himself as Jan was of herself, reconditioned emotionally, in his case, from the wreckage of the very act that had made him famous – and notorious – as an Omicron rookie all those years ago: arresting several close members of his own family for terrorism, including his mum and dad.

Strange, really. He'd talked about that at length with Alfreda, and she'd given him all kinds of honest insights and assurances that had assuaged his guilt at the time, but the effect had not lasted. The ensuing nightmares had persisted, always some vivid variation of being swallowed up by shame and a failure to protect those closest to him. But since saving Jan's life – and Stopper's – here on the Hesp, a little over two years ago now, he hadn't felt that same weight of responsibility to the job, that same need to qualify his family betrayal by proving himself the best lawman in the Bureau. No, he had different priorities now; they'd been seeping into his once impervious sense of duty ever since he'd escorted her to Med Lake following the hydra attack. Everything about that case, from the extraordinary alien contraband to his old mentor's betrayal, had shaken him, but thinking he'd lost Jan and Stopper there on that island inside the crater, seeing them crushed and lifeless like that, beyond all hope, had opened up something inside him he hadn't known before, a deep and cavernous capacity for love and grief, deep enough and cavernous enough to swallow tenfold the terrible pit that dominated his nightmares. And it was there, he felt, looking back, there in that infinitely empty place that heaved and swelled with primal urgency, ripping him like a soundless scream through the ribs of upturned hulls in a hurricane, that he'd known himself for the first time. Had truly known what it felt like to have nowhere to hide, no principles to piggyback on, no conscience with which to ward off those onslaughts of fear and doubt. He hadn't been Ferrix Vaughn in that moment. The old Ferrix Vaughn had died. And the person who'd emerged from the rainstorm on the island, seeing Jan miraculously alive, had been imbued with hope and all its mysteries. In some sense, ever since then, he hadn't really escaped the Hesp. Jan had always been there in his thoughts. And without his old guilt steering him, or his need to prove himself a bastion of lawfulness driving him to excel, he was caught between his old self and the new. Were they compatible?

What would Jan be like without her beloved Stopper? If she chose to leave Hesperidia – more than likely, if she lost her boy – what would she do? Where would she go? Would she want Vaughn to move with her, to stay with her? Options were not the problem; they were both smart enough and tough enough to make a go of pretty much any kind of life. But he'd never really thought about another career, and he didn't think she had either …

"Vaughn?"

"Yes?"

"What'll happen to those a-holes you marooned on the beach? I know you said Milady's injury isn't bad enough to ship her out to a med base, but I don't want her here either."

He sighed. "Well, I've tagged them all. They're officially under arrest until I can figure out what to do with them. And their craft is grounded. Beyond that, I guess it's up to that ranger guy to keep them safe till I get back – Bilulu, is it?"

"Bilali. I don't think he's up to it."

"That's too bad. He'll just have to do the best he can. He let them hire him, he can babysit them. A missing child takes priority. That's my end."

After a short silence, she replied, "I've missed you."

He turned to see if she was looking at him. She wasn't. "Yeah, I've missed you too. I mean it."

"I know." And now she did glance his way, but cheekily, from the corner of her eye. "I'd miss me too."

He checked his smile before it blossomed fully, or rather the gravity of their search checked it for him. "So, how've you been?" he asked. "Apart from, you know …"

"About the same. I'm thinking we might need a change of scenery. Me and Stops have both officially had enough

145

of sailing and tourists ... and waiting around for chump lawman boyfriends."

"Oh. Had a few since me, huh?"

"None that I'll ever tell you about."

He shook his head. "I feel their pain."

"Hmm. Speaking of wild animals, we're gonna need to find out exactly what these salvagers are here for," she went on, "before they cause some kind of ecological disaster. All that lumbering tech scouring my oceans – it's in violation of every preservation law known to mankind. Whatever they're looking for, they need to find it but quick. The big brass I leave to you; I know how much you love dealing with politicians."

"Yeah, I always try to shoot a few before breakfast. Does wonders for the constitution." Vaughn's mind scrambled to recall that pearl of a politician joke he'd overheard recently – Jan would love its dryness, if only he could get the wording just right – when the *Hopper's* automated switchboard voice awoke his headset with, "*PH7 secure ... two ... transmissions ... incoming.*"

He activated the autopilot and swung his pilot's seat across to the ancillary VDU on the portside dash. After inking in his Omicron ID, he quickly scanned the messages. The first was from Kraczinski himself, bootlegged through a sat net back-channel, while the second was an official long-range communique he'd simply forwarded by the same means.

The first read:

Hey Vaughn,

Hope you have some good news for me down there. I did a little digging and turned up some interesting info on the missing girl: DORCAS MOLLY TIERNAN, aged 9, is the daughter of Core Congresswoman MOLLY SCHAEFFER! Yes, that Congresswoman Schaeffer, the busty queen of filibusters. Tiernan is the girl's father's name — he died from rad exposure caused by an asteroid popper not long after she was born. Turns out the congresswoman was supposed to be taking her daughter on this Hesp safari tour herself when an emergency quorum was called, so she sent her sister along to babysit the girl instead: CAROLINE LAFAYETTE, aged 38, divorced.

As far as I know, news of the girl's disappearance hasn't left this sector. The assholes probably want it that way — no interference, right? But if you're thinking what I think you're thinking, that might be our ace in the hole. Bring Congresswoman Schaeffer into the game and suddenly it gets real interesting.

Let me know how you want to play it, bud. Give me the word and I'll deal her in.

Kraczinski

Vaughn didn't hesitate.

Messages received. Deal her in! Tell her we'll have a much better chance of finding Dorcas if the sat net is fully functional. And see if she can find out what the hell this salvage operation is about. Vaughn

He was figuring out exactly what he should tell Jan and what he should keep to himself when the second message flashed up on the screen. It was from Agent Sondergaard on Gilpraxia, scrambled with an extra layer of Omicron software encryption. Not just for his eyes only, but too sensitive to be logged on the official Bureau data stream. Intriguing. Vaughn leaned in close to read:

Agent Vaughn,

Just thought you should know, I've turned up some strange evidence in my investigation of the Moon Bridge bombers. Have you ever heard of something called THE SPEARHEAD PROJECT? *We ran a pattern trace through all of Rankin's encrypted comms to and from Gilpraxia, and this phrase kept coming up. We've also cross-referenced it with several data stream archives and it's cropped up in some unusual places, including a bunch of scientific correspondences, and even some government memos. It's all pretty sketchy so far, and I don't want to make any of this official until I can get a better handle on what is I'm dealing with. I remember two things you told me: never trust politicians, and always wait for the clear shot. If someone from government is involved with this, I need to be careful who I talk to, right?*

You've dealt with corrupt higher-ups before. How do you think I should proceed?

Sondergaard

Vaughn's first reaction draped him like an old, warm blanket. The kid was sensible after all, receptive to sound advice. Beneath the bravado, he knew his limitations and when not to push them. He'd make a fine agent.

Yet, several things about this case troubled him. They seemed to link intuitively but not in any way he could describe. Like jigsaw pieces to a blind man, the edges might seem to fit together, but without knowing the complete picture, the point was missing. Sondergaard was right not to proceed half-cocked.

And where had he heard that name before: Spearhead Project? It sounded so generic, it could be any of a thousand colonial construction projects or deep space exploratory missions; but still it rang a singular bell somewhere in his detective brain.

"Jan?"

"Huh?"

"Ever heard of a Spearhead Project?"

"Mm. Can't say that I have. Except … Spearhead, Spearhead … What is it?"

"Not sure. Something scientific and secretive."

"Okay, you've just narrowed it down to every R and D project ever," she said.

"Doesn't leap out, then?"

"Not as such. But my gut's telling me it's linked to something or someone off the beaten track. A case study maybe? I'm not sure."

"Off the beaten track? What do you mean by that?"

"Speculative science. Research a long way outside the mainstream. It's kind of like …" She sat up, rapidly clicking her fingers. "That's it! A long way! A long distance … for …" Jan grunted in frustration, then balled her fists and pressed them to her temples. "Gah! Running on empty here. I almost had it then."

"Almost had what?"

"Duh. If I knew *that* …" Her patronizing huff made him narrow his eyes at her a little. She could be infuriating when she was tetchy like this, when things weren't going her way. Especially when she was over-tired and refused to rest. "Where did that name come from?" she asked. "Spearhead – where did you hear it? In relation to what?"

Vaughn gave her a succinct account of his Gilpraxia mission, the moon bridge bombing, the null-g pursuit, the perp's mysterious vanishing act inside his hollow octagonal device, and Sondergaard's latest communique.

"The guy vaporized himself rather than get caught?" An absent remark, unworthy of her.

"I don't think so."

She thought for a moment. "No, no. Neither do I. Hey, can you not punch up Spearhead Project in your ship's data—hmm, sat net's still disabled, huh. Kraczinski could do it for you!"

"Not a bad idea."

Tapping her cranium with a fingertip – "Still ticking" – she resumed her lookout posture, while Vaughn swiveled back to his console, to message Kraczinski and Sondergaard. Jan was coming at the case from a totally different angle than him, but they were both stuck on the same missing piece of the puzzle. It was right there in front of them, he felt, a lilt of intuition away. She read the science journals; she was about as qualified as anyone could be in her field. If she'd only get some rest, she could probably join the dots for him in a blink.

Sunset on the equator practically was a blink. He'd forgotten how slippery the transition from day to night was. Almost before the notion had occurred to him a call came in over the rescue channel telling him it was useless to continue the search until morning. Miz De Brock had fulfilled her part of the bargain. Her three fliers had zigzagged over a considerable area and found nothing. It was time to call it a day.

"Copy that, Scout One. Send me your grid areas covered and you can head on back. Vaughn. Over."

"Copy. We don't need your permission. Scout One. Over and—hang on, hang on, I've got an incoming. I'll party us."

A woman's voice pierced the momentary static: "… the sand. Repeat. This is Scout Three. I have a probable sighting! Tracks in the sand in grid two-four-nine, the northern side of an isthmus joining several rugged islands. Two sets of tracks leading from the sea. One biped, probably human. The other possibly quadruped. They lead to a crater of some kind. Appears to be volcanic. Its heat signature is blocking my scanners. And it's too dark for an effective aerial search. Recommend a ground search and rescue. I'll continue circling the crater until you guys arrive. Over."

"Copy that, Rescue Three. Good work. Key us your exact coordinates and we'll rendezvous there. Rescue One. Over."

"Ten-Four. Sending co-ords now. Out."

Vaughn's words jostled and tripped over themselves as he figured out how to assemble them – almost the best news imaginable – for the only woman in his life. Instead, grinning, almost bursting with bonhomie, he accessed the recorded audio stream and hovered his finger over the replay button. "Jan?"

"Yeah, yeah, yeah. It's dark. So what? We keep looking."

"We're gonna need to stretch our legs."

"What are you blathering about?"

"Oh, don't take my word for it." He pressed play and put it on speaker.

"… *the sand. Repeat. This is Scout Three. I have a probable sighting! Tracks in the sand …*"

As she turned, Jan's eyes sparked with the flare of a binary sunrise.

* * *

By the time Vaughn had filled his rucksack with supplies for their pursuit on foot, Jan had summitted the crater three times at various points, desperate to penetrate the hothouse mist using the full spectral range of his spare omnipod goggles. Following the two sets of tracks – unquestionably

Stopper's and the girl's – she had mapped their likely route through the thick, sweaty vegetation, tracing the contours of the crater interior to a possible egress point a few miles down in the heart of the basin. Having circled that region a few times in the *Pitch Hopper*, Vaughn felt confident she was right. It appeared rocky and cavernous, and there was evidence of a river network, the moonlit slivers of its arteries barely visible at the bottom of precipitous ravines. Jan, Vaughn and Salino, the flier who'd discovered the tracks, all agreed that was where they would make for if they'd been marooned here. Possible fresh water. Shelter. A route to a potential way off the island: the maze of shallow sandbars and lush, dotted islets would not be a difficult puzzle for Stopper to solve once he'd determined they could lead him a north-trending arc toward his home in the Keys. The islets would stop hundreds of nautical miles short, but he didn't know that.

"I can't thank you enough," Jan said to Salino, whose ocular implants shone like cat's eyes in the pitch night. She was stretching against the fuselage of her craft, limbering up for this hike into the unknown. "You sure you won't get into trouble with your boss? We might be gone for some time."

"I figure I'm needed here more."

"What did she say when you told her?"

The tall woman shrugged her narrow, hunched shoulders. "I'm to wait for further instructions." She adjusted her breather. "Never did like killing time. We get little enough as it is. And the kid's got even less, right?"

"That's right. Maybe less than a day if she hasn't been careful with her regulator."

"So it's settled."

Jan nodded her approval, then re-checked the spare breathers, tapping the O2 gauges and blowing any pesky grains of sand or dust out of the filters. "What about the other flier?" She glanced up. "How long do you think Miz De Brock will let him stay with us, circling like this?"

Salino reached into her cockpit, flicked on their private radio channel. A minute or so later she hung the receiver up and slung the craft's orange survival bag over her shoulder. "Nothing further from HQ," she said. "I don't know much about Crowhurst, but I do know he's a man of his word. He'll keep circling till he runs out of fuel or he's given new orders. Not much imagination, but the guy's as loyal as they come. He's flown for her for years."

"Miz De Brock?"

"Uh-huh. Can't say I blame him. Lady pays higher rates than any employer I've heard of. And I've flown all over the OC."

Vaughn finished keying in the *Hopper's* security code, arming its powerful em defenses while he was away. "If you don't mind me asking," he addressed the gangly, somewhat solitary female figure striding out in front of him, "how much do you know about why she's here – your employer, I mean? What she's looking for?" After a few moments' silence, he added, "I mean I'm sure you've all had to ink a Non-Disclosure Agreement, but is there anything you can tell us? Anything at all?"

154

"I wish I knew," was all he could get out of her.

They were about a stone's throw up-beach from the two vessels when Salino's omnipod receiver began flashing. She sighed. "Crap. There's no uplink out here, guys. I'll have to take this back at the bird."

Jan and Vaughn waited while the woman jogged to her craft – her rangy stride and almost comically hunched back reminded him of an ungainly quadruped Jan had introduced him to on his last visit, one that stalked the swamps of the interior, facing downward at all times, questing for any critters that surfaced for a gasp of air.

Vaughn checked the time. Over four hours to go before sunrise. They'd have to flood their way with light, not just to see the path but to deter any night predators – a dazzling torch beam was usually enough to dissuade even the cockiest of hunters.

"He's changing his search pattern." Jan pointed out Crowhurst's flier now heading in the opposite direction, lower than his previous arc, out to sea. "Maybe she's recalling them."

"Bitch."

Then the ship about-faced and headed back toward the beach, keeping its lower trajectory, and Vaughn now reckoned Crowhurst was going to join them with the ground search.

"Well, well, I take back every bad thing I said about her," said Jan. "Ice Queen has a heart after all. Hey, with four searching we could split up. Two teams would have a much better—"

A hurtful hot flash lit up the beach like an exploding dawn. Salino vanished inside it, dark streaks of her flier shooting apart high into the night as flaming debris. The shock wave hit Vaughn and Jan a split-second later. It punched them off their feet and slammed them into the sandy bank. Winded him. The hard items in his rucksack dealt sharp, blunt blows across his back, but he couldn't tell if it was one blow or several when the pain began to swell.

He checked his breather for signs of a rupture, then checked Jan's. They seemed fine. She appeared unhurt but dazed, her darting, unseeing gaze quite normal after so severe a shock but it was still utterly unlike her. He tinted his visor, turned to the flames in an effort to figure out what had happened when a wayward streak of jagged light caught his peripheral vision. It came from the night, from over the sea. And even before the second shockwave hit, obliterating the *Pitch Hopper*, he knew they were under attack. He reached across to shield Jan from the second explosion. A blast of heat turned night momentarily to livid day.

Vaughn didn't have time to wrench the bag off his back to retrieve a larger weapon. No, the treacherous flier was circling again for a final killing salvo. He reached into his holster and tore the Kruger Mach IV out of its snag, not thinking, not aiming, his thumb instinctively rolling to the highest notch on the yield cycle, and snapped off a shot.

The night grew wings. Electric blue wings that dipped and flailed into a terrifying corkscrew meters above the black, molten-rippled sea. Crowhurst's ship slammed into the ocean. The fizzy sound of the splash barely registered through the twin infernos' roar on the sand. Electric blue still crackled across the shell of the submerging craft until it settled, its tail sticking diagonally out of the water not far off shore.

"You're bleeding out," Jan told Crowhurst without sympathy as she finished fastening the ad hoc tourniquet as high as she could above the horrible puncture wounds in his thigh. She and Vaughn had somehow managed to tie the ends of the pilot's severed femoral artery by the light of the burning ships on the beach. But one of the puncture wounds was higher still, near his groin, and despite their best efforts to stem the flow with constant pressure, it was a lost cause; the femoral had been nicked there too, and it was losing blood in a steady gush.

Rescuing him from the submerged flier had been a real struggle for Vaughn. Not just because a part of him wanted to let the bastard drown in his own blood, but because Crowhurst was hellish strong for such a wiry guy. He'd kept trying to slip Vaughn's grasp and swim away. But the more he'd squirmed, the more he'd ruptured his wounds. He had finally passed out for a minute or so on the sand, no doubt from the pain of them yanking at his innermost cords and stretching the ends so far that he could actually see them. After that he'd been docile, even when he'd come to. Now all he did was shiver and maintain a limp grip on Jan's forearm.

"Just did ... like ... like they told me." If Vaughn hadn't thumbed the volume wheel on the man's breather rig to a higher external setting, they might not have caught his whispered words.

"Who did?" asked Vaughn. "Who gave the order?"

"No. No. It's not what you *think*." He tried to sit up but collapsed again under a hurtful cavalcade of coughs.

"Was it Miz De Brock? Did she give the order to fire on us?"

"Not ... what you think."

"Why do they want us dead all of a sudden? After helping us for a full day, lending us two of their best fliers, what changed their minds?"

"Accident. All an accident." Crowhurst then mumbled an insensible string of words before they leaned in close enough to catch "I didn't mean to ... it was just ... there ... on my sensor ... just like they'd said ... that exact same ... pattern."

"What pattern?" asked Jan. "What is it you people are looking for?"

"The pattern ... underwater."

Jan shot Vaughn a tired, exasperated look that mirrored his own frustration.

"Come on, Crowhurst. You can do it," she whispered back. "Just tell us what you're looking for — what you spotted underwater. And we'll call your buddies to come get you, to come fix you up."

It was a dirty lie, and Vaughn only wished he'd used it.

"I only did ... what they paid me to do."

"I know," she replied. "It was your job. And it's my job to find that little girl, to bring her back safely to her folks.

Tell me what it is *you're* looking for and, who knows, we might still be able to help each other out."

"Spear …"

"What was that?" Vaughn pressed the ear of his breather rig to Crowhurst's speaker. "You said 'spear'?"

"Spear …"

"Spearhead? You're looking for Spearhead?"

"Spearhead. It's here. I-I found it."

"Yes, you did," said Vaughn. "It's your discovery. I'm sure there's a big reward waiting for you when you get back."

"Not what you think."

"Come on, you can tell us. Is Spearhead really the game-changer they say it is?"

"Not … not what you think. It's … older, older … than any of us."

"Yeah, but I bet you don't know *how* old."

"He was old even then. They never knew what happened … what really happened … when he … when he …"

Crowhurst's searching skyward gaze rested on oblivion, and he was gone. Vaughn went to remove the man's mask but checked himself.

"What's wrong?" asked Jan. "We should take that. He won't be needing it. We might."

"No. We need to disappear."

"Huh?"

He untied the blood-soaked tourniquet, balled it up and tossed it into the flaming wreckage. "They think we're dead.

So we're not here – we didn't survive the attack. Either we disappear or they come looking for us. It's that simple."

"Jesus, you're right." Stepping back from the body, Jan looked down at her footprints in the sand. "Vaughn, how do we—"

"Leave now," he told her. "Into the crater, just like we planned. I'll cover our tracks."

"But how?"

"The old way. Sweep them clear behind us as we go. It'll buy as some time."

"That won't work. It'll be obvious."

"Trust me. I work crime scenes for a living. The eye sees what it wants to see. Now go!"

She stayed silent as she tore up the nearest dune, carrying close to forty pounds of supplies and equipment, as though nothing in the world could stop her now. It was in these little moments, when he'd made the mistake of taking her for granted, that Jan never failed to surprise him. Women all across the colonies, in the most hardscrabble environments imaginable, had assured him they could take care of themselves, that they didn't need a man to look after them, thank you very much. And some of them might have been right. But Jan was the only one he'd ever perceived as truly independent, a law unto herself on the most lawless planet he'd ever visited.

She was a born survivor, like him.

Using his jacket, a couple of petrified branches of driftwood, a few clumps of alien kelp, and two grenades, he left four ghosts on the beach.

Chapter Ten

The furtive little critters skitter across the ravine floor with a hastiness that he feels too. But while they feed on uprooted vegetation strewn in knots or in long, vein-like streams that hiss steam, Stopper is focused on finding the quickest way across. Like the desperate scavengers below, he senses time is running out, that any move he makes now, any course he takes, is a gamble. It makes him tense, irritable. He snaps at any creature that comes near, sends it scurrying.

Dorcas follows him wherever he goes. She no longer whines or digs her heels in or even slows to catch her breath. The secret of the mask she wears, that all humans wear, weighs heavily on her, he senses. She is afraid, but she also believes that if she keeps going, if she keeps following him, he can lead her home. It emanates from her and infuses him, leaves him feeling twice his size, even in the slick and steamy depths of the ravine.

He's already decided it's too long for them to walk around, so he picks their way down and across instead. The rock floor is smooth, damp and slippery in patches, bone dry in others. The walls, too, are much smoother near the bottom and have been cut slightly deeper, slightly farther apart all along the canyon. Slow-moving plants with suckers on the ends of their fronds inch out of the shadows and appear to hose up any pockets of moisture near the walls. Fleeing critters find tiny hollows higher up. Meanwhile, the pungent salty odor spikes whenever he strides over one of the thick vines strewn lengthwise. He's almost certain they come from the sea, and that this was the scent he picked up back in the crater, which first led him to think that more non-drinking water lay in this direction: non-drinking water and the way home. It puzzles him, how the vines got here, but not enough to distract him from his crossing.

Stopper can't see a way up the opposite wall. He scrambles up a few times only to give up when it becomes too steep, but his trusty sense of smell tells him he's getting close. The scent of the monster he fought off not long since is faint yet discernible. It's up there somewhere, maybe lying in wait. Which means it has climbed up. More important than steering clear of its trap, he has to get the girl up there somehow. If the monster attacks he can fend it off again, even put it down for good this time. Ram it off the edge of the cliff. Rip its throat out.

Dorcas falls a few times in the slime, doesn't even bother cleaning herself before she gets up and soldiers on. She's in tune with him, grim and single-minded. Another promising ledge comes to nothing. He hops back down, pants at her a few moments until she catches up, then runs on to the next prospect. Meanwhile, a warm breeze jabs down at him, and on it the monster's scent grows stronger, more potent somehow, as though it's challenging him to make the climb and is so supremely confident it can best him this time that the anticipation has caused it to mark its high territory with a gusher that's meant to drive Stopper wild.

But the air bristles with other dangers. It seems to descend in a swell originating from some far-off place. Cooler, deadlier. It pricks his ears, dusts off the depths of his olfactory palette, leaving a hollow in the pit of his stomach. Whatever is approaching is immense and fast-moving and not something he can contend with.

He snarls, hunkers down. A keening wind presages the chill shadow of a falling sky as death sweeps in. Invisible death that thunder-rolls and breaks on unseen regions with a power beyond comprehension. The canyon behind Dorcas grays, yellows. He barks for her to run with him. She glances around and then obeys without question. The shadow spits at their heels, a cool mist that peppers his fur. Critters scamper up the vertical rock into holes he can't see, higher than he can reach. The plants with sucking fronds curl up and recede into cocoons in their dark crevices at the bases of the walls.

He sprints ahead until he sees a ledge he hasn't tried. It at least offers a chance at a way up. There isn't time for anything else. The rumble has grown to a roar, and the canyon itself now shakes, tingling his spine that tautens every time he pauses to look back.

He barks until he can barely hear his own voice. By now the girl is right behind him and he's begun the climb. Another bark, not his echo, registers from somewhere higher up. Barks distinct from the other and from his own follow. He glances up to see the over-sized eyes of several creatures peering down from the clifftop, watching him and Dorcas. The monster he fought is not alone. It has brought others. And that's not all. Another, taller creature stands over them, also peering down. He can't make out its features, only its slender, stooping frame and the big lump on one of its shoulders.

Dorcas hops up, loses her footing on an oily incline. Rather than slide back and try again, she inches up through the layer of gunk on her hands and knees, losing a step for every two she gains. They're frantic steps but she manages to follow him over three precarious sections in quick succession, where even he has to leap blindly. In her wide, darting eyes he sees the insurmountable threat heading their way. Droplets begin to trickle down the inside of her visor. The temperature dips suddenly. When she reaches, screaming, for a higher ledge, flat against the sheer rock, her toes and fingertips stretched to utmost, and can't make it … he knows she's in mortal danger. It's a calculation etched in the tragic losses borne by a million antecedents of his species and those lessons paid forward. She's simply not high enough. Stopper leaps down to her guard and barks senselessly at the tumult: a relentless surge of white water piles into the ravine behind them. It seems to bound and roll as it breaks again and again with frothing, crashing fury.

Spume and spray soak them in seconds as the wave surges by. But it doesn't sweep them off the rock ledge. Displaced air swirls and jabs impishly, threatening the girl's balance. But she holds firm. The noise is absolute. After the initial foamy chaos, the floodwater begins to smooth and streak, almost pouring by now, the white shapes rearing up on its flanks more like the rapids of a pre-existing river. But as he watches, those white watery shapes disappear and are replaced by others at different points on the wall. Higher and higher up.

The water is rising.

He snaps at the dark unyielding surface as it fills the ravine. Even as it thunders by it seems propelled from underneath too, an upwelling force that makes a spring tide in the Keys seem like Jan topping up his water bowl. He tugs at Dorcas's lifejacket, tries to inch her away from the water-line. She responds with a panicky attempt to claw her way up sheer rock.

All he can think of now is staying with her so he can keep her alive through this peril they can't escape.

A sudden swiping surge snatches her legs out from under her. It lifts Stopper completely off the ledge and sweeps him into the cold, cold flow. He kicks for all his worth and manages several of the strongest strokes he's ever swam. It drives him within paw's reach of the girl. She reaches. Grabs a fistful of his skin. It isn't enough to pull her close but she holds on until the force of the rapids does it for her. She's close, at least. Her gripping his shoulders like this reminds him of their endless swim the previous night. But this is harder, impossible to control. Currents from below keep trying to rip them down and apart. He struggles to keep his mouth above the surface.

Even through the roar he hears her scream.

A line with a loop at the end dips into the water up ahead. He can't decide if it's a rope or a cable but it's definitely not natural, definitely not a vine. It's braided. The loop is the perfect size for the girl to slip into. He doesn't know why he hates that idea so much but he does. And he can't believe it when she lets go of him and starts paddling *toward* it.

Instinctively he stays with her. She twists her body to make a grab and hang fast on the loop. One hand holding it, the other stretching to catch him, the girl thrashes to gain a better position. He doesn't know what she's trying to do but he knows the loop cannot hold two of them. It isn't big enough. He trusts her, though. Trusts her to save herself because she's grown so much since falling off the boat; she's reminded him more and more of his beloved Jan. All he has to do is stay close.

Water begins to surge against her and over her. The line is far from vertical; she's battered by the force of the flood. Fight though he might, he can no longer stay close. A hot dread strips his lungs as he pants and battles and wills the distance between them to shrink. But he's moving downstream and she is not. Suddenly the loop lifts out of the water with her attached and she gives another scream.

It continues to lift. She continues to scream. Somewhere around a bend in the canyon he loses sight of her. Then he goes under.

Chapter Eleven

The sun has long since set by the time the raging floodwater hurls him out of the ravine on the tongue of a shallow but forceful cataract. It pours into a vast underground lake, the far banks of which Stopper can't make out through the Stygian gloom. The downward force pushes and drags him deeper than he's ever been in water. His head feels like it's being crushed from both sides through his ears, and for the umpteenth time since losing sight of Dorcas he fights all-encompassing dread and panic with the only tool he has left: the desire to return to the way things should be: get back to the girl and get her safely back to Jan, so that *he* can be with Jan again.

He whines aloud in frightened little bursts when he regains the surface because his ears still hurt and because he's almost too tired to go on swimming. If shafts of blueish moonlight hadn't penetrated the rock ceiling, bathing the lake with an eerie, patchy glow, he would not know which way to swim. He also wouldn't be able to see the water spouts shooting high into the gloom at various points beyond the reach of the tumult, where the lake is otherwise gently rippled or flat calm. Distant noises accompany these breaches. They sound like the low-pitched snores of giants through whale-sized conches.

As he swims clear of the froth and the swirling breeze, he picks up the faintest familiar scent. Dorcas! Another few downwind sniffs allow him to mentally course-correct his paddling as he approaches a shore thick with deep, orange mud. The belly-trails and claw prints left by heavy creatures sliding into the water leave him hyper-alert. He doesn't sense any threats nearby, at least on land, but he's all too aware of the fact that threats from the water can erupt at any time without warning. Water is not his element. It's too unpredictable.

After struggling up through seemingly endless wads of the slimy orange gunk, he shakes himself off and begins the long trot over misty marshland dotted with petrified trees that lie half-slumped like the bowed skeletons of huge birds. The higher he goes, the drier it gets. But for the odd trickle of freshwater, which he laps up with relish, it's as still and quiet as he's ever known. In his experience such silence isn't a good sign. It suggests life is not welcome. In a world where all life is tenacious, where it can thrive in the most inhospitable places imaginable, an empty neighborhood so close to water is likely not an untenanted one. Stopper decides not to squat long enough to find out.

Piles of dry soil thick with the dug-up roots of dead trees lie scattered across the upper slopes of the hill. Each is roughly crescent-shaped and taller than him; they resemble the dens of large creatures he and Jan went searching for once, shy, skittish creatures that could burrow underground with incredible speed, their many reflective eyes shining up from the holes as they dug. But these piles are far bigger, as are the holes – no, more like tunnels – he glimpses in the ground at their centers. The danger he senses here comes not from sight or sound or even smell; it comes from experience, from a lifetime of patterns and intuitions he's gathered in order to guide Jan from harm.

Those same instincts guide him back toward the girl, to a wooded area high on the hilltop, then down, steeply down into the cleft between two peaks. It's still misty here. The wild flowers grow tall and straight, their stems ridged with sharp spirals like blood-red drill-bits. From here he can make out a trail worn through the top layer of soil to the bare rock beneath. It veers to the flooded ravine in one direction and winds down into a sheltered valley in the other. Dorcas came along this path. Her scent grows stronger as he sprints downhill. The other scents, just as strong, broil away inside him in tiny places he keeps separate. They are the enemies he must contend with. They took her from him, and if they're still with her he will fight them, one at a time if he can, all together if he must.

Large, dead creatures he's never seen before hang from trees, their eyeless, contorted faces showing pain and confusion as though they were caught in two minds just before they were killed: flee or fight? Their curved claws at the ends of long, powerful arms could shred a tree in no time, he reckons. But what killed them there as they hung like that? And why are there so many of them gathered here?

Stopper can't decide if this is some kind of ambush. Is their scent of death just a ruse to lure him or other unwary visitors in? Will the eyeless things spring to life when he's in their midst, and attack him from all sides?

There's no way around that he can see. The girl definitely came this way, along the trail snaking through the trees. She's somewhere in the direction of an opening in the hillside beyond. It's big enough to be a cave, could be a lair. He treads lightly past the hanging creatures. They don't stir. Puncture marks in their sides and necks are further proof that they are in fact dead, but he daren't dash, he daren't press the crispy soil underfoot any more than he needs to.

The cave entrance looms large through the wisps of warm mist. Several trails branch out from it. Clumps of bracken dot the outside walls of the cave. There are things underneath them, objects that don't belong. The ground is also littered with animal droppings, yet strangely they have no odor. As he nears, he's aware that the breeze has changed direction; it now drifts sidewise across his approach. The girl is inside the cave, he's almost certain of it. The hostile creatures are likely in there too.

Something blunt hits his nose. Not a powerful blow but it's hard enough to make him hunker down and snarl. He inches forward. Again his nose takes a hit. It doesn't so much hurt as puzzles him, infuriating his sense of composure. If he can't see it, how can it get through his defenses like this? He spins around, hops to one side, hunkers down once again. He feels the angry heat rippling his shoulders muscles while he readies himself for an attack on … on …

He howls his frustration, hoping to hear Dorcas answer him. Instead, the sounds of creatures inside the cave respond. Their growls and deep snarling voices overlap, but they're not unfamiliar. He barks again and again. The voices answer. Then the creatures pour out of the cave.

He recognizes their shapes from the one he fought off on the other side of the ravine. Only these don't have a single eye; they each have two. And there is no hump-like growth on their necks. In fact, they're so much like him he can't understand what he's looking at. Thinner, scrawnier, uglier versions of him: the familiarities excite unwelcome jealousies and challenges far too close to home. He recalls his parents, how they used to pin him down and hold him there, keep him in his place whenever he got too brave or too cocky.

These aren't like his parents. But their barks challenge him, tell him to get away or else. They're between him and Dorcas, and therefore him and Jan.

He rears up to tackle the fastest onrusher. His claws scrape against thin air. He tries again, this time pressing his paws on a barrier he can't see. Scratching it does nothing, doesn't even leave a mark. Biting does even less because it's like biting the glass window of one of Jan's flying cars. So he bounds around. Tries other ways in. Digging down into the soil in an effort to get *under* the wall gets him nowhere because the soil isn't thick enough before he touches rock. Getting in around the back of the wall fails because it seems to ring the cave completely. He tries everything he can think of, every *attaboy* trick in his arsenal. Always the same result. This invisible, confounding wall of nothing.

It keeps him out. But it also keeps them in. After a while they stop barking and just stand there watching his antics. There's no sign of the girl. One of them walks right up to an insect crawling up the nothing wall and, mouth open, tongue hanging, licks it. Saliva wets the air as the insect drowns and then disappears inside the animal's mouth. Soundless panting mists the air around that spot the way his own does when he's hot and tired inside Jan's striped ship after a long field outing and he's watching the wild zip by outside through the round window. For a moment he eyes the insect-eater as though he's gazing at his own reflection. He can't understand what he's looking at or why there's nothing between them, keeping them apart. Though he won't hesitate to rip the creature's throat out the first chance he gets, pricks of curiosity work away under his skin like the thorny darts shot from the tripwire plants. He feels he's been tricked somehow, duped by these animals and their presence here. They're hiding more than Dorcas from him. And they threaten him in ways he doesn't know how to fight. So he'll just have to set about them all – as soon as he can get at them.

They stare at one another. The others stalk in tight circles behind the insect-eater, waiting to see what happens next, who'll make the first move. Then they're distracted by something and their tails start to wag. Insect-Eater turns as well, and his tail goes berserk. He rears up to catch a hunk of meat tossed to him. The others are all feasting too. After licking his lips, Stopper hurls out his loudest, most vicious bark at the slender man heading his way.

The red face, cropped silver hair and glistening skin remind him of several of the older tourists he and Jan have had to put up with on those endless, boring sails. Only this man, though outside the confines of his cave home, is not wearing a mask. He's also barefoot and topless, his narrow shoulders and slightly saggy breasts pink. He doesn't have a threatening face, but right here, right now, he's the enemy of everything Stopper knows and loves.

He mouths something inaudible and retrieves a long, shiny black stick attached to a strap over his shoulder. The stick has a pointy end. With a slow, twisty push and much effort he manages to plant it *into* the nothing wall, so that its pointy end pokes through.

He smacks the other end of it with his palm. Stopper feels an actual prick this time, high up on his chest. He growls at the man, not knowing what he's done, only that he's done *something* sneaky and tricky and human. The other creatures stare at him wide-eyed, their tails still wagging. A tingly, almost gushingly cold sensation mushrooms from his chest to every inch of him. Confusion envelopes him and then evaporates like a heavy downpour kissed by the noonday sun. He feels himself fading, falling into a place with streaky lights. Somewhere in here, he hopes, Jan is waiting with a pack of Rip 'Ems.

Chapter Twelve

"So you've said. But the spectrometer readings trend toward the cave on the right," Vaughn pointed out. "All due respect to your gut, hard science disagrees. And your batteries are running low; these aren't." Tapping the rim of his visor was clearly meant to be a little charming, but Jan disliked his patronizing, take-charge gumshoe attitude as much as he disliked her know-it-all ranger counterpart. At rest, at leisure, they were such easy companions it was as though they'd spent a lifetime together and looked forward to several more. But in their respective professional guises, when their backs were up, an hour could feel like a lifetime. Neither had time for the other's pig-headedness. And both hated to be second-guessed.

"But you said the heat reading in there is twice as high, so it's more dangerous, and Stopper's instinct is to *avoid* danger," she reminded him. "Make your mind up, Vaughn. Or I'm taking charge of that thing," referring to his customized Bureau omnipod, which included state-of-the-art tracking capabilities that used a wider spectrum of light waves and a higher resolution of pattern recognition than the standard headset available commercially.

"You're tired, Jan, and you're making mistakes. You watch the wildlife; let me worry about the trail."

She snapped off a salute. Vaughn narrowed his eyes and marched into the right-hand cave. Millimeters under her prickly exterior she knew she was being unreasonable, that she was grateful to have him here and would show him that gratitude passionately and intimately when all this was over, but right now she couldn't help herself. A part of her *was* running on empty – recalling the names of plants and animals, ordinarily an instant encyclopedic facility, had become a dull mental constipation – yet the reserves of grit keeping her going ran bone-deep. And that grit did not play nice with others. Never had.

"Vaughn, wait up." She wiped the drips of moisture off her visor, leaving streaks. "I want to tell you something."

"What is it?"

"I'm—I'm sorry about your ship. The *Hopper* – I know what she meant to you."

He didn't reply.

"Maybe it's time for you to, you know, really think about it."

"Think about what?"

"Retiring."

He stopped. Near-scalding drips peppered the backs of their necks as they stood facing one another in the hellish mist reflecting the dazzling glare of their torch beams.

"I know you've been thinking about it," she added. "I have too – for you, I mean. You belong here. With me and Stops. The galaxy doesn't deserve you. We do."

Jan stretched the ends of her jacket sleeves over her hands and used them to shield her neck from the hot drips.

Vaughn didn't bother. "What makes you think I'm ready to give all that up? Everything I've worked for. My whole life."

"Because it's your batteries that are running low, not mine."

Vaughn didn't reply.

"Because three days without sleep and I can still tell you more about what you want than you can," she went on. "Because you feel aimless out there. Unwanted. And this feels like home."

"This death-trap?"

"I know you don't mean that. Vaughn, there are things you can say when you're tired that you can't even say when you're drunk, and this is what I'm saying to you: it's time to start over. Here. Make a new life together. You, me, Stops, and a world of wonders."

Vaughn was silent for a while, then he finally pulled up his collar to shield the back of his neck. "Come on," he said, resuming his march. "We've got a job to do."

Jan smiled to herself. He might be the most incorruptible agent anywhere in the colonies, but in Vaughn-speak, anything but a flat and instant refusal usually meant he was very much open to negotiation. And with a man like him, she knew, it was of the all or nothing kind.

The cool night air outside the cave refreshed her like a prolonged dawn dip in the sea.

Water trickled along the ravine floor below in moonlit slivers, though from the damp walls it was plain to see it had recently filled the canyon to over two-thirds its height. This baffled them at first – how could such a volume of water empty so quickly? – until Jan remembered something Ichi Nakamori had said about a planet's oceans being its circulatory system, all those hidden rhythms and cycles and current flows and layers people were barely aware of. As unpredictable as the sea could seem at times, those underlying rhythms and cycles generally ran like clockwork.

"It has to be a tidal surge," she said. "A violent spring tide overflow. Bit by bit, one surge at a time, maybe over millions of years, high tide has carved out this channel. So now it surges in at every spring tide or high tide and floods the channel for a short time until it empties again. I'm no geologist, but I'll bet smart money that's what Stops and the girl had to contend with when they crossed."

"Jesus." Vaughn turned over a slice of damp moss that had very recently been uprooted by something clawed. "I hope they weren't in there when it flooded."

She pretended she didn't hear that. "What can you tell me about this second animal? It's a quadruped, right?"

"Appears to be," he replied. "It may have tracked them. Its trace signatures are a lot like Stopper's prints, a little smaller, not as heavy. They fought here at the edge. The girl climbed down to that ledge …" Vaughn crept along at a crouch, watching the faint trace signature of her size 3 boots, "… then she climbed back up." He aimed the goggles' scan at the ground behind him. "The second animal ran away into the shadow of the cliff – big stride, bigger and lighter than Stopper's. Stopper and the girl carried on along the rim, staying close to the edge."

"Maybe they were looking for a safe way down and up the other side."

"Yeah, *if* that was before the tidal surge," Vaughn reminded her, then checked his pessimism. He was used to expecting the worst from manhunts. Tracking missing persons in the colonies tended to end with a condolence call and stiff drinks all round. But Stopper had defied an alien ocean to keep this girl alive. What was another wave?

"He's a great problem solver," he reassured her. "If there's a way across he'll have found it."

"Count on it."

But that way across was half a mile and more following the canyon, and he doubted a nine-year-old girl could have made it. The way down wasn't the problem; it was the climb up the other side, the only feasible route that he could find: several times he and Jan had to leap and scramble. Stopper had quite a powerful spring in his jump, so he could do it. But Little Dorcas would need a lot of help. Also, their tracks had ended partway down, which meant one of two things – they'd gotten across before the flood, which had washed their prints away, or they hadn't.

He said nothing to Jan and she didn't bring it up either.

Atop the far side of the ravine she crouched to rest. Studying the tracks in the top soil leading away from the edge, she said, "I don't know of any indigenous quadrupeds that could have made these. They're almost … canine." She let her chin sink to her chest. "But they're not his."

Vaughn crouched beside her and hooked a reassuring arm over her shoulders. "They might have climbed up further on. Maybe they didn't think this one was do-able."

She sniffled. Squeezed his hand. "Yeah. Maybe."

Half way through helping her up, Vaughn heard a thunderclap overhead. He threw her down onto the thin soil and lay flat on top of her. "Don't move, Jan."

Another thunderclap struck the sky, followed by a staccato *whu-whu-whup*.

"They're here?"

"Took them longer than I thought," he whispered.

"Doesn't change anything. You're law enforcement, right, on a search for a missing person? They can't interfere."

"That didn't stop them trying to nuke us on the beach. And they have the sat net. Right now, Omicron's just a letter in a dead language down here. "

"So we need to keep undercover. And you need to give me a weapon."

Vaughn shook his head – equal parts admiration and disapproval. As an agent he knew this couldn't end well, her scurrying about near so prominent a feature as this canyon, with an armada set to land and a squadron of contour-hugging spotter craft gawking down. It was only a matter of time …

On the other hand, this had been an inevitable part of his plan all along. Their only means of escape. Without it neither he nor Jan would ever get home. Miz De Brock's urgency in finding whatever it was she'd come here to find

179

had just bought them some time. She'd destroyed his ship. Now they just had to stay unseen long enough for him to steal one of hers.

If they didn't find Stopper's tracks *very* soon, they'd have to do what Jan would never consent to doing. For that reason, he thought twice about handing her a weapon. He could never persuade her to leave while she was armed. But nor could he risk leaving her defenseless on an island crawling with hostiles. What if something happened to him and she was left unprotected?

"Here." The handgun he slipped into her palm was his reserve, low-yield but deadly accurate. "The safety's on. In case of emergency—"

"Make holes in dear places."

"Something like that, only make sure they're not in *your* dear places."

"Vaughn, do I look like a tourist?"

"You look like someone who's going to keep herself safe, no matter what, so that this sorry lawman will have at least one person to miss him when he's gone."

She pulled her face. "Ugh, you do suck at sentiment."

"Promise me you'll stay safe and listen to me when things get hot."

"Promise me they'll get hot." Jan thumbed the safety on her weapon and threw him a wink. He rolled his eyes at her. "Okay, okay," she added, "I'll abide by the letter from the dead alphabet until we're out of trouble. But you promise me we won't stop searching for Stops and the girl."

"Copy that," he replied. "You have my word."

180

"And that's the only word in this galaxy worth a damn. I mean that. Here, help me up."

The white copses were bare, yet the thick, twisted shapes of the boles and branches provided a little cover from which Vaughn and Jan were able to follow the edge of the ravine, questing for the elusive pair of tracks. There were no more thunderclaps. Craft no longer *whupped* by overhead. They roved and crisscrossed in slow, deliberate patterns a few hundred feet up, their unblinking scanners painting the ground like ink-readers. After a couple of dozen passes along what appeared to be the full length of the canyon, they moved on and seemed to circle an area to the southwest.

Shortly after, Jan spotted footprints leading from the edge of the ravine into the forest. Human footprints. Two sets! She broke cover without hesitation.

"One's barefoot, adult," she pointed out. "The other's a child, size three?"

"Three, exactly." Vaughn checked and re-checked his angles to make sure they were in fact alone and no one was watching.

"And these are canine tracks … again. *Not his … again!*"

"But we know she came up here," he reminded her.

"Yes." Jan gripped him by the shoulder, pulling him to follow her. "And wherever she is, he'll find her. We know that for sure."

For her sake, she had to be right. But the more he thought about it, the more his own hope dampened. Why hadn't Stopper climbed out here with the girl? The sudden appearance of adult footprints suggested someone had helped her out, maybe lifted her out in the nick of time? The area was still wet, a lot wetter than its surroundings. So someone had been in the water and dripped a body-suit's worth. Most likely the girl. It was doubtful she could have climbed higher than Stopper on her own. So, if the girl was lifted out and Stopper wasn't, then he would probably have been swept away by the tidal surge.

All this he kept to himself as he tore after her along a misty trail through the dead forest. They soon trended downhill, where the footing became quite precarious due to the film of moisture covering a thin layer of spongy light-blue moss. The party had come this way – adult, girl, and what looked to be a pack of dogs – into a kind of hilly haven masked from above by floating mist and, as far as he could tell, inaccessible except by the route they were on.

"What in God's name …" He halted, took a few jittery backward steps. Palmed his Kruger and clicked the safety off. "Ever seen those before?"

Jan crept toward the hanging carcasses with a caution he wasn't used to seeing from her, at least as far as plants and creatures were concerned. Hell, they *looked* dead, but his experience of deceased animals extended to the odd house pet he'd encountered in the colonies and a large herd of gen-mod cattle that he'd found suffocated, all black and bloated, on a bio-dome ranch with a crapped-out atmospheric regulator. Grim scenes, but they'd been tragic, not threatening. This area was different. Like something from a nightmare. It was as though these corpses had been left here deliberately.

"Why hang them there like that?"

"I think they're scarecrows," she replied, inspecting the puncture wounds in the necks.

"They're what?"

"You know, deterrents. Farmers used to hang stuffed man-shaped figures in the middle of their fields to frighten the crows away from their crops. Birds are frightened of people, even their likeness. Whoever placed these here knows there's a creature – probably a dangerous one – that's afraid of them."

"I heard a story once, when I was little," he said, "about a woman who hung snake heads all along her fence to keep other snakes out. Don't know if it worked on the snakes, but it sure freaked *me* out."

"That's it exactly. Whatever repels pests and dangerous animals. Come to think of it, your example is better than mine. Nothing strikes fear into an animal more than seeing its own kind dead and on display. And there's another thing," she went on, looking over the rest of the nearest corpse, which resembled a large, eyeless white sloth with horrendously oversized claws, "I think these are juveniles."

"Doesn't sound good."

"There's no sign of any genitalia, which suggests they're infants. They're similar to Westinger's *suballuvial Ngeleii*," she said. "Powerful burrowers, nocturnal, subterranean. But these have webbed claws as well, and the beginnings of what appear to be gills around the thorax. Also, their overall shape is more streamlined, the longer tail and shorter, downy fur: they've likely evolved to become semi-aquatic. And they have no eyes at all – interesting. It's definitely a new species."

"Name it later. For now, stay close," he warned her. "Behind me."

Despite lingering on her discovery as she absently drew her own handgun, Jan didn't argue. She searched the way ahead and pointed him to the gray, wispy shape of a cave through the fog as he passed her. "This makes no sense, Vaughn. No human can live out here. How can they even *breathe*?"

"I don't know, but I'm pretty sure these fresh tracks belong to Stopper. Look, they're bigger than the others. And he came alone … from that direction." He motioned up a south-facing slope, from where the new trail clearly originated. "My guess is he saw the girl to safety just before the tidal surge swept in, but while somebody threw down a line to hoist her up, he was swept away. Somewhere, somehow, he managed to climb out, then made his way back here, following her scent."

"I believe you." She turned the volume of her external mike up several notches, and before he could intervene, she marched out into the mist and yelled, "Stopper!"

Vaughn yanked her back, wanted to rip the headset off her. "Of all the boneheaded, reckless … What did I say about keeping a low profile?"

She threw his hand away. "Give it a rest. He's here. He's got to be. *Stopper!* Sweetheart, where are you? We're here. Mommy's here."

"*Quiet!*" Vaughn glanced skyward, then spun to scan the entire area in one fluid glance. Alone … for now. He sprinted to catch Jan's run. If he couldn't disable her comms, she'd bring the entire armada down on top of them. But as he tried to restrain her from behind, her heel caught his boot and he tripped. On his way down his momentum flung him into the small of her back, knocking her off balance. Something solid stopped her mid-fall, but it wasn't a tree. Nor were they at the cave wall yet. They both fell in a heap.

Jan didn't get back up. The impact had knocked her cold. Cursing himself, Vaughn checked her pulse and her vitals and told himself it was just a straightforward concussion. In reality, he knew perfectly well there was no such thing, least of all out here, where each and every breath debited one's right to exist.

As he dusted himself off, he noted how the dirt particles either clung to or slid down a sheer, transparent surface otherwise invisible to the naked eye. The moment he reached out and felt the gentle buzz of static tickle his fingertips, he knew. The game had a new player. And the answers to all its riddles lay behind this photonic blister – an impressive home security measure. Stopper had found it. They'd found it. Miz De Brock and her hunters were close to finding it.

Before that happened he would have to find a way inside. Or at least somewhere safe to stow Jan until he could figure out his next move.

Somewhere safe.

The irony of those words was not lost on him as he hoisted her onto his shoulder and drew his Kruger.

Chapter Thirteen

Jan woke with pressure on her belly and a woozy, swaying motion that jerked her entire body, a rough kind of rhythm. Every second or third jerk was like an icepick to her temple. It brought tears to her eyes. At first she couldn't see anything but a smudge of colors, the way a shower screen blocks out the world after a steamy wash. A series of weak blinks and weaker groans later, she caught a glimpse of blue-green grass lying flat in long, streaming waves, all pointing the same way as though they were locks of hair blown dry and gelled down. She felt a breeze on her arms but it didn't even tickle the grass.

It dawned on her she was being carried. Then the rest filtered in slowly, memories falling into place and linking together like a slinky on a staircase. She wriggled when she remembered Stopper and the girl, how close they were.

Vaughn set her down gently, sat her upright in his arms. "Where does it hurt?" he asked.

"Right temple. Jesus." She palmed her head where the suction seal covered her skin near the throb. "How do you say hangover in an artificial breather?"

"Under your breath would be my advice."

He administered pain relief in an injection she neither watched nor wanted to discuss. She might be the scientist, but he'd seen to more injuries and saved more lives than a wartime medic.

Jan listened while he laid out the missing sequence of events that had brought them here: the fall, the invisible blister around the cave, the increased sky traffic overhead, and, most interestingly, his reconnaissance of the cave's entire perimeter via those handy little hover-bots he used to record his crime scenes – the germs. They'd located another cave, much lower in the hillside, in a cleft where two steep valleys met. He showed her the footage on a tiny wrist-mounted VDU he kept as a back-up in his utility baldric, but it was hard to make out, the device having limited image manipulation functions. Yet there was clearly a vast open space and water in there, lots of it. Maybe it was the sea itself.

The other thing the footage showed would not have been visible without the cross-spectral mapping capabilities of the germs. Some sort of sunken vessel, metallic, badly damaged, lay on the ocean bed at the water's edge, flush against the rock.

"That's where you were taking me," Jan suggested, "to escape the spotters, right?"

"Right. It's either that or turn us in to Miz De Brock, hope she holds off killing us long enough to get you fixed up."

"You wouldn't have done that. I know you too well."

"I gave it a passing thought," he said.

Jan rolled out of his embrace ready to get up, but the effort and the resulting cranial aftershock made her relent.

She sank back into his arms. "On second thoughts, I'm good right here. Forever and no regrets."

"Except one," he reminded her.

"Except one."

"Come on, I'll help you up."

Walking on eggshells wasn't her style, but the eggshell in her own head seemed to rattle whenever she tried to up the tempo. So they crept into the valley, hugging the steep hillside, umpteen rocky overhangs above providing a modicum of cover from the spotter craft. The germs returned shortly before Jan and Vaughn reached the cave entrance, having found a number of other passageways which honeycombed the interior of the island.

"They're great at picking out detail, but the one major thing they lack is instinct," he told her. "They can't see danger unless it's spelled out in neon letters."

"Which is why they pay you the big bucks, Hotshot. Am I right?"

"You're not wrong." He drew his Kruger and spun it on his fingers just like the gunslingers in those dopey OC outlaw movies. But he dropped it and hurriedly picked it up.

The cave, more like a gash in the rock, was barely big enough for them to fit into. Jan had done a lot of after-hours pot-holing in her rebellious teen days – mostly to find new dens so she could do all the things she wasn't allowed to do – but she'd forgotten how physically taxing it could be when the gaps were so narrow. With the added encumbrance of their breathers and packs, sliding down through the tight holes required more logistical wherewithal than either of them would have liked. As Vaughn had said, the germs were great mappers but poor storytellers: big on detail but no use when it came to conveying experience. The descent into the sanctum proved the hardest part of her entire expedition thus far. She had to lie down when they finally reached the shore of the underground lake, the muscles in her non-bionic limbs hot and wobbly, her temple pain as jagged as a cracked diamond. She took the bundle Vaughn lowered down and used it as a pillow.

Gone was her capacity for giddy excitement, that wide-eyed authoring of fresh discoveries, but even Jan had to admit that her first sight of the subterranean lake was magical. A kind of maroon glow bleeding out of the cyclopean silhouettes of stalagmites, and even more imposing stalactites that pointed down like the wisdom teeth of ever-patient epochs wary of the crunch at the end of time, filled her with appreciation, if not a little awe. It was a vast, self-contained world, likely with its own ecosystem. The wine-dark water sloshed, throwing up pink horses in this eerie, almost infrared light only a planet as secretive as Hesperidia could have hidden from human science. Only it wasn't a secret, not really. She'd find its source and record and catalogue it just as she would the countless unprecedented lifeforms dwelling down here, just as she'd done the hundreds, thousands of other discoveries.

But for a moment, just for a moment, it was fantasyland as only a girl of eight could dream, a cave of wonders and dreams and ebullient romance. Despite what was coming, she hoped she'd never forget how disarming this feeling was. It was everything she'd journeyed to the stars to find, once upon a time.

"Well, Doc, I have to hand it to you – this place rarely disappoints." Vaughn sat beside her on a sloping, slate-like ledge a few feet from the water's edge. "What are you going to call it?"

She smiled up at him. "This one's all yours."

"Really? Okay, how about … Bloodshine Lake?"

Jan rolled her eyes. Once a lawman …

"No good?" he asked.

"It's fine. Here, give me a hand," she said, struggling upright, "I have an idea how we can make these slippery ledges a little safer." She instructed him to pocket as much grit from the little beaches as he could, so they could spread it over the especially dangerous sections ahead. It was a rugged, winding course around the water to where the germs had spotted the submerged craft, and looked perilous. The grit helped their footing. Every now and then a noise would emerge from across the lake, a deep, unnerving noise that was part foghorn, part guttural cry, as though the voices of two distinct creatures overlapped in simultaneous communication.

Jan noticed the stem of a tall, pale, rubbery fungus, a species she'd never seen before, draw thorns as she and Vaughn passed. Its cap also ejected a dark cloud of gas whenever they ventured too close, within a couple of feet. She warned Vaughn to steer clear of them. Similarly, the barnacle-like crustaceans that formed a thick, ragged lip over the edge of any low ledges overhanging the water, produced tiny spines over their vulnerable parts when threatened. She'd seen this before in many, many organisms on the Hesp: quick, vicious defensive measures, often poisonous.

"I'm starting to think the little critters are more dangerous than the big ones," Vaughn observed.

"That's kind of the moral of self-defense, isn't it? The more vulnerable you are, the more prepared you have to be."

"Something like that."

"But we're gonna be okay, right?"

He turned to give her a reassuring glance. "Oh, we have a few tricks up our sleeves. And they still think we were blown up on the beach."

"I wouldn't bet on it."

"Why not?"

She stopped, let her shoulders sink into a bitter sigh. "'Cause they're waving to us, Vaughn. Look, ahead, right where we're supposed to be! They're here and they're waving to us. With bigger guns than ours."

"Stay behind me." He glanced down at the two jittery green dots on his chest, raised his hands above his head, then fixed his gaze on the two men across the water. "Whatever happens, do as I do."

"But we can't give ourselves in! Not yet. Not until we know what's going on. Not until I know Stopper's okay."

"Just … follow my lead."

"What if they're here to kill us?"

"They'd have done it by now."

"What if they're here to find out what we know *then* kill us?"

"I'm counting on it."

"Vaughn?"

"Mm."

"Watch your footing. I have a bad feeling about this lake – what's in it."

"Damn, there goes my master plan."

"You're kidding, right?" She swallowed hard.

"About having a master plan, yeah."

"It's just … those scarecrows, this water source, the absence of other animal life … and those noises we keep hearing …"

"I was thinking the same thing," he said. "And I need you to keep on doing just that, Doc."

"What? Thinking?"

"It might be our one big advantage. Your intuition. This is your home. They're tourists."

"Uninvited tourists," she added.

"Right, here we go. I'm going to try the old Omicron charm, flash the badge, razzle-dazzle 'em. Think it's worth a try?"

"Um, not so much."

"Me neither."

Less than a baseball pitch away from the two riflemen – they appeared as sleek as dolphins, wearing state-of-the-art amphibian gear – Vaughn slowed his pace and veered a little toward the water's edge. "Jan, when I say go, drop your pack and dive in."

"You said *what?*"

"Straight down. As deep as you can. Don't come up for at least a minute."

Her head wound suddenly began to jack-hammer. She realized it matched the rhythm of her runaway heartbeat. "And those bad feelings we had ... about what's down there?"

"Worry about them after we climb out."

"The badge and charm thing's sounding good about now."

"Okay, Jan ... start to your right and it's ready ... set ... *go!*"

She rushed her sidewise gamble and the momentum of her spin worked against her attempt to gain height during the dive. Jan entered the water shoulder-first in a tumble, instantly losing her bearings as she floundered upside-down, downside-up and every contortion in between. Fast-moving projectiles, no bigger than her pinkie, snipped past her. They left strings of fizz in their wake through the water.

It was warm like a tepid bath. Clearer than she'd imagined; the dark rosy light hacked silently at the surface and reminded her of one of those harshly-cut gemstones that, when twirled, splintered the light from torches in museum halls full of suits of armor. She glimpsed the shadowy outline of the submerged ship far below. It was bigger than she'd realized, bigger even than the *Pitch Hopper,* though its shape was tough to discern, being so mangled and overgrown with vegetation. A cluster of marker tags blinked across its roof.

Ahead, for she now had her bearings, a nib of blinding white light hovered for a moment before expanding like a lit fuse in slow-motion at the instant of detonation. A sudden shockwave drove Vaughn back and ripped a tunnel through the water in the opposite direction. Before the shock hit her, Jan closed her eyes, an involuntary reflex.

When she opened them, she was upside-down, downside-up again, but there was someone else in the lake with them. He sank and sank, twitching a little but otherwise dead, a huge cauterized chunk missing from his torso, and a leg gone as well, so that he resembled a question mark as he spun slowly to his grave. The cloud of blood and bits of flesh wavered in the ripples rebounding from the shockwave. It was then that Jan snapped to her senses.

Blood in the water!

But wait – had it been a minute? Vaughn had told her to stay under for a full minute. Weighing the immediate danger of the other rifleman if she surfaced too soon with the imminent threat of being hot lunch for whichever predator first sniffed the human chum – and there were *always* predators on Hesperidia – their hunting acuity was legendary – was a close call.

She trusted Vaughn.

A distant, barely audible tone caressed her inner ear, like one of those infamous swansong frequencies you heard when that part of your hearing died and you would never hear it again. She wanted to finger the itch it left, but Vaughn gave her arm a firm squeeze to let her know it was time to resurface.

The other rifleman was even more of a mess, she found. Vaughn's Kruger had obliterated him; there wasn't much left on the lip of rock where he'd stood, and the rest was on its way down to the blinking markers of the ghost ship.

"I'm not sorry," she said, "but that gun of yours still scares the hell out of me."

"I know. I couldn't take any chances. Been a long time since I used it in water." He dialed its yield setting back to its default. "There. Better?"

"A little." She fetched their packs, handed Vaughn his. "What I want to know is how they got in here before us. Something we missed?"

"Not sure." He scanned the shores of the sanctum. "Those were amphibious suits they were wearing. My guess is they either sailed a submersible in from the ocean or used propulsive diving gear."

"Either way, it's only a matter of time before the rest of them show up," Jan replied. "Trust me, that … plus *this*," motioning at the cloudy mess in the water, "does not end well."

"That cave was somewhere near here. And if I'm not mistaken …" He checked the digital vector-map the germs had made during their recce, "… it's between the crashed ship in the water and the mystery cave up above. *There*. There in the ribs of that alcove. A straight shot … straight up."

Jan noticed two things that didn't belong: one of them gave her hope, the other a shivery chill. A crude ladder climbed the cave shaft. Its wooden rungs had been hewn

196

from the petrified trees on which the scarecrow carcasses hung. So this *was* vertical access, a way into the heart of the hillside. On the other hand, they were being watched. A fish-egg camera rotated on its bracket between the second and third rungs, its lilac iris flared and trained on their approach.

At first she thought it might belong to the two divers Vaughn had just killed. They'd likely attached the blinking markers to the crashed vessel, so why not this surveillance camera as well? No. On closer inspection, it was encrusted with sediment, and its bracket was rusted; it had been here some time, perhaps even as long as the ladder itself.

"What do we do now?" she asked. "That shaft's bound to be booby-trapped."

Vaughn dabbed the button on the side of his breather to tint his visor. "Look closer." He dabbed it a few more times. Jan did likewise.

"I'll be a …" The darker her visor became, the clearer she could make out the flashes of light in the center of the camera's iris. Random? Again, she looked closer. There was a rhythm of some kind, sequencing. "Dots and dashes? It's telling us something in Morse Code?"

"I think so."

"You know Morse, right? All you Boy Scouts know Morse."

"It's been a while," he replied. "Okay, dot-dash-dot is an R. That's another R. Dash-dot-dash-dash is a Y. Then we have a pause, which means a new word. I-V-E, space, D-I-S-A-B-L-E-D, space, S-E-C-U-R-I-T-Y, space … CLIMB

… UP … AGENT … VAUGHN … AND … RANGER … CORBIJA … MONSTERS … COMING … HURRY."

"Wait – how does he know us?"

"Seriously? *That's* your question?" Vaughn glanced at her askance. "Only a zoologist wouldn't crap her pants at the word monsters. Me, I'm not waiting for a second invitation. I'm getting the hell up this shaft."

She yanked his hand away from the rung. "Easy, Bub. If you're going to crap yourself, at least let me go first. Boy Scout etiquette."

Vaughn laughed a nervous laugh, then swallowed a lump the size of a pool ball as she brushed past him to start her ascent. "Never did like caves," he whispered. "Don't do anything up top until I get there."

She called down, "Then move your ass." The thought of finding Stopper up there left her feeling nimble and weightless and, well, grateful. Yes, grateful to this mystery intruder, *if* Stopper was up there and unharmed. It had been a hell of a journey to find him. Almost as epic as his had been to keep the girl alive.

No more surprises, she thought, imagining Hesperidia itself listening. *Just give him back to me and we'll be quiet from now on, I promise.*

Chapter Fourteen

The far-off *pat-pat* of remnant morning rain dripping from leaf to leaf before the hot overhead sun bakes it into steam, wakes him like a trusty old friend. He knows the patterns well, the sequences of sounds and smells that cycle through the days and nights at his home in the Keys. They tell him when and where he is. They tell him a thousand little things in the service of a precious few: is there anything awry, anything new, anything that might threaten Jan and him in their safe compound on the island he's marked every inch of?

Here the smells do not match that *pat-pat* sound. The smells do not match period. He forces his eyes open but only for a misty moment. They're heavy and damp and the air is thick – thick and dull, like swamp water. He sniffs wet rubber, something metallic, but worst of all the reek of his own salty, unbathed odor. In licking his dry lips his tongue slides across a slippery surface. Again, he forces his weary eyes open, again they see only the glob of a steamy window.

Is he lying against the wall he could not see? What happened to him? Dear memories of the girl slither through limp inkling bubbles that can't quite grow into thoughts. He recalls a forest, tracks in the dirt, dangers unknown. A deep breath tickles his insides, sends vines of sweet sensation reaching up behind his eyes, where he sees colors, where part of him wants to drift into them. Another part, the part that hasn't slept – not really – fights the rush of easy, empty defeat. His task is not yet completed.

He stirs but can't lift his head. Limbs and muscles feel wrapped in warm, leafy lianas. Every effort leaves him panting into the rubbery swamp air. A blink seems to clear the mist. Another deep breath sees its return. The more he blinks and breathes, the more the inklings swell into full, lucid thoughts, the more he realizes he's inside somewhere. Indoors *and* inside glass. He's breathing against a window, and each breath heats up the glass house. An occasional slight breeze touches his coat but not his head, so only his head is encased in the glass house? That thought would ordinarily panic him but Stopper is too weak to panic. His curiosity grapples with it instead – strangely relevant recollections – the creature he tracked, the pack of creatures behind the unseen wall, the man with one big eye he saw from the bottom of the ravine, the man with two eyes he saw approach him from behind the wall, Jan's mask, Dorcas's mask – visions, ideas that seemed jumbled, trying to rearrange themselves, join themselves together so he can understand them, but to no avail.

"Stopper?"

The sound of her voice always did make him want to solve *attaboy* problems. If only he was back home. If only she was …

"*Stopper!* It *is* you!"

His wagging tail repeatedly *pings* against something hollow and metallic. He fidgets and pants and delves deep for the dearest, whiniest bark he's ever given.

"Ohmygod, where have you *been*? I didn't think I'd ever *see* you again. My boy, my beautiful boy, what have they done to you? Come here, you *good boy! Good boy!*"

He sees her faint outline snuggle up to him, feels her arms nestle around his neck and imagines her smell as real and magnificent as ever it was. Her words break into sobs. He never did like that sound, but he's too happy, his world is too complete for anything but blissful licks against warm, slippery glass and his dream-come-true.

The sound of another dear voice hikes his excitement up through another few layers of tiredness. He's almost fully awake now, though the resistance mounts, dragging him back down into the sleepy fog as he hears "Good for you, Stopper! Good for you, boy! You made it." Vaughn patting his side and rubbing his belly is another dream fulfilled. He loves Vaughn like he loves no other human except Jan. That these two are here together, showering him with praise and affection like this … he can't imagine ever being happier. He can't imagine ever leaving them again.

As the tiredness and the excitement overcome him, the vines of sweet sensation reach once again. This time they take hold, and this time he doesn't fight them. He feels himself settling into a place he knows well, into a sleep he'll be happy to wake from, a place where nothing else matters, except …

Dorcas. If only Dorcas was here too …

"First guess? He's been drugged. And the bastard that did it is behind all this." Jan inspected the breathing apparatus attached to the back of Stopper's neck. "It's an old rig, decades old, like the standard Goldilocks re-breather they used to furnish colonists with, only this has been adapted, reshaped. Look at the patchwork seams, the re-soldered connections. Somebody's improvised the hell out of this thing. It's feeding him pressurized Hesperidian air to keep him alive in an oxygen environment."

"So our mystery guest is an ally after all. He saved Stops's life."

"To be confirmed." She checked the sleeping dog's pulse against her wristwatch, didn't appear alarmed by the count. "He tranqed him. That could have gone wrong in so many ways. No, whoever did this is on my shit list until he proves otherwise."

On the other hand, Vaughn was becoming increasingly inclined to give this person the benefit of the doubt. Not only had he probably saved the girl from the flooding canyon, not only had he gone to these extraordinary lengths to keep Stopper alive, he had also invited Jan and Vaughn up into his sanctum at a time when hostiles were gathering in force.

Spotting an adjoining tunnel, he said, "I think I'll have a look around, see if I can find the girl." He realized he hadn't holstered his Kruger and was about to suggest Jan accompany him, for her own safety, when the sight of her cuddling her boy, whispering sweet words, told him her rescue mission was at an end, that she would stay put until he woke, even if the planet imploded.

She called after him: "Vaughn, be careful. We still don't know what we're dealing with."

"I know. Stay alert."

"There's no need for that," a deep, gentle male voice answered from the entrance to the tunnel. A dazzling blue light blinked behind him, lending him an intermittent, almost saintly corona as he stood watching them. In the gaps between flashes his appearance was contradictory: old but bolt-upright, wiry but strong-looking, unkempt but not bedraggled as one might expect a reclusive cave-dweller to be, and sunburnt. His face was sharp and sleek; that, together with his short, spiky silver hair, gave a vivacious edge to his otherwise avuncular air.

Despite being one of the most astute profilers in the Bureau, Vaughn couldn't pinpoint the man's age – anything between sixty and seventy-five. A fierce radiance in his blue-gray eyes suggested intelligence, hyper-alertness.

He wore a ratty old blue waistcoat that had once adorned a man of high station. Underneath, a durable survival suit, long-sleeved and a good fit. He'd cut off the legs of both this suit and a pair of cargo pants below the knees and wore them now as shorts. Why he walked barefoot Vaughn couldn't figure out, as the cave floor was damp rock. But his tracks outside had also been made by bare feet, which was insane. Maybe he just didn't have any shoes? Again, that notion didn't fit. The innovation he'd displayed in all other aspects of his survival plight thus far was next-level.

"Who are you?" Vaughn stiffened his posture but lowered his weapon when he satisfied himself the man was unarmed.

"A fellow survivor. Pleased to meet you, Agent Vaughn and Doctor Corbija." It was a soothing voice, completely unguarded. The words themselves, however, were not.

"How do you know us?"

"Oh, I've been listening in for years. If it weren't for the rangers here, I wouldn't have known humans still existed. And though I've never personally tried it, I'm a big fan of Alien Safari."

"Who are you?" shouted Jan. "How did you get here?"

"If you'll both be so kind as to follow me, I'll endeavor to explain." He stepped to one side and gestured down the passageway that Vaughn now saw was blocked by a grav-lev trolley. Old and battered, it nonetheless floated with remarkable poise a steady few inches off the floor, with no sign of the wonkiness that bedeviled their equilibrium after long use. Its flashing hover lights still worked like a charm, too. The man lifted a pair of compressed gas canisters into it and made the effort look easy – no small feat. Then he pressed a pre-set vector function on the trolley's dash for it to guide itself back to wherever it had come from. "Please," he motioned again, "we don't have much time."

"I'm good right here," answered Jan, pulling up a manmade wooden stool from a nearby workbench.

"He's perfectly safe, I can assure you."

"You can't make that assurance. No one can. He won't be safe until he's back home with me."

"Jan, maybe we should …" But Vaughn didn't even bother finishing when he saw her lay her head next to Stopper's. "Let's go," he told the man. Still he didn't holster his sidearm.

The narrow passageway, slick with moisture and ribbed with aborted stalagmites that hadn't been able to stand upright and had instead congealed with the walls, quickly grew in height as it arced to the right. All of a sudden it opened up into a chamber the size of a lighthouse, with a roof over a hundred feet high, jagged and spangled with glittering sediment. The echoey acoustics lent it an ancient, almost mythic air of gothic mystery. This was where the man had made his home, evidenced by the ship's bunk he'd set in a nook just to the right. It was protected from a potential through-draught that, when the photonic blister wasn't sealing the cave, might carry air from outside into the trio of passages dotting the far side of the chamber. Steady light emanated from two of them.

At first Vaughn didn't notice the girl lying tucked up in the bunk. She was so small and the light was so dim in that corner of the chamber, it was a pleasant relief when he saw her shift position and tug the blanket, exposing the pink of her bodysuit. He covered her up and left her to sleep.

"Is she—"

"Sedated? Yes, but only mildly. She was suffering from insomnia and refused to sleep until I'd told her my story.

My *whole* story. She's bright as a button. I have to say one of the hardest things about being marooned is that lack of contact with kids. I've missed my granddaughter something rotten. The quirks. The messiness. The total disregard for what the future holds. Children are so present in the moment it's infectious to be around. Dorcas brought all that back, if only briefly, when I tried to tell her my story earlier."

"Tried to tell?"

"You have to understand," the man went on, "that keeping oneself a secret for so long rather bifurcates one. On the one hand the paranoia, the ceaseless vigilance. Not only being marooned but having to actively stay hidden even when the means of rescue arrives. But on the other, the need to just *tell someone*. Tell them your secret, but more importantly tell them you *still exist*. Consequently, I made rather a pig's ear of telling my tale because I was in too much of a hurry to get it all out. In opening the sluice after so long I let all the unnecessary parts flood out too. But more than that, I suppose I've just forgotten how to talk to children."

Vaughn glanced around the chamber. It was a well-ordered, utilitarian abode, with practically no effort made to add comfort, apart from the bed. He'd clearly salvaged every last item, coil of wire and engineering mechanism from the wreckage of his ship. Anything he hadn't found a use for he'd stored and catalogued on shelved scaffolding he'd carved himself from the trunks of trees. This stood against the primary wall, dozens of tiers high, the uppermost shelves only accessible by a ridiculously tall and sturdy-looking ladder. The grav-lev trolley could rise that high, Vaughn knew, but only under maximum power-consumption. Where was he getting his power?

Into the wall above his reading desk he'd carved crude portraits of people, male and female. Next to each he'd tacked a paper profile with wrinkled pages of information. As Vaughn inched closer, he discerned some of the names: Corbija, Juanita, XZ; Bilali, XB; Jelicho, Ed, XZ; Bilderbeck, Alexander, XB; Vaughn, Ferrix, Det. (OB).

"My own long-term investigation, Detective. I'm afraid it's all rather sketchy." The man chuckled at his own pun, and Vaughn felt a pang of sympathy.

"You seem to know a lot about us. You've been monitoring our comms?"

"Yes. As often as possible."

"How long have you been here?"

"Before I answer that, Detective Vaughn …" The man gave a squeal of delight, covered his face with his hands and spun around on his heels. It seemed both out of character for someone so stiff and proper and yet completely plausible, given what he'd been through. "I can hardly believe it … *the* Agent Vaughn, here in my office, interrogating me. You're not at all what I imagined. Ten, fifteen years younger. Much less intimidating in person. I'd like to shake your hand before we go any further, if that's all right?"

Vaughn indulged him, noted his stronger-than-average grip. "Pleased to meet you, Mister …"

"Oh, Threlfall. Joshua Acton Threlfall. That's my name."

The woman whose jaw Jan had almost broken back at the cove was called Threlfall – he'd logged her tag – Imogen Jacqueline Threlfall.

"How long have you been here?"

"That's … complicated."

"How so?"

"Well, a man of your singular talents, you've no doubt divined some … peculiarities so far?"

Vaughn looked around again, delved deeper into a few of the more remarkable aspects of this habitat. Most prominent of all was the abundance of—

"Expound your thoughts. Please. I'd love to hear how a great detective's mind works."

It struck Vaughn how evasive Threlfall was being, how he'd dodged this question – the most pressing question of all – several times already. But it might just be playfulness, him bigging up the truth for his own excitement, the denouement to his long, arduous survival plight. It was a watershed day for this mystery castaway.

Vaughn played along. "First, there's far more equipment here than a ship of that size could have carried." He pointed up to the scaffolding, of which even the highest tiers were full of machine parts and odds and ends. "Second, the photonic shield. There has to be a significant power source to maintain it, and my environmental readouts haven't picked up that kind of rad count – unless you've encased the reactor somehow, which, again, is more heavy equipment. And third, there's currently a massive salvage operation underway; it's here, in fact. For someone who monitors comms so diligently, you must know they're coming for you, or for something you possess. The fact that you're not panicked by that knowledge, even though you've gone to extraordinary lengths to keep your existence on Hesperidia a secret, suggests you have a viable means of escape."

But what escape? Unless one of the tunnels led to another ship, he wouldn't get far on foot. Yet if he had a ship capable of reaching orbit, why hadn't he used it before now?

The word *Spearhead* kept latching onto his threads of reasoning. It seemed to twine at least a few of them together, though to what end he couldn't fathom. Sondergaard had first mentioned it in relation to the terrorist bombings on the moon bridge. Then Miz De Brock's pilot assassin, Crowhurst, had burbled it during his final agonizing moments on the beach.

Spearhead.

It was important not just to De Brock and her sister, but to ISPA itself. A Core congressman and umpteen sub-committee delegates were here to retrieve it.

Spearhead.

What could it possibly have to do with destroying the Gilpraxia Moon Bridge? With terrorists wanting to sabotage a peaceful commercial venture? And what *had* happened to that slippery bomber who'd jaunted out into space and performed a feat of prestidigitation inside his octagonal Sphere of Doom? It gave a whole new dimension to escapology, that was for damn sure!

Spearhead? Escapology? A scientific secret …

"How much do you know about teleportation?" he asked Threlfall. It was the least practical theory imaginable – everyone knew it was impossible to coherently transport more than a single particle or molecule the quantum way – but right now it was all he had.

"A clumsy word," came the nonetheless telling reply.

"You have a better one?"

"Not in any language you're conversant in, Detective."

"What then? Alien?"

"Universal."

"You mean mathematics."

Threlfall quirked a smile. "Precisely. You don't disappoint, Mr Vaughn. I can see why she likes you."

Vaughn didn't reply.

"I've one more thing I want to show you, then I'll tell you my story, my whole story from the beginning. I promise." He fetched a container full of turquoise liquid from a rucksack he'd left on his desk chair, offered it to Vaughn. "Care to wet your whistle first?"

"What is it?"

"Purified water with a little flavoring: it's quite pleasant, I assure you. And it will allow you to do me the courtesy of removing your breather while we talk, man to man, as it were."

"What about alien pathogens?" asked Vaughn.

"I'm still here, aren't I?" Threlfall sighed, then added sharply, "What more will it take to impress you? A photonic defense system, airlocks, an oxygenator," counting them on his fingers, "water filtration, re-breathers adapted for canines for oxygen *and* native air, a geothermal generator, a radio receiver built from scratch, remote CCTV surveillance, sanctuary for years. Let me tell you, *no one* else could have achieved all this on his own." After a grunt of frustration, "Why not add a decontamination chamber to my DIY list, then, along with a sauna and a pizza oven and a holographic escort service? Christ! I might be a genius, Detective, but I don't have a magic wand."

"I believe you." Vaughn slid his visor up and took a swig of the marzipan-flavored water, then fixed his breather back into place without taking a breath. "But I just don't trust this planet. Thanks for the drink, though."

"Have it your way."

He stopped by another alcove, where he'd cobbled together a makeshift command console from the crashed ship's dash and other spare components. It was all old tech, a lot older than Vaughn. Threlfall checked the live-feed image on what appeared to be the last working monitor on an ancient multi-screen VDU; it showed the camera's view at the bottom of the ladder: the underground lake. The lights and water wakes of numerous amphibious craft confirmed Miz De Brock's team was closing in.

"That photonic blister of yours is about to get a workout. You've turned it back on, I presume?"

"The moment you and Ranger Corbija passed through the airlock."

"And it's strong enough to keep these people out?"

"More than strong enough, whoever they are."

Vaughn blew warm air across his damp face as he followed Threlfall. The rest of him was starting to feel the heat too. No doubt the geothermal power source was close by. An industrial strength cable followed the right-hand tunnel downhill as it wound in a jagged crescent to a kind of antechamber just above sea level (according to Vaughn's altimeter gauge), neither as tall nor as big as the main sanctum. One side of the room had completely caved in. Dozens of elaborate metal convex panels along the walls and the pile of rubble, and some even hanging overhead, supported by brackets bolted to the rock, formed an impressive octagonal framework. It had the appearance of an unfinished dome, but the gaps between panels were always at regular intervals, as though they were part of the design. Scorch marks here and there hinted at crude attempts to re-forge the metalwork, though most of it was so smooth and unblemished that Vaughn wondered how the hell it could have survived the crash without more damage.

The octagonal shape cast his mind back to the peculiar objects he'd seen on the moon bridge, one of which the bomber had mysteriously vanished inside. Again, the word *Spearhead* thrust itself to the fore.

"This is a teleportation device," he concluded. "This is how you've been able to fetch all these supplies. This is how you plan to escape. *This* is what they're after. Only …"

"Only what?"

"They already have this tech. A perp made an extraordinary getaway a few days ago, slipped through my clutches, by climbing into a smaller version of this, only his was solid."

"How much smaller?"

Vaughn held up his hands about four feet apart. "And he did it in null-g, without a suit."

Threlfall caressed the surface of one of the panels, then kissed it. "They've progressed as far as human science will allow. As far as my own science has got them. No, this is not teleportation, Agent Vaughn. That concept belongs to twentieth century pulp nonsense. This is something else entirely. This is an ancient means of traversing the dark sea to its farthest shores, celestial gulfs mankind has scarcely dreamed of, navigable only by me. This, dear Detective, is my gateway to the cosmos."

Intrigued, but hardly won over by all the pontificating and grandiloquence – ways of speaking that had always had the adverse effect on him – Vaughn let the man bask in his own glory. He'd worked so hard here for so long, this chance to finally share his accomplishment, whatever it really was, had to be of profound importance to him. And when all was said and done, he had given sanctuary when Vaughn, Jan, Stopper and the girl had badly needed it.

"You'd like to know how it works, I take it?" Threlfall's lips trembled with prideful emotion as he unmagnoed a compartment at the front of his utility belt.

"I wouldn't mind."

Retrieving a cylindrical beige bar about a foot in length, with a straight, shallow bend at one end, Threlfall could barely hold back his tears. "This ... *this* is what they've come for."

The object's translucency only became clear when Vaughn shone his head torch on it. The scientist recoiled at first, then slowly relented. Strong light passing through it revealed an elaborate geometric pattern running as a kind a fluid spine inside. The pattern appeared infinitely complex.

As Threlfall held it up, gazing, mesmerized, into its secrets, the cave began to tremble. The muffled sound of heavy drilling, if Vaughn wasn't mistaken, seemed to be coming from the other side of the collapse.

"Hold on a minute," said Vaughn. "I thought you *didn't* have a magic wand."

Threlfall arched an eyebrow at him, twitched a smile, then stuffed the object back into his belt.

"In case you didn't know, these aren't retirees panning for gold outside," Vaughn added. "They've brought industry. One way or another, they'll get in here, even if they have to undermine this whole island."

"Industry, huh?"

"Backed by Congress. And your own kin."

Vaughn had expected more of a reaction — well, *some* reaction, at least, to the news that the man's family was here

– but Threlfall simply nodded and strolled away, back up to the main chamber.

"Did you hear what I said? Your relatives are here: two young women with lots of influence: Edith De Brock and Imogen Threlfall."

"You'll have to bear with me, Detective. I'm going to have to tell you my story while I make final preparations." The scientist quickened his pace. "I've a few loose ends to tie up before I leave."

Following hot on his heels, Vaughn reiterated, "Edith and Imogen? Who are they? Nieces?"

"I don't recognize the names. My family, you say?"

"They're fully grown. Thirtyish."

No response.

It didn't add up. After so long spent in isolation, a man would do anything to see his family. Unless he was telling the truth and he had no knowledge of them at all. Which meant he'd been missing for over three decades?

"Why don't you start from the beginning," Vaughn suggested. "The abridged version. And does your escape route have room for us – me, Jan, the girl and the dog?"

"Not the dog, I'm afraid. He's been bioengineered to breathe Hesperidian air. Where I'm going, I won't be able to make any more, so he'll have to stay here."

"Then that rules all of us out."

"Nonsense, Agent Vaughn. You'd throw away three human lives for one canine? Brave though he is, that's crazy logic."

As Vaughn helped him load several more oxygen canisters into the trolley, he replied, "It's called loyalty. A family needn't be defined by blood. One of us stays, we all stay. We'll take our chances here."

"Have it your way." The old man, spry as someone half his age, clambered up the scaffold ladder and retrieved a small stack of books he'd tied together with cord. "Here. Catch this." He dropped them into Vaughn's waiting arms. A few of the titles were: *Rendezvous with Rama; Light Reefs and the Dark Sea; The Aeneid; Into Perihelion.* His desert island reads? Some people preferred paper books, that tactile feel of turning pages and running their fingers over inked text. Vaughn wasn't one of them, but he could see the appeal. Especially for someone who led a solitary life, an actual book would be a friend of sorts, an intimate.

"How do we get out of here once you've gone?" Vaughn asked him. "How do we disable the blister?"

"The coupling is built onto the generator. I'll have to show you. Now then … where were we? The last oh-two tanks filled and ready. Food and water have gone ahead. Weapons are waiting there as well. Ah yes, mustn't forget these." From behind the scaffold he fetched a military-grade Kursk N-71 sniper rifle – a model not in circulation since the last commerce war, over a century ago – and a tranq stick. "I'd say a few more trips with the trolley should do it. Then I'll fetch the dogs and bid you *adieu,* Detective. This place is really starting to shimmy. They're more tenacious than I'd imagined. I was rather hoping you would come with me, you and Jan. You're both so resourceful. I feel like I've got to know you well these past couple of years."

"Not well enough if you think we'd ever consider leaving Stopper. But thanks for the offer." He paused while the old man configured his own breather. "Where is it you're going again?"

"Ah, ah." Threlfall's impish finger wag irritated Vaughn. This man had what the powers-that-be wanted. His secret had precipitated this wild alien goose chase that had very nearly cost him Jan and Stopper, and killed the little girl, not to mention his own dice with death back at the beach. And now Houdini wanted to up and vanish, just like that, taking his little magic show back on the road and leaving them to face the snow-haired hellcat and her full claws-out invasion? Maybe he should *make* this joker stay to face the music. *Make* him hand over the teleportation wand or whatever the hell it was. Place him under arrest for … something. Vagrancy. Owning an illegal firearm. Hell, how about crimes against fashion.

But at the back of his mind, the Golden Fleece fiasco kept gnawing at him – corrupt ISPA officials bending the rules to obtain something extraordinary they wanted for "research." The more powerful the secret, the more far-reaching its implications, the more they had to have it, for "research." And Threlfall's was an absolute doozy, no question. He'd kept it under the radar all this time for a reason, and not just for the patent. These people were willing to kill for it; they'd proved that. If he'd learned anything from his mentor Saul DeSanto's treachery regarding the Fleece, it was that sometimes great discoveries needed to be introduced a small miracle at a time, off the radar, so that good people could use them where they were needed most, for the right reasons, and when the time was ready, *then* use them for the benefit of all.

Yes, he'd much rather Threlfall continued his research in secret than let the war-mongers get their hands on it and blunder its application in some weaponized bloodlust first-strike on the enemy. The overriding point being escalation: once ISPA started using it in that way, it would only be a matter of time before the enemy got hold of that tech and used it against humanity, only in a bigger, better and badder form. That had been the Finaglers' *modus operandi* since before the current war had even begun.

Either way, this day probably wasn't going to end well. The least Vaughn could do was hear the guy out before deciding on his next move.

"Why so reticent?" he asked a self-amused, muttering Threlfall. "I thought you were eager to share your story. Now you're going to disappear again? It might be a while before you have a chance to tell the truth about what really happened."

"Maybe. Maybe not. If everything goes to plan, I'll return with knowledge that will make this discovery seem like a toddler's first kite flight. But to answer your question, Agent Vaughn, I'm reticent to share specific information like dates and coordinates because you've refused my invitation. Which by default makes you a rival, a part of the establishment that betrayed me. So out of necessity this will be an even more abridged version of the account than I was going to give you.

"It began well over a century ago, when I was invited to join the Hartdagen Initiative as a young physicist – a prodigy, they all said – for a research project at Mars's North Pole. What I thought was a geological expedition turned out to be something truly extraordinary. A man named Thorpe-Campbell – no doubt you've heard of him …"

"The famous athlete and pioneer?"

"Yes. And he made his greatest discovery there, under hundreds of feet of ice: a portal to an ancient transit system, buried for millions of years."

Vaughn had had direct experience of the mysterious goings-on in that region: no-fly zones, missing persons, classified logistics operations. He'd even investigated the murder of a field guide and his two children in Bowman's Reach, a town not all that far from the polar region. One of his few unsolved cases, in fact. But he had no idea they'd found something so … unprecedented. "What kind of transit system?"

"The kind that spans galaxies, maybe even clusters of galaxies. They called it the Star Binder. Thorpe-Campbell had already made several journeys through it when I arrived, and he was on the most ambitious expedition ever undertaken at that time. So I immediately signed up for the next one. I couldn't *wait* to see what was out there. What else was waiting to be discovered. Little did I know I was going to find, on only my first trip out, one of the rarest artefacts of the whole enterprise."

Threlfall gave his belt a gentle tap. "I believe this is one of the original tunnel-building tools used by the ancients. It's somehow able to summon a temporary adjoining arm that branches the main, permanent transit system. The Star Binder, as you can infer from its title, is like a network of tunnels running in and out of space-time. It links countless suns and draws gravitational energy from them to maintain its integrity. When I left the Initiative decades later, they were nowhere near to understanding the full scope of its physics. But after studying this artefact, which I kept a secret from them for years, I was able to effect a temporary, localized tunnel to transport complex matter at the macro level and keep its integrity intact. It was one of the most significant breakthroughs in the history of human science."

"It's nothing like warp gate tech, then?"

"Nothing at all. Warp gates fold space, instantaneously transporting vehicles from one point to another. A significant discovery, yes. But they have to be built on a very large scale, and they can only operate in a vacuum. Plus, they're ruinously expensive. The further you want to jump, the more energy it takes. That's why they're mostly installed by corporations for commercial ventures, and why long-distance space travel is so prohibitive for anyone who isn't rich or in law enforcement."

"Your method works on a smaller scale?" asked Vaughn.

"Smaller, more private, and infinitely cheaper. The stars themselves provide all the energy for transportation. All I have to do is prime my departure device before each journey. That's why I had to be so cagey with my research, why I never told anyone about the artefact. Even the little I've gleaned from its secrets has brought about a quantum leap in human physics. First, I tested it on several short-range solo trips through the Binder, refined it, perfected it. Then I was even more careful when I took out a private patent for it, away from the Initiative's prying eyes. Or so I thought."

"They stole your patent?" The notion didn't surprise Vaughn in the slightest.

"That wasn't the word they used. I forget the exact legal phrase; it had a smug, sinister ring to it. But yes, they seized my lab, my prototype pods, and reams of equations I'd solved where no one else could. If that's not theft, I don't know what qualifies."

"The legal phrase was probably 'eminent domain,'" suggested Vaughn. "It gives ISPA the right to take private property for public use under exceptional circumstances. But from what I understand, they'd be obligated to compensate you."

The note of naked disgust in the old man's scoff hinted at a darker, lonelier journey than Vaughn had anticipated. The government had forced him to turn rogue, perhaps to go into exile to finish his work. It had left him bitter, vengeful and single-minded.

"I took every last clip they offered," he said. "I leased a brand-new research lab on an outer colony moon, light-years away from the one they suggested; there were several other labs already established there, each privately owned and run and just as jealously guarded as mine. I bought a first-rate ship to take me there, with all the equipment and supplies I needed for an indefinite stay. And most importantly, I took the one piece of private property exempt from ISPA's eminent domain – everything in here." He tapped his head. "You see, unfinished equations aren't like crossword puzzles with missing letters. You can't infer what isn't there. It's more like the mathematics of music; notes alone mean nothing, but together, in harmony, with both form and abstraction and an end result you can conceptualize …"

There he broke off, seemingly able to sense Vaughn's wandering attention.

"What happened next, Professor?"

"Where was I? Ah yes, the Finaglers started attacking the colonies; worse, on one of my sojourns through the Binder, I spotted them camped outside my outpost. It was becoming dangerous. So, under fleet protection, we were all escorted back to the Inner Colonies; but we were attacked en route and most of the convoy of scientific vessels was destroyed. I managed to fend them off with some improvised counter-measures – scientists can be dangerous enemies, you know – and in a last-ditch gamble I entered the damaged warp gate and rolled the dice on a vector-less jump. I wound up near the Herculean system, and had just enough power to reach the only Goldilocks planet, L-Twelve. Never was much of a pilot, though. I crashed in the middle of the ocean, and started leaking radioactive fuel onto the sea bed. It was only by a fluke of fate that I sank into a deep-sea thermal current strong enough, with the help of the last joules of energy from my engine for propulsion along the way, to whisk me here … wherever here is. My last port, or so I thought. A dormant volcanic island in an archipelago of them: that's still all I really know about this place.

"To cut a long story short, I made this my base of operations. One of the canines travelling with me at the time of the crash had a litter of puppies, some of which are still with me now. I let them out now and then for exercise. They don't normally go very far, but one of them must have heard your dog. When he didn't come back, I went out looking, and that's when I saw the girl … "

Something distracted the old man, so Vaughn finished for him: "You saved her from the flood. That tells me a lot about you."

"Anyone would have done the same."

"Not in my experience."

The worry lines of Threlfall's frown burrowed deep into his sun-kissed brow, making him look his age. Vaughn's gambit – to impress upon the castaway that by rescuing Dorcas he'd re-joined humanity in all the ways that mattered – seemed to pay off. The old man was seeing himself objectively, perhaps for the first time in ages. If he kept looking, he might be able to see through his obsession, his mania for secrecy, the lonely end he was heading towards.

The drilling stopped. The cave no longer trembled. Silence seemed to coax Threlfall out of his reflection as he grabbed an old, modified re-breather from its hanger on the wall and put it on. Then he retrieved a long coil of damp climbing rope from the scaffold – probably the same one he'd used to save Dorcas – and made his way back down to the Star Binder apparatus, at the center of which he'd carefully arranged his tanks and equipment. He was now going to fasten it all together, Vaughn reckoned.

"I'll make this the last supply run," he said, scanning the chamber and the rubble. "Then the dogs can go through with me. They're already fast asleep in their cocoons. But I'm afraid … I'll have to ask you to return to your ranger friend, Agent Vaughn. I can't allow anyone to see what happens next. Not even an incorruptible lawman. I'm sure you understand."

"Perfectly."

But there were a few things about lawmen that the old man couldn't know. With a deft, practised unclasping of his baldric's rib pocket, Vaughn released the germs on his way out. They glided soundlessly to the walls, their hive AI coordinating them to the nearest nooks and shadows, the least detectable vantage points, where they awaited further instructions. Vaughn inched them into position at the edge of the tunnel, so that he had a clear remote view of the entire chamber.

He went up to check the ladder camera, to see why the intruders had stopped drilling. An animated confab was underway on the bank of the underground lake. More people than he could count. Most were dressed like the two riflemen he'd shot from underwater: uniform drysuits, rebreathers, retractable fin-boots: all expensive and pristine. But there were several at the heart of the gathering who didn't conform. Two were women, slim, white-haired, young. One, he was almost certain from the athletic posture and the jazzy customized wetsuit, was Imogen Threlfall. The other had to be her sister, Miz De Brock. She wore black leggings and a fleecy gray jumper a couple of sizes too big for her. The contrast between the two women was stark, bolstered by their opposing positions in the confab. Miz De Brock's uniformed employees and compatriots surrounded her and ringed the whole gathering, while Imogen's posse, including Bronston, stood by her side in tight-knit formation, weapons drawn but not aimed. Though neither woman appeared to speak, their rivalry was palpable, and many others were joining in the discussion.

When he looked closer, Vaughn had to do a double take. Then he sighed, convinced he was just getting punchy, that the long search had taken its toll on him. He took a deep breath, lifted his breather and rubbed his tired eyes until he saw afterglow blotches. Then he looked again, concentrating hard.

"Sonofabitch."

He *hadn't* been mistaken. Fastened to the baldrics of two men stood slightly apart from the rest, the unmistakable shape and luminosity of the Omicron badge was the last thing he'd expected to find down here.

But had Miz De Brock brought these agents with her? Was the Bureau itself complicit in this murderous salvage operation?

He tensed for a moment, the first wrinkles of outright anger he'd felt in a while threatening to ripple through him.

Congressional corruption he could stomach; that political mating ball was notorious for contorting the rules to accommodate its own slithering sleaze. But the Bureau was supposed to operate independently. An investigation, once assigned, was intractably the province of the agent responsible, superseded by no one until he or she relinquished that responsibility by official inked consent. Which meant that these were rogue agents, because the Bureau would never assign them bodyguard duty – that wasn't an Omicron role – and any Bureau personnel visiting this sector would have to check in with its supervising officer first. And Kraczinski hadn't—

"Son of a *bitch!*"

The big guy unclipped his badge and flashed it directly at the camera, then gave a breezy wave. Why hadn't Vaughn clocked him straightaway? That bulk. That slob. That boozy, bloated, brash, beautiful wife-bane bag of stubborn and potato chips, Kraczinski!

And who was that with him? Younger, leaner, the cocky posture, the impressive stand-my-ground-and-take-on-all-comers confidence, and he was arguing with several people at once – no, several *politicians* at once. That had to be Sondergaard.

More interesting still, they had a man in cuffs. Shorter than the rest, maybe under five feet. Vaughn instantly deduced the link: the bomber who'd jaunted outside the moon bridge had been roughly that height, and now Sondergaard had him. He'd somehow tracked him here and notified Kraczinski and now they'd crashed the party to arrest him.

Well, well. If he was right and that was the bomber, it changed everything. By association, it rendered Miz De Brock and this whole congressional treasure hunt subject to Omicron investigation. Which they were clearly having none of. No surprise there. The last thing politicians and corporate untouchables ceded was power, control.

It left Vaughn's colleagues in a sticky spot. They had the right of law on their side; the others, however, had greater numbers and superior firepower. And Miz De Brock, possibly with the permission of her friends from Congress, had already tried to kill one Omicron agent. Him. That made it highly likely, no, *inevitable* that they'd do it again, because they knew Vaughn and Jan were still alive and there was no way they could let them live now.

Christ. Jan was right. One way or another, this wasn't going to end well.

A bright, rose-colored glow lit the tunnel he'd just left. He brought up the germs' live feed on his portable VDU, but all he got was static. The germs, too, weren't responding. But they'd recorded everything they'd seen up to the blackout. He rewound the footage and watched Threlfall's every move.

Switching on the artefact appeared simple enough. By pressing both ends of the bar at once and then twisting the angled section to straighten it, the translucent spine inside lit up. At the moment this happened, dozens of glyphs located equidistantly around the metal panels began to glow and rotate. Their electric blue hue intensified to a brilliant luminance. This was when Threlfall stepped outside the perimeter of the apparatus, still holding the artefact. He stood almost on the spot the germs had arrayed themselves around; luckily, he didn't notice them.

From out of the panels' luminance grew a kind of membranous, transparent film that reflected, at a massively exaggerated size, the items Threlfall had piled in the center. It started out as a perfect shimmering blister with the full octagonal dimensions of the device, then began to shrink. As it did it quickly morphed into the collective shape of the items, becoming a mimetic skin that didn't quite cling to them but hovered a few inches around. The items appeared completely untouched and unharmed, even when the skin levitated them off the ground. Something opened up in the roof of the device. Several of the panels dimmed and then vanished, as if the top of the octagon had been sliced off. There was a blinding flash. Then static.

Vaughn timed the whole operation from first activation to blackout at just over twelve seconds. As he switched off the VDU and put it away, he realized his hands were shaking. The implications of this thing – something so unprecedented and alien it was almost indistinguishable from magic – frightened him. He hadn't the first clue how it worked or what, or even *when*, existed on the other side. How long did the journey take? Was it instantaneous? Would special relativity take its toll? A plethora of questions bombarded him, but the thought of Jan and Stopper, not to mention the little girl lying sound asleep across the chamber, refocused him on what really mattered here. On what he must do. Thinking like a detective and thinking like a man in love were by definition so opposite they bordered on schizophrenia. But not here, strangely enough. Not now.

Here they saw eye to eye in a way that shocked him, revealing a solution that hadn't occurred to him before and otherwise might never have. It had only a slim chance of success. But it was a chance.

Chapter Fifteen

"Channel seventeen. When I say 'Over and out', I want you to reactivate it right away," he told Jan, whose weary, puzzled expression switched to one of aloof resignation. As her fingers hovered over the coupling switch that turned the photonic shield's epicentral emanator on and off, she flicked Vaughn a cheeky wink.

It was so cute and irreverent, so utterly Jan, he decided right there that he never wanted to forget it.

"If you won't tell me what you're up to, what else can I do?" she said. "Threlfall in on this?"

"He's the key player."

"I don't hear him."

"You only need to hear three words. What are they?"

"All night long, baby."

"Jan."

"Over and out. Jeez Louise, you always like this on the job?"

Vaughn leaned in and stroked her upper arm, partly to wipe away a few wood shavings that had stuck to her while she'd been dozing with Stopper, and partly just to touch her, to make sure she was real.

"Do that again," she said.

He did, and their gazes, though separated by the smeared glasses of their visors, connected like they had the very first time they'd met in person, in the *Pitch Hopper's* airlock, moments after his initial touchdown on Hesperidia. Everything had changed since then, everything except that unspoken connection. He knew now that no matter what happened, they would always share it.

"You hum when you ruminate," she said. "Did you know that?"

"What? I do not."

"You were doing it just now. I can never make out the tune, but you definitely hum, Omicron. Is it me that brings out the music in you? Say it is or you'll be the one who's over and out."

Vaughn quirked an eyebrow. "You know what? You do bring out the music in me. No wonder I can't carry a tune worth a damn." And he sprinkled the wood shavings onto her frizzy black hair.

She didn't bother batting them off. Instead, her eyes slowly turned up and she pulled a goofy face.

"Okay, this is it," he said. "Remember, when you've reactivated it, go straight back to Stopper and the girl and stay hidden with the other dogs. It's best that nobody else sees you."

"What are those weird cocoons the other dogs are in? They freak me out. They're almost like … I don't know, cryo-pods, something for long-duration space flight."

"I'll ask Threlfall. Till then, keep your head down, okay?"

"Affirmative. Go do your agent thing."

He left the chamber at a jog. Leaving her alone like this, even though she wouldn't be alone for long, stung him in tender places because it reminded him what a massive gamble he was about to take. He focused instead on the sequence of events, the only sequence of events, that might possibly see him beat this trap.

The CCTV monitor showed no significant change below. They were still arguing, posturing, and most of the players were still armed. If the two white-haired sisters hadn't been rivals, Kraczinski and Sondergaard would likely now be dead; fortunately, the treasure seekers were divided, and it had muddied their resolve. At least for the time being. The presence of congressional representatives had probably also helped stay any summary executions, especially of lawmen. Politicians, as a rule, didn't like to get their hands dirty.

But Miz De Brock's flier *had* tried to assassinate Vaughn and Jan on the beach. Vaughn had no choice but to attempt an intervention.

Having already deactivated the photonic shield – Jan was only waiting to reactivate it – Vaughn hurried through the airlock and climbed down the ladder. Arm outstretched, he aimed his Kruger lakeside as he descended the final dozen steps.

At someone's shout of "Got him! From the cave!" all gazes whipped in Vaughn's direction. He stumbled when he landed, but quickly found his footing on the wet rock. The points of colored targeting beams assaulted him like angry fireflies jostling for position in a frenzied mating ritual. It dazzled him. He had to tint his visor.

"Vaughn, is she okay?"

It was Kraczinski. The big oaf bulldozed his way through the crowd, but Bronston stuck the muzzle of a handgun into his neck, stopping him.

"You're not going anywhere, Ten-Ton."

"I guess not. But I can still break you in half right here."

The big guy wasn't exaggerating.

"What's the move, Vaughn?" shouted Sondergaard. "We'll back whatever you got, you know that."

"I know. First, we all come clean. We all say why we're here and what we want. Then we figure out who gets what, so that we can all walk away from this."

"You have no authority here, Agent Vaughn. Our operation is endorsed by the Core Congress; you and your colleagues are interfering in government business."

The man's voice had a familiar ring to it, forceful but measured, practiced. "Which one are you? Haneke? Epsom?"

"Congressman Epsom."

Was that title supposed to impress anyone who didn't kiss ass for a living?

"Well, congrats, Congressman. That's the one thing you've got right so far."

"Meaning what?"

"Meaning my colleagues have every right to be here. You relinquished any authority when you abetted a fleeing terrorist suspect. Until you've all been questioned on that

233

count, you're in Omicron custody. Then there's the matter of conspiracy to commit murder – Salino, one of your fliers, was killed when another of your fliers, Crowhurst, fired on us back at the beach. Just before he died, Crowhurst admitted he acted under orders. Now, I'll ask again, why are you people here and what do you want?"

Murmurs burbled all across the gathering. Behind, in the water, bubbles surfaced at various points between the berthed submersibles, roughly over Threlfall's sunken craft. The divers would be searching every inch of it, but they'd find nothing of value down there. Gentle waves now lapped at the floating vessels and the rocky bank. Farther out, rippled rings began to appear on the surface with the frequency of droplets preluding heavy rain. Was there a storm outside? Rainwater percolating down through porous rock?

"Mr Vaughn, I think you know more than you pretend." Imogen Threlfall, the white-haired beauty whose chest and jaw Jan had badly bruised the day before, held on to Bronston as she added, "And it's too late to play any more of these games. It's my sister you need to arrest. *She's* the one who—"

"Shut up, Immy! You're the one who's been playing games. You had the crash coordinates all this time. This would have all been over now if you hadn't sneaked in and stirred up a hornet's nest. *You* brought Omicron into this."

"Oh? And who's in league with a terrorist bomber again? Who is that? I forget."

The diminutive escapologist in question tried to make a run for it, but Sondergaard collared him and roughed him into submission.

"I know all about Spearhead," Vaughn announced. "Professor Threlfall told me everything."

"You're lying," Miz De Brock shot back. "He's been dead for over a century."

"Who is he? Your great-grandfather?"

"Try backing up another generation," said Imogen, "and see how ridiculous your claim sounds then."

"I claim nothing. I'm simply stating a fact. Your great-great grandfather survived the crash, and he carried on his research here. Who do you think erected the photonic shield?"

"Let's say we believe you, which we don't," answered Edith, "why would he stay in hiding all this time? This planet has been settled for years. Why would he not approach one of the rangers or call for help? A man who can erect a photonic shield and create enough oxygen to breathe all this time can certainly figure out a way to signal for help."

"Perhaps he didn't want to be found?" Vaughn proposed. "I mean anyone who'd go to the lengths you people have to find his crashed ship must want something he has badly enough to kill for it."

"Oh? And what is that?"

"You tell me. What did you think you'd find on board his ship?"

Epsom stepped forward. "The answer to his disappearance, of course. Professor Threlfall was one of our most valued scientists, and through an old recording of a distress signal, we were able to triangulate his final vector coordinates before he vanished." Typical congressman, versed in the political art of saying absolutely nothing in as many words as possible.

"I see. And if he agrees to come out and tell you all about the crash, you'll leave it at that? You'll respect his right to stay here and continue his research?"

"Let us speak to him, and we can decide from there," replied Epsom with oily reserve.

It was the opening Vaughn had been waiting for.

"Don't do it, bud! Don't give these pigs an inch," yelled Kraczinski. When Bronston again pressed his gun muzzle into the big guy's blubbery throat, Kraczinski deftly reciprocated. The two men clashed visors like stags locking antlers. The entire gathering shuffled away.

It was time to defuse this before someone got trigger-happy.

"Kraczinski, stand down," Vaughn said. "We need to let this play out."

"We should call for back-up. Take them *all* in. Let it play out with the law."

Bad idea. The odds of that sparking a rash action from one or more of these mercenaries was just too great. These people had crossed the line, their employer had crossed the line. No way were they going to roll over and face the music, not to mention forego their bonus of a lifetime, when they had the upper hand like this.

"It's okay, bud. I think this is the best way. Trust me."

It would pain Kraczinski to unilaterally stand down from his stalemate, but he did it anyway, even holstering his sidearm while his opponent's weapon was still buried in his neck.

Imogen gave Bronston's shoulder a gentle squeeze. "Scott, you too." He relented.

"Okay. Now there's only so much room in there," Vaughn began, "and the old man won't want thirty armed strangers trying to squeeze into his private quarters. Remember he's been living in isolation for a long time." He caught the sisters' shared eye-roll reaction. No, they didn't believe their great-great-grandfather was still alive and in this cave; and yes, they knew Vaughn was up to something, that he was attempting to dupe them with a ruse they both saw coming. Maybe there was an old man in there, but it wasn't *their* old man. Couldn't be. And they would play along until they saw their game-winning move.

Epsom and a younger, much shorter man conversed. The latter gave an order to a group of men behind him. Was this Haneke, the other bureaucrat? The two sisters orchestrated their respective posses until a small contingent from each of the three factions jostled forward through the cramped gathering.

Following Imogen Threlfall were three of the men Vaughn had fought and incapacitated on the beach, including Bronston, who had a black eye and a busted nose.

The others had assorted injuries they wouldn't soon forget. Accompanying Edith De Brock, a tall, hard-looking woman named Kincaid – it was sewn onto the breast of her suit – led two icy mercenary males out of the ranks. Finally, Epsom and Haneke, the two congressional reps, dragged a few worried men along with them.

Thirteen visitors in total. More than he'd have liked, but tempers were already frayed; it was time to get this over with.

Vaughn motioned for his two Omicron colleagues to join him. No way was he going to be trapped on his own with this many hostiles. And when Sondergaard reminded him he still had a shackled suspect, thirteen became sixteen. *Sure, why leave a known terrorist off the itinerary?*

As Kraczinski passed, Vaughn whispered, "After the airlock, follow the passage straight until you find the girl and the dogs. A room near the far exit. Jan will join you. Whatever happens, stay with Jan!"

The big guy patted his upper arm and they touched visors. Then a second time – a full-on reckless headbutt that damn near cracked Vaughn's glass.

"Shit, man. What the—"

He saw the crowd was pushing against them and that Kraczinski had just been rammed from behind. What was this? An attempt to swamp them? Overwhelm them?

A separate fracas caught his gaze out near the water's edge. Two men were pulling a colleague out of the water. But it was a struggle, as though one of the submersibles had pinned him against the rocky bank. Another two men went to help. It worked. They pulled him out … but not all of him. His legs were missing from just above the knees. Jets of blood spurted from the red-cabbage stumps, and if his external mike had been switched on, his screams would have awoken the whole lake. The whole wine-dark, rippling, bubbling …

Oh, Christ!

A sleek, pale form scythed up through the gloom, throwing a sleeve of pink water in a shocking arc across the would-be rescuers. Before Vaughn could make out its full shape crouching on the bank, the heads of two men dropped from their shoulders.

A second sleeve scythed up, then a third. Two more pale, glistening forms leapt out onto the rock. The other two rescuers burst apart as they spun, thrashing and trying to hold in their vitals. The wounds had sliced them diagonally from hip to shoulder, almost cleaved them in two. Everything was spilling out.

From a few brief glimpses before the firing started, Vaughn clocked something that appeared to be a cross between a crab and one of the eyeless sloth monsters Threlfall had hung as scarecrows outside his cave up top. Only these were three, four times as big! Rangy, agile quadrupeds that crept sidewise, amazingly low to the ground on sinuous limbs that were crustacean-like in their length but sloth-like in their flexibility and sharp claws. Pale, practically albino down covered them from head to claw.

The stampede to escape up the ladder created a deadly bottleneck. Vaughn knew he'd be crushed if he didn't get up *now*. And then there was his plan – a plan gone to hell. No way could he leave them all down here to die. But—but he couldn't let them *all* up. That would be as a good as killing himself and Jan and the girl and his two Omicron colleagues.

Christ, he didn't know what to do except climb.

Pulse blasts blazed the lakeside behind him as he followed Sondergaard and the bomber up. Screams, more screams. How many overlapped? In the snatches between deaths and death-dealing, he heard phrases like "demons" and "sea cockroaches" and "They just keep coming; there's no end."

He remembered his own warning phrase to Jan, telling her to reactivate the shield. It was now or never. He switched his comm channel to 17.

"Jan, over and out."

There was no reply, just static. Was something interfering with his signal? Had she switched to the right channel? He might have to shout. But would she even hear him through the tumult?

"Jan, do you read me? I said over and out."

Static. He switched back to external comms, and, careful not to give her name, shouted: "Over and out! Over and out!"

If she had got his message, the soundproofing of the photonic blister should have drowned out the screams and the splashing and the rips of pulse artillery below. But chaos still snapped at his heels as he neared the top of the ladder.

"Over and out!"

The panicky yells and swearing and screams of agony were nearer than ever, not further away. They didn't taper, they crescendoed! To the thumping staccato of pulse shots was added a horrible new cacophony: the creatures' claws scraped, clicked, sliced, gouged, and cracked wood as they forced their way up.

Vaughn pulled himself up onto the ledge, then leapt aside to let Kraczinski climb up and roll away from the chute. He didn't know how many had made it up before them, but they'd wisely moved further inside the cave. The tall woman, Kincaid, fired a downward shot as she summitted. Vaughn gave her a hand, then yelled until it roughed his throat: "Over and out! Activate the shield!"

Another two men scrambled out. They turned and aimed their weapons, joining Kincaid and Kraczinski in a defensive line. But Vaughn said to the big guy, "I've got this, bud. Go find Jan. Protect her with your life."

Kraczinski thought for a moment, then slapped his old friend on the arm. "Don't let any of those bast—"

Before he could finish, a pale limb whipped up and drew a curtain of blood-spray and flesh from the back of the next man to summit. With a desperate plea for help contorting his gaped mouth, the poor guy was yanked soundlessly down out of sight.

Every weapon trained on the open shaft quivered, Vaughn's Kruger included. It wasn't like him. He didn't rattle in a firefight like this. But then again, he'd never had so much at stake in a firefight before.

The first creature tore into view and sprang up along the left-hand wall, propelling itself past them even as their combined volley punctured the rock like fisted knuckles. Four of them ducked in time, but the man on the end caught a claw through the neck. The creature ripped him open on the move and sped off up the tunnel, toward the other survivors.

Vaughn instinctively thumbed his Kruger's yield wheel to its maximum setting. No way could he let this thing get loose in the main sanctum. He snapped off a shot that tore into the roof and the wall, slicing slate edges free like razor blades. The pulse blast ripped at least one limb off the creature. But it was soon out of sight.

"No!"

He got up to chase it. A residual blast hit him from the opposite direction, head-on, stopping him but no more, like the press of a strong, sustained gust of wind. The creature hurtled back, writhing and mangled against the wall. Vaughn fired again, as did the others. Several shots came from inside the sanctum as well. The monster evaporated in a cloud of flash-boiled blood and chunks of flesh.

He was in that meta-alert, almost out-of-body state of hyper-awareness as he watched the clawed end of a dismembered limb fidget—*tap, tap, tap*—against the tunnel wall; whorls of disrupted air rolled through the blood-mist; the flesh chunks slapped and slid and fizzed as they fell on mayonnaise-coated rock; and the whole grotesque scene seemed to hiss its own disgust.

Despite his heightened cognition, Vaughn neither heard nor saw the second monster climb up from the shaft and leap. But Kincaid did. Her rapid series of shots plucked it from the ceiling and drove it back toward the hole. Kraczinski soon joined her. Vaughn ran in to help them finish it off. The thing fell, dead, into the shaft. He wasted no time in dropping a grenade in after it. When the explosion had settled, he peered down and, satisfied that the carnage would not be added to, that Jan had reactivated the shield after all, returned Kraczinski's arm slap. To Kincaid he almost said, "I wish you were on our side," but this was no time for making new friends.

Kraczinski had to have lost a few pounds in sweat alone during the last few minutes. He nodded his assent and jogged his way up the tunnel, keen to fulfil his promise of guarding Jan and the girl. It was one of the things Vaughn had always liked about him. The big guy knew when to set his ego aside; he knew that even though this planet fell under his jurisdiction, he didn't have all the facts pertinent to the current situation. In short, he trusted Vaughn implicitly and would back his play to whatever end.

The others, in their panic to escape, had torn down the airlock's tent sheeting and sealant plugs. Having waited in the workshop, where Stopper had formerly been sleeping, they now migrated to the main sanctum and assembled in front of the scaffold.

No sooner had Vaughn joined them from the tunnel when Kincaid pressed the hot muzzle of her weapon into the small of his back. One of her colleagues darted out from the alcove where the little girl had slept, demanded he hand over his Kruger. He hesitated. Checked to see if Sondergaard was still alive. He was, though he'd also been disarmed. The bomber in his charge was now without cuffs. Vaughn performed a quick head count: *fourteen*, including himself.

Things could easily spiral out of control in a hurry if he gave them space to strategize, to take advantage of their supremacy. Handing over his weapon, he said, "I promised I'd take you to the old man, and I never break my word."

"So we've heard," replied Edith De Brock, now brandishing Sondergaard's sidearm. "Then take us. The sooner I get what I came for, the sooner we can leave this treacherous planet behind. And Vaughn, any tricks and you and your colleague will line the walls of this cave, just like those sea demons. You've been warned."

Vaughn didn't reply.

He could practically feel the laser sighting dots twitch up and down his spine as he led the party down the right-hand tunnel to the lower chamber, where Threlfall's device stood in the gloom, the cold perfection of its panels poised in eerie contrast to the hot mess life had wrought in the caves.

The static lights were out. Several inquisitive torch beams inspected the remarkable apparatus and its intricate design. At its center, Threlfall lay motionless on the ground. Only he wasn't dead. Imogen confirmed he was still breathing. When asked what had happened, Vaughn crouched beside the old man's body and, placing a finger over his own mouth to ask for the group's silence, said in a low voice, "If I'm right, it's important that no one makes a sound. No one disturb him. I think he was trying to escape, and it must have gone wrong."

Imogen reached into Bronston's rucksack, retrieved a portable med-kit. She pulled out a smelling salts spray. "Then bring him round. What are we waiting—"

Vaughn grabbed hold of the thumb-sized cylinder. "You people have no idea what you're dealing with, do you. What's at stake here."

"What do you mean? What went wrong?" whispered Edith De Brock. "Is the artefact still here or isn't it?"

Vaughn shrugged. "I'm pretty sure he kept it in there," motioning to Threlfall's belt, "but after what it's done to him, I'm not touching that thing."

"What? What did it do to him?" Subtle cracks were beginning to appear in Edith's icy delivery: puzzlement, now genuine concern. She stabbed a glance at her sister, whose returned glare mirrored those same emotions.

"I thought you people would be able to tell me what this thing is," Vaughn whispered. "I'm only a lawman."

"For chrissakes, *he* must have told you something." Bronston's stature might be twice that of the bomber's, but as a man he was diminishing fast.

Vaughn answered, "Yeah, he did. He said it's the greatest achievement in all of human science. And that where it takes him, no one else must follow. Not until he's finished his research."

By now the entire group had huddled in, hanging on every word. Only one man stood apart, guarding the exit.

"You think he activated it?" asked Edith. "You must do, because you said it might have gone wrong. But if he activated it, why's it still in his belt?"

"I don't know if it *is* still in his belt," replied Vaughn. "All I'm saying is I'm not opening it up to find out. Something that powerful, who knows what it's capable of."

"The great Ferrix Vaughn. Omicron's finest." She thought for a moment. Flashing him a cruel, defiant grin, Edith reached for the belt. Paused. The weight of her obsession seemed counterbalanced for a moment by the gravity of what it might lead to. Whatever she thought she knew about this artefact, it was all theory. She'd never seen it, talked to her ancestor about it, witnessed the effects of its *alien* mechanics.

"Maybe we should wait, Edith." Wise words from her younger sister.

Yet … they'd always been rivals for a reason.

"Don't you think we've waited long enough?" Edith slowly unmagnoed the clasp. "This is our legacy, Immy. Yours and mine. It belongs … in the family."

As she lifted the bar out, it seemed to snag on something inside the pouch. Imogen reached in and helped her pull it free. The tip of the bar exploded into a searing red flare that burned as bright as a sun, blinding all who caught its shocking brilliance.

At the same time, behind his back, while no one had vision, Vaughn twisted the ends of the real artefact and counted to twelve …

Chapter Sixteen

When the red sun rises, follow the bluebird home.

The words conjured burnished imagery in his mind's eye, of alien vistas and architecture so opulent and vast they overwhelmed him, summoning bittersweet tears. But why? He knew he'd heard those words and seen those sights before, and that they were important. But he was too groggy to remember where or when, or why they contained such strong emotion.

Beneath it all, a distant mountain's monotone snore rumbled endlessly on …

The snap of a gunshot wrenched Vaughn to his senses. He was one of the first to his feet. Instinctively upon seeing the various weapons arrayed around him, he slid the artefact up his sleeve, as though the thought had survived his blackout intact but incomplete, waiting for him to finish his magic trick. No one seemed to notice. They were all too busy trying to figure out what the hell had just happened.

A dusky pink-orange light stole in between the device's concave panels. It refracted off gently spinning flakes that floated across empty space where the rubble had been; the flakes resembled transparent insect wings that had been torn off and tossed to the breeze. There were hundreds of them, and the kaleidoscopic lighting effect was eerie and childish at the same time.

As the light source rose, Vaughn discerned the corona of an occluded sun. By this time his eyes were adjusting to the gloom. The silhouetted edges of a structure began to show, straight and arched edges of a dark, tall structure that dwarfed the device a hundredfold. This building had a roof, but it was too dark to make out.

Outside the structure, opposite the sun, a spindly walkway climbed forever into the night. There didn't appear to be anything holding it suspended, so he guessed it was attached to some other structure much higher up.

Even more bizarrely, breaks in the curtains of mist that swept across the walkway allowed snatches of dusk-light through. They revealed a world of immense cataracts, where white water fell from summits his vision couldn't reach to depths his imagination couldn't fathom. The distant, thunderous rumble might be this world's only sound, its only abiding memory.

The dispersal of stars around the eclipsed sun bore no resemblance to those he knew, those his ship's navi-computer had relied on to get him from point to point in the dark sea of space. Here he had no reference. And if he was *that* far from home, how much of a toll had general relativity taken on his journey through the Star Binder? He'd endured it in a single sleep, but how long had he been asleep? Time-wise, how far had that dislocation separated him from Jan? Hours? Days? Longer?

As a rock-hopping lawman who liked to roll solo, he was no stranger to isolation, even for fairly long durations, but this was something new. Something frightening. The prospect of losing *time*, actual, measurable time, not just the shrapnel cost of warp gate jumps, shrink-wrapped his chest and left him hugging his elbows, conscious of each and every precious breath.

He almost dreaded waking Threlfall in case the answers to these questions were too big for him to deal with.

"What is this?" Kincaid, so cool and effective during the sea creatures' attack on the cave, now stumbled about over Threlfall's supplies like a drunk on an escalator. She sat on a hemp crate in order to get her bearings. Pinpointing Vaughn with her sidearm's sighting beam, she yelled, "Shitheel! What did you *do*?"

"He did nothing. It was me."

Everyone looked across at Threlfall as he sat up among the crates of supplies, nursing a sore head.

"Then you!" Kincaid's busy infrared found the old man's visor, dazzling him as it magnified through the glass. "What did *you* do?"

"I …" He struggled to his feet and made his way round to Vaughn, who was standing at a sunward facing gap in the panels. "I think I know what happened," he announced to the group; then quietly to Vaughn, "For Jan?"

Vaughn gave the slightest of nods.

"Bold move, brother," said the old man. "Sedative, was it?"

"Sorry about that."

"You may have just killed us both."

Vaughn didn't reply.

"One of you explain right now or I execute both of you … right now." It was Bronston's turn to assault them vigorously with his laser dot.

"Really? You want to kill the only two people who might have an inkling of what just happened or how to undo it?" Joshua Acton Threlfall was a cagey customer all right. It was difficult to know which side he was ultimately on. *So far, his own,* reckoned Vaughn. But in this high-stakes game of Cydonia Face, the old man could see everyone else's cards while no one, not even Vaughn, knew what he was holding.

"Everyone, holster your weapons," ordered Edith De Brock. "Keep calm. We need to work the problem. Right, Immy?"

"Right. And … be careful what you wish for. I just wanted to say that."

"Meaning what?"

"I don't know. It just seemed apropos … on any number of levels. Scott, put it away. This is the great Professor Threlfall. He doesn't take orders. Am I right, Professor?"

Old Threlfall studied her for a few moments. "You know, you're a lot like Sian was at your age." And to Edith, "But I don't see any of her in you. No, you have more of Cora, even the drab taste in apparel."

"Cora was our great-grandma," replied Imogen.

"My daughter. My little girl. She was all grown up when I left. For years I've been trying to remember where she was the last time I saw her, whether she seemed happy. She had a young son about six years old, Wesley, who played the holo-keys every chance he got. I always wondered if he kept it up, like she did. Cora had played the oboe in college, even performed two full seasons for the Io Philharmonic, but she put it on hold to start a family. It's not the choice I would have made at that age, but she always did go her own way. A family trait, if I'm honest. Tell me, did they keep it up?"

"I believe she went back to it for a while, before the fragmentia …" Edith began to pensively massage her throat as she stared in wonder at the old man. "How is this possible? You … alive after all this time, and you've hardly aged. Spearhead always had amazing potential, but we'd have to be talking hundreds, thousands of light-years of travel. I'm struggling to—"

"This is bigger than Spearhead," her sister cut in. "This is out of sight. But I think the pertinent question is … where *are* we?"

"Oh, I never did think up a name. The career podders used to brag about how many outposts they'd gamed and named. It became a kind of hierarchy, tallying discoveries as if they were goals scored in a season." Addressing each member of the group in turn, Threlfall seemed to grow in stature and confidence as he spoke, and was soon gesticulating like a self-amused headteacher recounting an absurd social practice from his youth. "Then they started measuring it by total distance travelled through the Binder. The oldest podders had millions of light-years. We used to call them the Big IFFs—Intergalactic Frequent Fliers. They were so dislocated, some of them, so out of sync with Core time as we know it, they experienced a psychological phenomenon known as 'skipper's due,' or 'the skew,' as we came to call it. No sooner had they started to catch up with the years they'd lost than they'd be back out again, skipping over more years. That loneliness drove a few of them insane. It gave others a sort of messianic complex, seeing everyone they knew grow old and die while they hardly aged. They couldn't re-engage with humanity in any meaningful way, so they just kept going back out, living out their immortal quest. The Binder itself *became* their reality, how they measured time and success and everything else. I know some kept journals, and let me tell you there's nothing in the universe more pompous, more narcissistic than a podder who believes his own hype.

"Me? I just wanted to know. What was out there. What interstellar civilizations had wrought long before we existed. What had become of them. Where that technology might lead us. And fate led me here, on one of my earliest pod expeditions. At the far side of that bridge into the clouds is the Binder port for this system. It's how I first arrived here. It's also the only way back into the true Binder, and it's where we need to go."

"Why can't we go back the way we came?" shouted one of Edith's mercenaries.

The old man folded his arms and widened his stance. "Because I say so."

The sound of weapons being cocked all around the supply pile had Vaughn choosing the best crate to duck behind. The targeting beams danced across Threlfall's closed arms and his natty waistcoat.

"Go ahead," he said. "But none of you will see home again if anything happens to me. I didn't invite you here. Agent Vaughn tricked you all, just as he tricked me. Fortunately, I know what kind of man he is, so I know why he did it. Unfortunately, *he* knows not what he's done, the ramifications of it. And as for the rest of you, know this: you are nothing to me. I, on the other hand, am your everything. Do as I say and you might one day see your homes again. Do otherwise and you will die here. Sooner than you think."

"We know of the Binder," replied Edith. "We've gleaned rumors of it from Hartdagen dissidents; we've heard of its huge reach. But it's always been one of the galaxy's best-kept secrets. That was until a salvager named Karajian visited the site of your evacuated laboratory on Brahe-Six, way outside the safe zone. He found that the top few floors had been completely destroyed in the attack, but some of the sub-level labs had only suffered moderate damage. He was able to rescue enough prototype equipment and cutting-edge research data stored on hard drives to make him a billionaire overnight. It took ISPA's R and D division months to sift through it all. Including one of your hard drives, Professor."

"Impossible. I wiped my OS's memory before I left, and I brought all the quad-cores with me."

"Evidently not. We found blueprints for a transportation device far more powerful than the one you'd patented—"

"The one you people stole from me."

"The one *they* stole from you," Imogen cut in, jabbing her thumb at the congressional delegates, who wisely kept mum.

"Be that as it may," her younger sister continued, "what we found in those files suggested you'd not only cracked the equations to theorize interplanetary meta-space transportation, you were actually building a device to achieve it on Brahe-Six. The notes mentioned an artefact from which you'd extrapolated hundreds of algorithms, and on which you'd based your coupling design and various other innovations. But the data was incomplete. My sister and I took it to some of the leading privately-run physics laboratories in the colonies. None were able to build your new device. So, as a last resort, I took the data back to ISPA."

"Yes, and signed a co-opt contract for any future patents arising from it," Imogen again interrupted, this time with a touch more venom. "After what they'd done to Father. After everything he'd told us about them, how they were the Threlfalls' sworn enemies, how we'd been fighting those patent claims for generations. And what do you go and do? Sell us out all over again, to the very organization that tried to scupper us in the first place! Honestly, I don't have the words. Restoring a family legacy by betraying it to those who'd done it the most harm … if that isn't the definition of crazy …"

"And yet here you are, Immy, neck-deep in it with me. At least I was up front about every move I made. I offered to bring you on board as a full partner."

"Traitor!"

"I offered to compensate you as a silent partner. But no, you had to cling to a hundred-year-old vendetta that didn't benefit either of us one iota. You had to go on tilting at windmills and hiring auditors to screw with me and private detectives to try to entrap me and anyone I did business with. Restoring a family legacy by blackening it at every turn with your whiny, pathetic tantrums … if that isn't the definition of crazy …"

"I'll tell you what *is* the definition of crazy," snapped Sondergaard. "Travelling light-years through a wormhole to the far side of the galaxy and *still* not being able to escape women talking shit. Seriously, save it for that late-night talk show where they settle all disputes with a pillow fight. Or better yet, you could restore your family legacy by persuading Professor Batshit over there to show us how to get the fleck out of Dodge?"

Vaughn, expecting a blizzard of insults and threats to descend on his unarmed Omicron colleague, was surprised by the silence that followed. The faces were fearful, inward-looking. The glare of pink-orange sunlight seemed to squeeze out from the left side of the eclipse in molten form, casting the shadows of vast, concave pillars across the interior of the great hall. As day opened up this alien world, the sky took on a grayish, lime-tinged color, shiny and metallic, as though an epic storm had just passed. Other moons roamed in orbit, but they were non-reflective, either dark brown or jet black. As the primary moon and the sun it had eclipsed appeared to follow precisely the same arc across the sky, only at slightly different speeds – the moon was quicker – solar eclipses would be frequent here.

"Of those who say nothing, few are silent. But the older I grow the more I listen to people who don't talk much."

No one dared answer the old man's cryptic quote.

"The question you're all afraid to ask," he added. "What's *your* skipper's due? How much time have you lost?" Addressing Vaughn, he placed a gentle hand on his shoulder. "For a two-way journey, here and back, the minimum time you will have lost … is a little over nineteen years."

Of the four gunshots in the aftermath of Threlfall's shocking announcement, three happened in such quick succession and so unexpectedly that Vaughn was only able to piece together the sequence of events later, based on what the others told him. He was on his knees, fighting the urge to vomit when the first shot rang out. A suicide. One of Haneke's aides, a married man in his forties, whose wife had a rare degenerative neural condition and had been told that, despite several experimental operations to slow the effects, she had, at most, another five or six years before the paralysis reached her lungs and she would die.

On seeing this suicide, the aide's colleague, a close personal friend who had helped the struggling couple pay their astronomical medical expenses, saw red and flipped. He took a snapshot at Threlfall, grazing his visor – the scorch mark would be indelible. Whether in a panic or with extraordinary cool-headedness, Edith De Brock responded a couple of seconds later with a shot right through the middle of the shooter's chest. He died before he fell. If she hadn't done that, either Vaughn or, as he later admitted, Sondergaard would have probably done the honors before the man got another shot off. For chrissakes, killing Threlfall was killing every last one of them!

The fourth shot rang out hours later. Another suicide. One of Imogen's men who, as it turned out, had left neither family nor partner nor even a pet behind. He just couldn't see a way out of time's abyss. And despite Threlfall doing his best to reassure them that he did have a potential way back to the Core colonies, it did nothing to assuage the loss, the desolation, the sheer imperceptibility of having nineteen years stolen away in the gap of a single sleep.

Some, including Considine the bomber, and Epsom, raged until their throats were hoarse and they'd thrown or kicked nearly everything that could be kicked or thrown. Imogen and Bronston held hands for a while, then held each other in silence away from the group, perhaps finding solace in the fact that they'd at least shared this sharp swerve in fate. They were castaways in space and time, but they were together.

For that reason, Vaughn couldn't stand to look at them.

Nineteen years.

When he got back—*if* he got back—Jan would be in her fifties. Maybe graying. She'd never color her hair or wear make-up to hide her ageing, he knew that much. But would she still be on Hesperidia?

Nineteen years.

Stopper would no longer be with her. Vaughn would not get to see the big rascal grow old. He would not get to say goodbye. The deep, welling sadness inside him spread to hidden regions that he was sure hadn't felt emotion before, hadn't felt at all. He hoped they never would again. But it was a sadness that fused, tightened, sealed itself in. He couldn't get past the idea that he'd seen Stopper with Jan what seemed like moments ago; *that* was his reality. Telling himself that scene had unfolded almost a decade and millions of light-years ago ... was a stitch his mind couldn't quite make. That needle carried no thread.

He sat with his back against a crate full of he-knew-not-what, staring out at the half-lit dawn of a world he'd found at great loss. Unimaginable loss. The realization of that loss radiated outward in tremors that got shallower, more cerebral the further his thoughts were from Jan and Stopper. Had his parents, jailed for life after he'd arrested them, died behind bars? That old guilt clawed through him again, reopening wounds that had only ever healed superficially, the thinnest kind of skin that could be rubbed away by a stray childhood memory, or seeing other families together. He hadn't seen any member of his own family for years – now decades. What about colleagues? Kraczinski?

Had the big guy managed to get Jan off the island and back to her home in the Keys? Would *he* still be alive, or had his appetites gotten the best of him by now?

Then there was the Bureau. Was Agent Vaughn technically still an Omicron agent? Had he and Sondergaard been declared dead? If so, who had turned up at their funerals? An entire chapter in the history of the colonies – the war itself, politics, scientific advancement, social revolution, the Pacintic Cup finals, news of every kind, upheavals, prodigies born, luminaries passing, new gadgets, new drinks, new movies, new words, new *worlds* – had happened without him.

Even if he did somehow make it back, would he recognize this new time? Would he be able to reintegrate? Hell, had he ever *been* integrated? A loner lawman who'd never stayed long in any one place. The *Pitch Hopper* had been his home. Then it had been Hesperidia.

Like self-perpetuating aftershocks, his thoughts kept shimmying out into the consequences of this dislocation. He tried to convince himself there was an exciting aspect to it. A chance to start over. To catch up on all the important things that had happened in his absence. To be the subject of awe and wonder when he reappeared. But all those thoughts and theories and flights of fancy had the same epicenter. And every time he felt it, he felt her. The one thing he really, truly missed was the one thing he dreaded being without if he ever made it back. No, if his life didn't include Jan then maybe he shouldn't go back. Maybe he should go on with Threlfall into the infinite mysteries of the Star Binder.

But if he didn't go back, he'd never know for sure whether Jan was there waiting for him. She'd lost Stopper, her boy, but would she leave Hesperidia while there was a chance Vaughn might return to that island cave someday? If it had been the other way around, would *he* stay and wait for her return? He felt confident he would. At the very least, he'd leave her a means of transport off the island and instructions on how to find him.

Hmm, she would always wonder, she would always live in hope. And even if she couldn't bear to live on the Hesp without Stopper, she would see to it that if Vaughn ever did reappear, he'd be able to find her.

As he hugged his knees again, he let the bitter tears mist his view of the breathtaking vista – a panorama of waterfalls that fell into eternity. He'd never felt so fragile, pared-down, helpless. The dark sea between him and everything he cared about seemed uncrossable. By saving Jan, he'd almost certainly lost her. It didn't feel heroic; it felt like a betrayal ... of her, of the promises he'd made, of the only dream he'd ever wanted to see made real.

There were no do-overs in this life. But even if there were, he knew he wouldn't hesitate to make that same decision again. The lesser of two evils was a choice many people struggled to see through. Not Ferrix Vaughn – pragmatic bastard to the end. Being decisive was his curse. Professionally, it had made him a legend. Personally, it had cost him everything.

"Ladies and gentlemen, you need to listen carefully."

The unpacked crates and neatly positioned machine parts and supplies arranged around Threlfall, outside the device's paneled perimeter, surprised Vaughn. He'd been vaguely aware of the work effort — the old man had recruited several others to help him take inventory — but how had they shifted, opened and sorted every last item in so short a time? He'd been lost in his own memories, watching the transient rainbows arch across the vast falls. Time had no meaning here. Things had no consequence. They just were.

"If I could give you more time to take all this in, believe me, I would. But consider this: I sent ahead enough food, water and oxygen to last one person several weeks. There are now eleven of us. So while we should be able to complete the work needed for a crossing far quicker than I expected, we'll also have to ration supplies with ironclad discipline. We can't afford to waste anything, especially time."

"Okay, but what are we building with all that stuff?" asked Kincaid, whose curt middle-fingered refusal to help earlier had sparked a mini fracas. She'd come out on top, of course, leaving two men sprawled out on their backs, nursing contusions. Spying her technique had left him in no doubt she was ex-Phi, combat-trained to the nth degree. And the saying went that the only time a Phi ever gave an inch was to his barber.

"We're modifying my pod," replied the old man, "so that it can climb up the exterior of the bridge undetected. There's no other way to reach the Binder portal."

"Undetected by whom?" The first sensible thing Haneke had said.

"By the Finaglers, of course. They watch one in three Binder portals that we know of, and that was a century ago. For some reason the Star Binder itself won't give them access; it seems to know their intentions are hostile. The same thing happens if you try to bring anything with mass destructive capability through, unstable radioactive isotopes for example. It's much more than a transit system. There's a phenomenal artificial intelligence coursing through it. The Finaglers will do anything to gain access, to get control of it, which is why they leave a ring of sentient probes around the portals, to monitor any activity, so they can capture unwary travelers and torture them for any Binder intel they might have.

"Like I said, that was a century ago, and the sentient ring is still up there, hovering. The moment a sentient detects anything bigger than itself approaching the ring from outside, it will destroy it. I've flown drones up there with wave-jamming signals of every kind, and none of them have made it through. The only method I've tried with any kind of success, the *only* method, is to bend light around the drone. In other words, to become completely invisible."

"How the hell do we do that?" someone asked.

"Smoke and mirrors – a nanotech variation of my own design. If any of you understand polymorphic particle robotics, I'll be glad to explain along the way. Otherwise, you'll just have to trust me."

As Vaughn scanned the dumbstruck faces of his fellow castaways, he knew exactly what they were feeling. This was a realm of gods and magic. Science of the impossible. Threlfall had missed decades of human scientific progress, yet he was still operating far beyond the limit of known Core physics. He was both shaping the future and surfing its wake. His persistence and ingenuity were almost superhuman. But he had the touch of death about him, too. A fearlessness Vaughn had seen in many a perp with nothing to lose. That, together with his propensity for grandiosity, did not bode well for anyone around him. He was on the trail of the gods, so what could the lives of mere mortals, and strangers at that, matter to him? He would use them as long as they were useful, then jettison them as soon as they became a burden.

That was Vaughn's impression of the man. Not that he could do anything but listen, obey, and hope he was wrong.

"My pod is waiting on the level beneath us. It hasn't been touched, as far as I can tell. With any luck we should be able to complete modifications and have it ready to begin the ascent in a matter of days. There's no point attempting a trial run because, quite frankly, there's no plan B. We get everything right the first time or else. But don't worry, I'll triple-check all the modifications before we launch.

"Now, a quick word about arms. I can see most of you carry a firearm of some sort. That ends now. In such a precarious predicament, and in light of the volatile emotions it will inevitably throw up, I'm going to have to demand that you give up all lethal weapons. I won't be carrying one either. Only Agents Vaughn and Sondergaard will be armed from now on. I don't know much about the twenty-third century, but I know integrity when I find it. Vaughn has more of it than the rest of you put together. And if he vouches for Sondergaard, well, that's good enough for me. Anyone who objects will forfeit his seat for the return journey. It's that simple. And that goes for any order I give. This isn't a democracy. This is the opposite of a democracy. The sooner you get with that, the sooner we'll be underway."

He reached into one of the food crates and retrieved a mintato, one of Hesperidia's most common vegetables, very light green, almost white when ripe like this one, about the size of a pepper. Vaughn had never liked their taste, somewhere between, as the name suggested, mint and potato. The old man tossed it to Kincaid, who caught it one-handed. She studied it for a few moments, then tossed it on to Bronston. He lifted his mask and took a bite. After several loud crunches, he gave his verdict: a slow, sarcastic thumbs-up that left Imogen and several others sniggering.

"You should know, the first-class meal comes with a side order of toe-cheese," joked Sondergaard.

Nervous laughter did the rounds until most of them wore a smirk – blackly comic, self-aware, advertising that they were finally starting to come to terms with the absurdity of the whole thing. The quips soon came thick and fast:

"Now that's what I call a greengrocer's: a billion light-years and still fresh."

"Yeah, pick one that didn't drop from something's ass-end and win a prize."

"It's all yours, Bubba."

"Anyone up for a pizza? I'm buying."

"With what?"

"The old man's pension. Geezer should be richer than a pharaoh about now. Am I right?"

"Not about anything. Ever. Numbnuts."

"Anyone else craving a Hershey bar in the worst way?"

"Only someone who doesn't know what real chocolate is."

"Don't tell me you're into that Swiss crap."

"Nope. Cadbury's. All the way. I'll die happy if there's a Dairy Milk in one of those crates."

"Same here, for a Chinese chicken curry with egg fried rice."

"You're weird. I'll go with Mexican."

"Just think, though, it will literally take us ten years to find a decent taco."

"It'll take a lot longer than that. Seeing as there's no such thing."

And so on … until heads started to drop in somber reflection and the quips became more and more puerile and desperate. Threlfall let it play out. He even smiled at some of it, though he seemed to be watching events unfold from some remote place, weighing up the group and the individuals in it for reasons known only to him. A kind of fluid experiment to figure out who might work well with whom, or how he could use this levity to his advantage over the coming days. Finally, when the laughter dried up, he said, "I think it's time now … to show you exactly where you are and what we're dealing with. The pod is this way. Each of you grab a machine part and bring it with you. Whatever you can manage. Don't worry, they're lighter than you'd imagine. And the clock is ticking."

Then he put them to work.

Chapter Seventeen

The hiss of compressed oxygen venting from the nozzle faded to silence as Vaughn rotated the tank's valve control, closing the aperture. He'd gotten quite adept at refilling breathers with this old school method. Conserving O2 was the key, keeping leakage to an absolute minimum. And as Congressman Epsom had a serious hand injury – not being much in the way of a tool-smith, he'd somehow managed to solder his left forefinger and index finger, fusing them together with fourth-degree burns – Vaughn had had to fill his breather for him.

Epsom thanked him and asked how he was holding up. The group's vibe had grown somber over the past couple of days, and Epsom, as the highest-ranking official, had taken to dispensing pep talks on a one-to-one basis in an effort to lift morale. The problem was, morale wasn't the issue here. They'd never had any to begin with. It was an uneasy truce. The only thing holding this group and this work effort together was the old man's promise of getting them home. They would do whatever it took to help him make that happen. The rest was navel-gazing.

Vaughn told him he was glad to see everyone pulling their weight, and that he was optimistic about the ascent. It seemed to satisfy the politician for now. Vaughn decided to head down to one of the lower tiers for some solitude. He'd made an abortive attempt to update his voice log the day before, and he didn't want to leave this part – arguably the most important – to the last minute. Sondergaard was already well underway with his update. They'd agreed on a dual approach, for maximum fidelity. Even if one of them didn't survive the journey home, the other would have his report, and ISPA would have corroborating testimonies from two Omicron officers.

The soundless, spiral elevator alighted him on the lower arboretum level, one above the metalworks lab and two above the smelting tier. It was amazing how quickly they'd got used to the layout of the complex, or maybe not, as the alien builders had fashioned it into such an efficient, intuitive operation, it just made sense on every level.

He picked his way through the overgrown clumps of golden grass and exotic shrubs. The balcony on the far side offered the best view he'd found anywhere. He switched on his voice log as he approached the open air.

"Unknown date. This is Agent Ferrix Vaughn, Omicron Bureau, badge number seven-dash-three-one-hotel-zulu-niner. We're on day three, Core time, after the displacement event. My previous log entry described the events immediately preceding and following the displacement. Work is well underway on modifying Professor Threlfall's transport. He calls it his pod. How can I describe it? About thirty feet in length, cylindrical, but with a spiral-ridged exoskeleton. Think of a cross between a maglev passenger car and a drill-bit. Threlfall says that design was supposed to make use of the Star Binder's gravitational propulsion, but it will be obsolete once he gets back to Alpha base, wherever that is, and shares his discoveries with the Initiative, whatever that is.

"He's a genius, no question. The way he's figured out how this alien tech works, and how to use those secrets to modify our own science *and* make it practicable, all on his own, is pretty remarkable. I've never seen anything like it. He's spent a fair amount of time here on previous trips, plundering tech and ideas, which he took back to his cave laboratory on Hesperidia whenever he needed to replenish his oxygen. There's no oxygen here, apart from in the water itself. But electrolysis requires equipment we don't have.

"This complex appears to serve several functions. It used to be a deep-water drilling and mining facility. That ore was extracted, refined, smelted, and fashioned into thousands of the light metal panels Threlfall used to make his device. They're stockpiled on the third level. It all has to do with the Star Binder, he says. Creating an annex transit system. I don't understand the scope of it, to be honest. How can anything span entire systems and galaxies and galaxy super-clusters without us actually being to see it? It's like the song says: 'I'm analogue, a dream inside a digitalic enterprise. I'm always Now in Never-Was and Never-Will-Be skies.' Old song now, I guess. But this facility, as well as the one across the sky bridge, was abandoned a long time ago. We don't know why exactly. Threlfall thinks it might be related to the Finaglers' presence. I'll come to that in a minute.

"Agent Sondergaard and I have been tasked with keeping the peace. I hesitate to say 'law and order' because this is Threlfall's show. He's calling the shots. We might have the semblance of Omicron authority, being armed, but he can take that away from us at any time. We're no longer the masters of our own destiny. It feels strange, not to have that freedom to come and go as the badge has always permitted.

"I'm speaking from a balcony on the fourth tier, more or less under the sky bridge. Both the bridge and the facility itself are made of some unknown material. It doesn't exist on our Extended Periodic Table. Like the refined metal ore, it's incredibly light and incredibly dense at the same time. We've had a number of accidents so far with our cutting and welding equipment, but not one of them has damaged or even marked the floors or walls of this structure. That, more than anything else, embodies the alien-ness of this place.

"Threlfall tells us the bridge is actually hollow, probably a tunnel for freight, but the previous residents sealed it so well he hasn't the first clue how to break in. It would have made this whole goddamn ascent so much easier, but there you go. In a few days' time we'll have our very own *Flight of the Phoenix*. All things considered, I'd rather be sunbathing with Jan in the Keys.

"What else? Ah yes, the Finaglers. You know all about their underhanded methods and their pathological opportunism. But here's something you might not know, and it could prove decisive in the future, if they ever gain the upper hand in the war. Admittedly, it's speculation and

271

hearsay at this point. But Threlfall has no reason to lie to us that I can tell, and his stories about the podders and the Initiative and the checkpoint colonies do ring true. There always was something mysterious about Rupes Tenuis at the Martian North Pole. It wouldn't surprise me at all if one of the portals to the Star Binder was buried there in the ice.

"Anyway, this is what I've surmised so far: Finaglers have been desperately trying to gain access to the Binder for as long as they've known about it. How long that is is anyone's guess – hundreds, thousands of years? Maybe longer? Insofar as Threlfall is aware, they've never managed to get in. The Binder itself has a lethal AI security system that seems able to perceive destructive intent. Put simply, if it thinks you're up to no good, it won't let you in. If you try to bring weapons or materials of potentially mass destruction in, it'll close the portal tighter than a rich guy's sphincter on Tax Day. And if it perceives you as a direct threat to it, it'll vaporize you on contact. Threlfall says that last part has never happened to any of the human podders he knows about. But they've found Finagler skeletons at quite a few of the portals on their expeditions. And Finagler surveillance equipment – alarm systems, deadly sentient devices and such – are apparently commonplace at these sites. All this suggests those bastards are not about to give up on the Binder any time soon. Also, we have access and they don't. As I said, that could become a crucial factor in the struggle."

Vaughn considered leaving a warning message about the artefact he still had in his possession. It was powerful beyond belief – perhaps, if Threlfall was right, one of the original tunnel-building tools of the ancient engineers. What if it didn't have those same security protocols that the main Star Binder network had? If the Finaglers got their hands on it, were able to use it like Threlfall and Vaughn had, they might not *need* access to the main Binder. They could sneak in and out of anywhere they chose. Rout the Core defenses with impunity. They could achieve total supremacy on a scale that dwarfed mankind's worst nightmares.

So it was probably best to keep it under wraps as much as he could, to make no mention of it. If they made it back to the Core colonies, he would have to decide what to do with it. Maybe bury it. Maybe destroy it if possible. Handing it over to ISPA was dicey because they had a habit of using new tech recklessly, in daring raids that drew the attention of their Sheiker and Finagler counterparts, who in turn went to extraordinary lengths to steal that tech. They usually improved it, too, before using it against ISPA. That proliferation was clearly building to a tipping point – something so decisive and lethal that one side could sweep the other side out of existence. Was this artefact it? If Edith De Brock, Epsom, Haneke or any of the others knew he had it, what would they do, or more importantly what *wouldn't* they do, to take it from him when they got back?

He resumed his voice log: "In the event of a hearing, so ISPA can find out exactly what happened here, I'd like to talk about the conduct of the people involved. For the record, I consider them all guilty of multiple crimes, but those may not all be relevant after the conclusion of this dislocation event. It may exempt them, it may not. Professor Threlfall is the outlier, as he didn't collude with them in any way on Hesperidia. It's not for me to judge his actions. And Agent Sondergaard has performed his duties with distinction throughout this ordeal. I'd like to recommend him for the Nisus Award for conspicuous bravery.

"As for me?" He watched as a lone, upstanding green stem without a single leaf or blossom, bobbed this way and that under a swiping gust, then returned to its stubborn, rigid posture. It was unlike all other plants in the garden: it stood apart, flush against the raised edge of the soil bed, exposed to the elements, the first to bear the brunt of whatever this world threw at the arboretum. There was a foolishness in that, but also a magnificence. A sad one. Because while it stood upright, it stood alone.

"It's been the greatest honor of my life to serve in the Omicron Bureau. I'll never stop admiring the dedication of the men and women who wear this badge, and the sacrifices they make. I'll do my utmost to live up to my oath until every one of these castaways is delivered safely to a human colony, wherever that might be. After that, it's my firm intention to retire and start a fresh—"

"Vaughn?"

The urgency in Sondergaard's voice wrenched Vaughn out of his self-reflection. He signed off his voice-log and sprang to his feet.

"Ah, there you are." Sondergaard glanced warily across the many unidentified forms of vegetation. "Someone mentioned you like to hang out here. Makes sense. After Hesperidia, I mean."

Why hadn't Vaughn made that connection?

"Here, I want to show you something." The young Dane raised his arms over his head as he brushed past a spiny, frond-bearing shrub. He hurried to the balcony and gazed up into the mist. "That asshole has made a mistake. Spectrum pre-set fifteen. Inclination thirty-four-point-eight-two degrees. Magnify and scan the underside of the bridge."

Vaughn switched on the omnipod function of his headset. His goggles lowered into position. Controlling the digital interface with blinks and eye movements was second nature, and he was soon tracing the perfect fluorescent line of the bridge through the clouds until it became no more than a faint green spindle pointing the way to nothingness. At inclination 34.82 he winked his right eye, then held it closed until the magnification zoom and automatic focus enlarged the smooth, eye shape of the bridge.

Perfect. Uniform. Smooth. Or was it?

He noticed the anomaly moments before Sondergaard asked, "What do you see?"

"Something sticking out. Large, cylindrical, about the size of a skybus. Maybe it crashed into the bridge? I don't know. But it's at zero angle to it. Pierced through it from inside?"

"Or from the top, and it went all the way through? Either way, it's going to stop us dead. The old man's vessel pretty much hugs the bridge right round with em stabilizers, not much room to spare. And his light-bending tech — that's totally dependent on the shape as well. He's looking at a complete re-design …"

"Or …" Vaughn knew what was coming next, but he wanted the rookie to suggest it anyway. This was Sondergaard's discovery. He should take all the kudos.

"Or we set precision charges and blast our way out of Dodge."

"*Blast*, you say?" Threlfall had swapped breathers with Vaughn briefly, long enough to spy the visible dimensions of the obstacle. But he didn't know how to work the omnipod properly — that tech hadn't been invented in his day — so he trusted the agents' assessment instead. "I'm no demolition expert," he said. "Do you think you can clear it? I can maybe extend the em gap to a couple of feet *at most*. Anything jutting further than that will give us eccentricity, possibly destabilize us altogether." The old man flashed the whites of his eyes. "Fascinating. Fate has taken another hand, it seems. So I couldn't have done this alone after all." After a long moment's pause, "What do you gentlemen have in mind?"

"Agent Sondergaard has a plan," replied Vaughn.

"More like a theory," added the Dane. "We'll need to bring together at least two highly unstable elements: whatever goes into the explosives … and the bomber."

"Bomber?"

"The squat guy with the bald head, avoids Vaughn and me like the plague."

"The man you arrested? Considine?"

"Professional terrorist," said Sondergaard. "Suspected of numerous corporate heists, black-ops incursions to destroy Sheiker installations. And Vaughn and I caught him red-handed fleeing the Gilpraxia Moon Bridge after a serious bombing."

"Almost caught," Vaughn corrected him.

"No, *actually* caught – just a couple of days later. Before this Fate you keep mentioning flipped us all the cosmic finger."

"And you think you can get him to do it?" asked the old man.

"What choice does he have? What choice do any of us have?"

"Very well. Go fetch him, and we'll see what kind of explosive he suggests. One thing we're not short of here is rare chemical compounds."

"Done." At that Sondergaard jogged back to the elevator, leaving Vaughn with Threlfall. It was late in the day; the sun had begun to bleed into the cloudy depths of the cataracts. There was no horizon here, only mist and the mysteries behind it.

"Now that we're alone, there's something I want you to know. It's important," said the old man. "Neither of us have mentioned it, but I'm perfectly aware you still have the artefact. I don't blame you for doing what you did back in the cave. It might very well have been the only way to keep your Jan alive. Who knows? But I'll need it back now. Sondergaard has spirit, but he's not you. And he'll need you out there on that bridge. Where the obstacle is … it's borderline for sentient detection."

"You mean there's a good chance we might be seen?" Something walked over Vaughn's grave.

"Probably not – it's not quite at the red zone, as I call it – but to be honest it's such an unlikely thing to have happened – remember I said the bridge is incredibly hard to breach – I doubt that object got there on its own."

"Sondergaard and I had the same thought: that the Finaglers put it there. What we want to do is plant the explosives, haul ass back across the bridge and then detonate just before we all start the pod ascent. That will give the Finaglers almost no time to react. By the time they get here, we'll be at home plate. And even if the blast alerts the sentients, they won't be able to see us passing. What do you think, Professor?"

"I think I was right to trust you." He gripped Vaughn's shoulder with a firm, paternal hand. "And that's why I'm telling you this, away from the others. In case something goes wrong and the pod fails, use the device to get home."

"But I thought you said … it won't let us return through. You told us that as soon as we got here. It's why I've never—"

"It might have power enough for one. You brought over a dozen people through that day, and that was after I'd sent several batches of supplies. It wasn't built for extensive use like that. You were lucky it had enough juice to carry everyone through. But it's been slowly recharging ever since. By the time we make our ascent, it should provide an emergency life-line for one person. You're the only one I'm telling, Vaughn. I can't let you keep the original artefact, but I can use it to prime the device to take you home if all else fails. That's all I can promise, I'm afraid. The others either make the ascent with me or they die. And anyway, I have plans for some of them."

"Meaning what?"

"The Star Binder doesn't give up her secrets to just anyone. I aim to find as many artefacts as I can before I die. For that I'll need people with vision. With a willingness to leap across voids and leap again, to sound the depths of the dark sea and cast their mortal lots into it, to stake their claims and conquer dreams, to—"

"I get the idea, Professor. So long as you give them the choice, it's all good."

The old man showed his palm, clicked his fingers. Vaughn retrieved the artefact and, after a moment's hesitation, pressed it into Threlfall's callused grip.

"There goes my billion-clip lottery ticket," said Vaughn.

"Money." The old man blinked. "Do they still have that?"

Vaughn rummaged inside one of his baldric pouches, plucked out a couple of old clipped five-credit discs. They were each about the size of a draughts piece but half as thick, dirty, still smooth. He flipped one at Threlfall, who caught it.

"Make a wish," said Vaughn. "This is the biggest damn wishing well I ever saw, but it'll do."

The old man grinned, closed his eyes and tossed his disc into the mist.

Vaughn's followed a few moments later.

* * *

First light on the eighth day, the morning earmarked for the ascent, was a pallid gray excuse for a sunrise. In fact, it augured in the worst weather they'd seen on this perennially wet world: a full day of rainfall so torrential, with winds so spiteful, it reduced even the most rational members of the group to bouts of superstitious fretting. The hundred percent humidity had not been a problem before. Constant fresh breezes had kept the facility temperate, and no one's breathing had suffered because they all had to use tank oxygen. Spray from the waterfalls, borne on the breezes, had also watered the plants of the arboretum and, collected in tarp pockets – one of Threlfall's earliest innovations – replenished the group's drinking water. The big question now was: how long would the downpour last? Rainfall on some colony worlds was known to last for months, even years.

If it didn't end soon, the launch would be impossible in these conditions. For one thing, it would spoil the invisibility trick; Threlfall's panels might be able to bend light, but the rain would still bounce off them, revealing the full, exact dimensions of the craft. And there was no way they could walk out there to plant the explosives in these high winds.

The only dry place was inside the pod, but it was so cramped in there – it had comfortable quarters for four people – Vaughn decided to wrap himself in a tarp and hunker down in the arboretum, pretending, like Sondergaard had said, that he was back on Hesperidia, that miraculous world of pure, unbound Nature. Among these alien plants, he felt closest to Jan.

In the middle of the night the thunderous noise receded like a wave of applause into the back rows of an immense auditorium, where it merged with the rumble of the falls, leaving that familiar, now almost comfortable background cushion of sound. Vaughn uncrumpled himself from his tarp cocoon and wearily made his way back up to the pod. All he'd managed was a few power naps; they'd have to suffice, for at sunrise, if the weather held, he was going for a hike.

"Jus' a feckin' minute there, Chief. Lady's got somethin' she wants to say." Considine, the bomber – though that probably wasn't his real name – Sondergaard had discovered umpteen aliases flagged on his ISPA Person of Interest record – spoke in a coarse outer colony accent with an unwavering note of contempt for everything and everyone, except for Edith de Brock. It was unusual, the level of adoration she inspired in those who worked for her. They weren't just loyal to a fault; they practically worshipped the ground she walked on, typified by the way

Considine shoved aside men much bigger than him to clear a path for her. He was her little bulldog, vicious and deceptively smart. The others gave him a wide berth, the same way they did Bronston, who was his counterpart on Imogen's side, equally loyal and equally intimidating in the service of his mistress.

Though he was eager to set out, Vaughn didn't want to risk causing any more friction. Considine had already made it clear he wouldn't be taking orders from any lawmen on this expedition – they wanted his expertise, they'd have to bite their feckin' tongues and let him do the job the way he feckin' wanted. Vaughn sighed and waited to hear what Edith had to say.

"I wanted to wish you luck, detectives," she said.

"Thanks. Conditions don't look too—"

"And to add that we appreciate the risk you're taking, given how dangerous it is." When she motioned for her sister to join them, the entire group, save Threlfall, pressed in close. "So dangerous, in fact, that Mr Considine is venturing far above and beyond where a man under arrest should have to go to save the lives of others, least of all those who've put him … under arrest."

Vaughn's lips tightened into a thin line. "Where are you going with this?"

"We think he should be granted amnesty. If we make it back to civilization, he deserves to be a free man with a clean slate. It's the least he deserves if he's able to pull this off."

"But that isn't our call to—"

"Ah, ah," Vaughn interrupted his younger colleague. "It's agreed. If this works, we promise not to say anything more about what happened before the dislocation event. Right, Agent Sondergaard?"

The rookie flashed him an appalled look, then Vaughn detected a subtle un-creasing of his brow, as though the young Dame had just glommed the irony in the phrase "We promise not to say anything *more* about what happened."

They'd exchanged voice logs not half an hour before, full testimonies covering everything from Gilpraxia to the Star Binder. They needn't say anything more to anyone. Those files were enough to bring everyone here to justice.

"Okay. I second that," said Sondergaard.

"And for the rest of us as well. We each get a clean slate. No charges," added Edith de Brock.

"We won't say another word," replied Vaughn.

"On your oaths?"

Both agents assented.

"Very well. It's settled. God speed, all three of you."

Considine clasped her hand with both of his. "We'll see you shortly, darlin'." Rucksack slung over his shoulder, he strode out onto the rain-minted bridge and growled to Vaughn and Sondergaard, "Let's get this feckin' show on the road."

The irony of them again following the Gilpraxia bomber out onto a bridge over nothingness was not lost on either of them as they exchanged a knowing glance.

"Déjà vu, huh?" said Sondergaard.

"Something like that," replied Vaughn.

A few of the others waved them off. Threlfall was busy tinkering with the em brackets he was about to pulley into position around the shape of the bridge – the two halves, waiting to be clamped together underneath the walkway, resembled spider legs hanging in mid-air. Some of the convex light-bending panels were already attached to the pod. There were over a hundred of them, all told, enough to form a streamlined shell masking the pod and the entire circumventing bracket. It was an audacious plan, but the old man had total confidence in his design.

From further out, Vaughn glimpsed the tripod legs of the facility for the first time. Each consisted of two immense bars twisted and braided together; he imagined them being superheated that way, like the strongest medieval swords used to be, in some colossal forge built by an alien Hephaestus. But even so, they didn't appear thick enough to be able to support the structure's weight. He couldn't see the lower sections because the elusive lake or sea was, as ever, shrouded in mist.

It wasn't long before the entire facility disappeared. The passing of the storm had precipitated a rise in temperature, and that meant evaporation, more than enough to transform the region into one big rising cloud of vapor. By the time they'd walked a kilometer, it was a total whiteout in every direction. And it was a good thing they were roped together, as Considine had a habit of marching ahead at an imprudent pace, ignoring the slick, curved surface and the every-present threat of a cross wind. They'd agreed not to use the radio comms out here in case the sentients picked up the signal, so Vaughn tugged the rope whenever the errant bomber got too far ahead.

A little over an hour after they'd set out it was Considine's turn to yank on the line, waking Vaughn from a daydream about a gin-and-lime cocktail and a waitress he'd once seen fight off a stalker with a broken champagne bottle. He looked up and shivered. They were at the breach!

Threlfall had flown his invisible drone out here a couple of days ago to give Sondergaard's germs a piggyback. The latter had gamed most of the breach, inside and out, and had determined that while the foreign object had probably fallen from orbit, it was not a part of a comet or a meteor or any other naturally occurring space body. Rather it had been sculpted from a single giant mineral rock that was harder than diamond, into an obelisk shape, like a smaller version of the Washington Monument. It had crashed into the bridge at an oblique angle and, despite piercing right through, had become lodged in the phenomenally tough bridge structure.

Sondergaard unpacked the hoisting cable and handed one end to Considine, who fixed it to his harness without even looking. He was a professional demolitionist, and this was his show. He gave no acknowledgement of any kind to the two men who were about to hold his life in their hands; he merely perched on the edge of the upper breach hole, watching them thread the cable through their respective safety harnesses until they were confident the feed/hoist system was workable – there were no footholds, so it was lucky Considine was relatively light. Vaughn and

Sondergaard positioned themselves either side of the breach, took the strain and nodded, first to each other, then to the bomber.

Using his hands and feet almost like an insect's for balance, Considine slid-crawled down the glassy face of the cut-diamond obelisk on his back, the rucksack filled with explosives following a meter or so behind on the cable. It was only a shallow decline, but the edges appeared razor sharp, so they fed him the line at a slow, steady rate until he shot a pulse of electricity through it – his signal for them to halt. Another pulse cued them to resume. Two quick pulses would tell them to hoist back up at a similar slow pace, while three would signal he'd set all the explosives and was ready for the express elevator the hell out of there.

It was such a crude, improvised effort compared to the usual over-planned, tech-heavy Omicron team operations, Vaughn soon grew acutely aware of his own brute strength, and how it had so often made the difference in the countless tight spots he'd found himself in throughout his career. Sure, intellect, instinct, adherence to procedure and the rule of law: those were core attributes for any lawman; but when it came to the crunch, as it so often did, one person's physical capabilities compared to another's had decided more outcomes than anything else in the gritty dark corners of the colonies.

More than that – here was that Hesperidian paradox again. Creatures ordinarily hostile to one another, even natural predators and prey, suddenly working together for mutual survival. It had puzzled him when he'd first encountered it with Jan on safari – all those disparate species clubbing together, closing ranks to ward off a greater threat to their ecosystem – but the more he'd thought about it, the more sense it made. They were enacting it out here between the three of them, as was every member of Threlfall's workforce. All for one and one for all was not some chivalric ideal. It was much older and deeper than that. Jan and Stopper had merely represented the best of it, an unlikely partnership that had crossed worlds and species for mutual dependence, while for everyone here, it was more of a utilitarian truce. A means to an end.

There was no better problem solver than a mutual survival instinct.

The cable went slack a little over twenty minutes in, telling them Considine had reached level ground and was moving around freely inside the tunnel. Vaughn and Sondergaard rested, limbered up. The big question now was the explosive. While the old man and the bomber had concocted a combustible chemical compound that would burn hot enough to vaporize any known rock or mineral, it had not been tested on such a big scale. Would it be enough to break apart the obelisk and remove the jutting section? Or might the force of the blast be *too* strong, destroying the already compromised bridge? Did Considine really know what he was doing with so many unknowable variables in play? Faith was an intrinsic part of any mutual survival plight, but damn it, trusting their lives to this Humpty

Dumpty with a death wish was pushing absurdity to its limit.

The clouds continued to rise all around. On Hesperidia, there was a ubiquitous bird in the equatorial regions that flocked in sometimes crazy numbers to the rainforest canopies in the aftermath of a heavy downpour. He couldn't remember its name, but Jan had explained how it loved to luxuriate in the warm, steamy mist evaporating from the forest, in that specific, scent-rich climate between the cruel blows of a storm and the baking heat of day. He'd never seen one up close. He'd never wanted to until now. But he promised, if he ever did make it back there, to pay a lot more attention to the life around him. For here there was none – not a single bird or insect since he'd got here. If it hadn't been for the arboretum, this would be a dead world. Perhaps beyond the mists of the cataracts it was teeming with life – life that would astound even Jan. The empty ache in his bones told him different, however. He was a long way from that garden world. He was a long way from—

A prick of electricity flashed the amber LEDs on the cable wheels attached to his and Sondergaard's harnesses. Then a second. After the third, the automatic voice command, a woman's, confirmed: "Start emergency hoist."

They each took the strain, straight-backed, and began with a concerted pull that didn't seem much of an effort. A high-pitched whistle made Vaughn look round. It reminded him of one of those Chinese rockets people sent up at New Year's celebrations. Nothing there. Sondergaard suddenly took the initiative, pulling twice as fast. Had he seen something Vaughn hadn't? Again, the whistle, only this time its Doppler effect had a different trajectory. A pale purple light shot out at forty-five degrees under the bridge, seemed to swizzle into the mist like some kind of supersonic curlicue. Another whistle, short-lived, made the bridge shudder. Two more increased the vibrations.

Considine scrabbled up onto the lip of the breach. He waved for them to back off, yelling "They've feckin' found us! Run!"

Vaughn and Sondergaard drew their Krugers. Considine retrieved the detonator from his backpack. The three of them were still bound together by the cable as they jogged clear of the hole.

"Get into the mist! They might miss us," suggested the bomber.

"Did you plant all the explosives?" asked Vaughn.

"Most of 'em. Enough of 'em. Ah, feck, they nearly blew me in half."

It was only then that Vaughn saw there was a large chunk missing from Considine's side. The wound was cauterized, but it was doubtful he'd survive the hike back to the facility. He'd lost at least a couple of vital organs.

"What are they? Finagler ships?" asked Sondergaard.

"Feck do I know? They came out of nowhere. I—" He sank to one knee, tried to brace the pain in his side but his hand passed right through, finding only thin air. "Jesus. I never even felt it happen. It just itched and … what a feckin' gyp. You guys need to get clear. I'm gonna blow this feckin' thing so it … yeah, come get me, you bastards!" A ribbon of purple energy whistled inches over his shoulder. Vaughn ducked, trying to locate its source through the mist.

"We need to get him back," Sondergaard told Vaughn. "We can't leave him like this."

"No! You need to get the others out," answered Considine. "Make sure *she* makes it – you know who I mean." He tossed Vaughn the detonator, then turned to Sondergaard. "Guess you're not such a prick after all."

"Yeah, we'll see about that." The young Dane started toward him, clearly determined to carry him to safety. If Sondergaard's mentor could see him now, he or she would be bursting with pride. The kid was a spectacular lawman, but unless his luck changed, no one would ever know.

A blast hit the bomber mid-chest and sent him wheeling, disintegrating into the mist.

"Sonofa—"

More blasts whistled by, the torrid heat of their wakes scorching flesh whenever they passed at close range. Vaughn and Sondergaard returned fire, but all it seemed to do was give the attackers pinpoint targets.

As per firefight protocol, they lay flat on the bridge.

"Vaughn, what do we do?"

"I'm thinking."

The neck and fuselage of a swan-shaped craft appeared for a few seconds, then vanished back into the cloud. Vaughn guessed it was a manned craft; it certainly appeared bigger than a drone, and was similar in design to Finagler fighters from a few decades ago he'd read about, those that had fought in the Battle of Perihelion.

There was no way two handguns could contend with one or more of those.

"Brother," he said, "we need to jump."

"We need to *what?*"

"Trust me, there's no other choice. We're not making it back to the pod, and we can't beat these things."

"You don't know that. Vaughn, you've got the detonator – you can make it back. I'll hold these things off as long as I can. We need to try."

It was a valiant gesture, but not pragmatic enough. In moments like this, an Omicron agent had to be ruthless in weighing the consequences of a course of action. It told him that if they both died here on this bridge without triggering the detonator, no one was making it off this world.

"I'll never make it," he said. "We don't blow this thing now, it's game over for everyone."

"Ah, shit! You had to ruin my big hero moment."

Vaughn helped him up, and Sondergaard unhitched them from the cable.

"Pray to God this works." Shuffling toward the precipice, the Dane gave Vaughn a firm go-ahead nod.

Vaughn unclasped the protective lid, uncovering the detonator switch. Another shot whistled in. It struck the bridge right next to Sondergaard's boot. He leapt away, scalded but unhurt. Perched on the edge, he formed his finger and thumb into the okay signal.

Vaughn held his breath and flicked the switch.

There was a moment's pause. Then a yellow-orange flash licked skyward like a nuclear forked tongue, wrenching apart as it approached its apex. A hurtful crack of static followed. A shimmy underfoot almost tickled. Then the real shockwave rolled silently through the alien tension of the bridge with a violence that felt pent-up for millennia and now unleashed. It threw Vaughn off his feet. When he landed, he was sliding down the slick slope to the edge. He instinctively tried to stop his momentum, but it was too wet and he was sliding too fast and there was no hope for him up here anyway.

He fell into thin air at the same time as Sondergaard. They glimpsed each other for the last time for a split-second in mid fall before the clouds rushed in.

Chapter Eighteen

He held his rigid posture with maniacal focus, face down, arms and legs apart for balance like one of those far-leaping monkeys Jan had told him about. The wing-flaps of his survival suit – one either side from elbow to hip, and one from his crotch to his ankles – had deployed first time. He hadn't used them since his days as a cadet. Truth be told he'd never liked them; they were a poor apology for a parachute, and unless you could see exactly where you were going, they could guide you miles off course from only a moderate height.

Wet tissues of cloud parted for him wispily, expectantly, as though they were counting down to him hitting bottom. It was impossible to tell how far he'd fallen or how long he'd been gliding. With mist this thick, he'd have a split-second to reposition himself for the water entry. Any moment now. With only the dessert layers of cloud to gauge his relative motion, and the air resistance pushing against him from underneath, it didn't really *feel* like falling. And for a beat or two he did wonder …

The dark surface bled through the final tissues of mist. He clenched himself for the tumble. A life-or-death maneuver with no margin for error. The water seethed and raged but there were no waves. It was more like the rapids of a great river. *Christ,* if there were rocks near the surface, he was dead! Nothing he could do about that.

Vaughn tucked himself into a ball and rolled forward, folding his arms in last. Then, legs together, he extended into a vertical pencil dive.

His posture was more or less spot on, but he'd folded in his flaps too early. He picked up speed as he fell like a stone. *Ah, hell.* Using his arms again for balance in order to stay vertical, he took a deep, unnecessary breath. His feet smacked the water. He tucked his arms into his sides but not quite in time. The force of the impact jerked his left arm up and outward at an awkward angle. It felt as though it had been ripped out of its socket. The pain split him in half for several sickening moments, then receded into a hot, nerve-ringing throb in his shoulder. At first he thought he was paralyzed on his left side, but as he eased himself up to the surface with gentle kicks, he adjusted his diagnosis to a dislocation of the shoulder. An old injury he'd suffered several times. He knew how to fix it, but not whilst swimming. Until he could, he'd have to swim with one arm.

The fast-flowing water had a muscular undertow that dragged him under periodically but not more than a few feet deep at a time. Each time he went under he hit something whiskery and rubbery. He decided to cling to it, and as the current pulled him he slid along it, shaving brown clumps of moss that, when held in his fist, resembled kindling that had just caught fire, turning a deep orange, then an even deeper red. On closer inspection he saw that they were tiny crawling creatures. Vaughn didn't wait to see the end result of the color change; he threw them away and kicked for the surface. From then on, any time he was pulled under he tried to either avoid these seemingly endless, colossal, white rubbery vines or use his boots to surf them. Sections of them arched up above the surface into the mist. They leaned and swayed with the current, and there were strange, fiery-colored webs festooned on them, with the even stranger shapes of fish and flying creatures hanging lifeless in the tangles.

Visibility remained horrible on the surface as the rapids thrust him further into nowhere.

"Sondergaard! Do you read me? Come in, Agent Sondergaard! This is Vaughn. Where are you? Over."

He repeated this message at frequent intervals, partly to keep his hopes alive, partly to keep himself company and distract him from the nightmare raging all about. He never got a reply.

It struck him he didn't know for sure which way he was being pulled – he supposed it was away from the cataracts, out to sea, but what if it was the other way, into some kind of chasm or vortex where the great waters fell? Was he travelling toward or away from the facility?

The next time he spoke the name "Sondergaard," it reminded him of the Dane's clever idea to survey the integrity of the bridge. To see where the human eye couldn't – through the mist. *Spectrum pre-set 15*. The omni-goggles.

After adjusting the setting, he looked up. Most of the left side of his field of vision blazed as an incandescent green blob. It left him even more disorientated. Then he recalled the high magnification he'd last used for spectrum 15. It hadn't reverted to its default, so he blinked it back manually. And as he drifted on the current, the gaps between the legs of the facility yawned more and more. Above, the spindly bridge was still intact. Thank God the blast hadn't destroyed it altogether.

Vaughn was about to zoom in on the breach, to see if they had in fact cleared the way for the pod ascent, when it suddenly hit him how quickly he was travelling past the facility.

Either he swam for it now or he might be swept away forever.

Kicking as hard and fast as he could, he helped to propel and guide himself with a one-armed crawl stroke that would have been difficult to maintain in calm water, let alone fighting upstream against the unrelenting rapids. Lactic acid began to bite at his good shoulder. He pulled on until it hurt even more than his dislocated one. In terms of progress, each stroke lost him the equivalent of five. The current did not want him to escape. He had this one chance to grab hold of a spiral rail that followed a curiously pocked staircase up one single bar of the giant braided leg, and it didn't look like he had—

"… aughn, if you're … live … lis … careful … when the red … ises … blue … home."

"Threlfall?"

He pulled even harder, though his rhythm was labored. His strength was leaving him.

Got to climb up, he thought. *Got to get higher to improve the signal. Maybe they haven't left yet. Maybe they're under attack!*

"Vaughn, if you're … alive … fully … when the … sun … bluebird home."

That last phrase lit a memory inside him – words he'd heard at the tail-end of his unconscious journey through the Star Binder. Words and a breathtaking vista, familiar somehow. It kindled one last spark of energy, flooding him with hope.

When the red sun rises, follow the bluebird home.

A premonition? A promise? Was there more to the Star Binder than the old man had told him?

He leapt up to grab the rail. Missed. He threw his arm out in a panic. Crooked fingertips clamped around the rough bar – possibly the only rough part of this whole structure. An alien safety feature? He was still half in the water. The rapids bounced him, threatened to tear him off. He managed to heave himself up just enough to crook his elbow around the rail. From there he climbed onto the staircase – nothing more than elliptical hollows less than a meter wide, cut into the giant, twisted bar at equidistant intervals – and wasted no time in starting his ascent.

When he finally reached the bridge, the pod was not there. All the supplies had gone. Not a sign of life was left. A part of him, perhaps the best part, was thrilled at the idea of them having made it safely across. He'd helped them achieve that. He'd given them that chance, fulfilling his Omicron oath.

Another part of him tightened up with doubt, an all-too realistic suspicion that he'd failed, that the obstacle had not been fully removed by the blast, and that the Finaglers had not fallen for the light-bending trick after all.

And yet another part of him, perhaps the lesser, selfish part, was disappointed that they hadn't waited for him. He'd risked his life for them and they hadn't reciprocated. He should be used to that. It was always part and parcel of being a professional lawman. But none of that salved the pain in his shoulder, nor comforted him at the end of what had been a hellish ordeal, nor offered solace for what lay ahead – loneliness the likes of which few had ever known.

Finagler craft flew by with pattern-less persistence. He had to expect them at all times, which meant he had to stay hidden whenever possible. Once or twice he thought he heard a clanging noise coming from the bridge, where the pod had set off from, so he kept to the lower levels. Threlfall had hypothesized that they were afraid to enter these facilities. Whether they were looking for him in particular or they simply suspected there were other creatures holed up here – had they even identified them as human? – it didn't matter. The more they flew by, the more he believed his fellow castaways had made it across. The Finaglers were trying to solve a mystery here. They didn't know *what* exactly was going on.

Spectrum 15 confirmed his theory, at least in part. The jutting section of the obelisk was no longer there; the blast had done its job! As for whether the pod had made it across unseen, he would never know.

Threlfall's garbled message never transmitted again.

All he could do now was wait. For night-time. For the world to turn. For the red sun to rise.

For a while he listened out for Sondergaard's return, half in hope, half with trepidation, because the old man had left a one-way, non-refundable ticket for only a single passenger through the Star Binder. How could he possibly leave a fellow agent behind to die, especially one so young and full of promise? Yet that was the thing with magnanimity – it had its limits. In the heat of battle it was different; instinct made those choices. Given sufficient time to reflect, how many of those selfless acts of sacrifice would heroes choose not to carry out? As much as he wanted Sondergaard to survive this ordeal and make it home safely and go on to have a thrilling and illustrious career, he wasn't ready to give up his own chance at happiness, of seeing Jan again.

For a while he lay stiff under a wing of the flexing, water-filled tarp, just watching the phantom lights of Finagler probes circle the facility behind a thin layer of mist. Their random changes of speed, height and luminance made it impossible to predict which floor they would survey next, or how many times they would circle it before moving on, or how quickly they would fly by. The odds of Vaughn making it to Threlfall's device without being spotted were virtually nil, so it would have to be a non-stop, one-shot bolt at the last possible moment. He couldn't afford to wait up there, in the open hall, for the sunrise. He would have to arrive at the precise moment the device activated. The problem was, the old man had not given any specifics.

Exactly when *was* this bluebird going to appear? And if the clouds didn't thin overnight, would he even be able to tell when the sun actually rose, the *moment* it appeared above the horizon?

For a while he thought of what he'd eat at the first restaurant he came across. The tastes were vivid; they made him salivate. The flavors of drinks he imagined somehow manifested in the drips of condensation he tongued from the inside of his visor.

For a while he suspected the old man had lied about the extent of the time skew. A decade's worth of dislocation was just too far-fetched. Too unbelievable. And if he'd lied about that, what else had he lied about? Maybe the device had been capable of taking them all back immediately; it hadn't needed to recharge at all, and he'd instead recruited them for an insane god-chasing endeavor with no intention of returning them to Core space or another occupied colony. And maybe he'd lied about this sunrise, too. He'd broadcast his message for the others' benefit, so they'd think he was being kind to the poor suffering agent out there, lending him hope. It was a sham. *He* was a sham. They were all against Ferrix Vaughn, had been from the start. Hell, the whole universe had conspired against him – he was the butt of its sick cosmic joke, hiding under a tarp at the edge of nowhere, trusting his fate to a haiku prophecy that made no sense. None. There *were* no birds here, blue or otherwise. What the hell had he been *thinking*?

For a while he just hated.

The phantom lights peered and spun and left eerie glow-wakes in the night mist.

For a while he wanted to drift to sleep, perhaps forever. But he daren't.

For a while he imagined an identical tower on a far shore at the other end of this wet world, and another Vaughn, looking back, wondering the same thing: did he, like the unseen river flowing between them, really have a choice where he ended up? One's nature had its own currents, its own predestined course. Had he always been meant to end up here? Had this spot at the edge of nowhere been picked out for him long ago, when it was clear who and what he would become?

For a while he wondered, unafraid.

Then he realized the edge of nowhere was no longer black. It had begun to bleed, not with a gush but a slow, almost imperceptible blot. A touch of beetroot spread across the mist. It was most evident in the phantom lights' glow-wakes as they shot by.

As he uncrumpled himself from his stiff posture and threw off the wing of the tarp, he felt horribly exposed. Reckless and resolute at the same time. His head swam for a few moments, then several waves of frightening lucidity forced him to lock onto his bearings. He bolted for the elevator. Ignored the phantom lights as best he could, despite the fact they were hovering now, all of them in concert, following his silent ascent. How long before this place was crawling with Finaglers? If he ran flat-out, did he have enough time to reach the device?

A molten red pinprick winked low through the clouds on the opposite side of the hall. The mood of the mist seemed to thaw, gunmetal gray kissed by the light of embers and awash in a ravishing heat. This was it! He kicked too hard into a sprint, stumbled heavily on the wet hall floor. Somehow, he regained his balance and reached the center of the concave panels in a single breath. The clouds over the bridge were dotted with approaching craft. Already he could hear a frantic clanging coming from the tier below, from the bridge roof. Armored troops disembarking? Some kind of weaponry or machinery being unloaded?

The red sun rose. Nothing happened. Through the parting clouds he beheld a sumptuous alien dawn, a vista so vibrant and spectacular it painted the architecture of the facility, this vast pillared hall, in a new, thrilling light that would have astounded Vaughn if he hadn't seen this precise image before. In the moments prior to waking from his Binder sleep, he'd seen this vista and heard the words of Threlfall's prophecy as clear as anything he'd ever seen or heard. This was more than déjà vu. It was a premonition made real – a moment in time given him to witness days before it had come into being.

Silhouetted swan shapes swooped into view above the bridge, hovering behind the phantom probe lights that still hung there, watching his every move. Dawn light inched across the panels of the device. It seemed to tickle some sort of electric blue luminance from the alien glyphs carved into their surfaces. To Vaughn's surprise, he found he could discern English lettering within the complex glyphs. In sequence, they read:

TOUCH THE BLUEBIRD TO FOLLOW HER HOME

Vaughn spun several times as he scanned the panel lightshow for signs of a bluebird. He couldn't see one. What did it mean by 'touch'? What was he missing? This was a one-time getaway deal, a life-or-death contingency pre-programmed by Professor Threlfall.

Why weren't the Finaglers attacking? No doubt he'd make a valuable prisoner; despite his ignorance of all things Binder-related, he knew a lot about the Core defenses, fleet deployment protocols, the whereabouts of ISPA HQs right across the IC and OC. If abduction was their plan, how were they planning to lure him outside?

No, don't get side-tracked. Stay on mission.

The full disc of the sun now blazed over an endless ocean bespangled with islands of prismatic gemstones, more colors than his eyes could take in in one gaze. It began its shallow arc across the sky, lighting more panels as it went. Soon the electric blue glyphs covered half the apparatus, which triggered a sudden rousing of the other half. At the moment all the panels were lit, they started to project blue particles toward the center space, where Vaughn was standing. The particles crackled gently like fur static as they touched him and coalesced.

He stepped back. The image forming in mid-air did not have wings per se, nor a beak; no, it was another kind of

Bluebird, one that had flown around Earth, the fastest Bluebird that had ever flown. It was Charlie Thorpe-Campbell's famous orbital racer – the iconic Ram-runner, never beaten! Professor Threlfall had later followed Thorpe-Campbell into an even more astonishing endeavor – the Star Binder – so it made sense that the old man would idolize this symbol of man's endurance.

Follow the *Bluebird* home.

When the vehicle was fully formed, a sparkling sapphire hologram, Vaughn held his breath, extended a hand and touched his ride home.

The thought of taking a cosmic trip in the ship belonging to one of his boyhood heroes made him smile. A secret smile for a secret trip. He stepped into it, closed his eyes as a splash of liquid light shrank around him, magnifying his surroundings, the great hall, to a scary, cyclopean dimension. The static rush started to infuse him, to undermine his control. He wanted to scream with fear and excitement and the pride of having an unimaginable tale to tell the boy inside. The boy he'd missed. He wanted to scream but it wouldn't let him.

So he whispered it with all his heart instead, clean across the cosmos.

Chapter Nineteen

The beam from his head torch roved across the rubble of the collapsed wall. It found the panels' darkened contours, the heavily insulated power cable, and finally revealed the cave's full dimensions. As far as he could tell, nothing about it had changed. Threlfall's device hadn't been touched. That notion struck Vaughn as rather implausible. If nearly two decades had passed, surely someone or *something* would have interfered, if only to trash it: an earthquake, a stampede of amphibian monsters, meddling scientists. Instead it was untouched. No time appeared to have passed here in his absence.

He hiked up the winding passage to Threlfall's main chamber in a daydream, an impression of quiet awe holding him at arm's length from the reality of what he'd done, where he'd been, that he'd returned against all odds.

The storm damage in the sanctum was extensive. For a few horrible moments he was trapped between the two worlds and their twin realities. The recent storm on Wetworld had been a doozy; he'd lived through it. That continuity was merely in his head, then, but it was eerie all the same. Tangles of damp yellow fronds, cages of knotted bracken, shreds and wads of paper, broken electrical equipment, smashed furniture and scaffolding: a hurricane had howled through here recently. Gone was the old man's neat troglodyte abode. In its place lay the aftermath of a wrecked carnival. A huge, once-colorful drape hanging over the scaffold had been torn to pieces, but the top section remained, pinned against the cave wall by debris, its frayed edges fluttering in a constant breeze. The word WELCOME was visible, the rest covered by layers of dirt and grime. Rummaging through the carnage, Vaughn retrieved a few other pieces of the torn canopy and, after scrubbing away some of the grime, managed to piece together:

WELCOME HOME VAUGHN!
PARTY AT MY PLACE – BRING OWN BOOZE
CALL YOUR FREE TAXI ON CH. 17 VHF
Years meter left running: 1̶ 2̶ 3 4 5 6 7̶ 8

That ache he'd felt through most of his time on Wetworld flared up again, weighting his chest with soggy, wrung-out regret. Weariness. Defeat. Jan had clearly kept coming back here. She'd waited, hoping. Then, sometime in the eighth year, she'd given up waiting and hoping and coming back here. Was that when Stopper had died? Had she decided enough was enough and left Hesperidia behind?

There was more debris down the left-hand passage, more old, soiled shreds of canopy and wrecked electronic equipment. He didn't have the heart to sift through it, to piece together more evidence that would only break *him* to pieces. It was as he'd feared: time had taken her from him, her and Stopper. It had taken his chance at a new life.

He wandered outside into a brilliant sunny day. No photonic blister to stop him. No marauding amphibians. No welcome of any kind. It was as though he'd never existed, as though time had stopped counting him among the living.

He didn't even see the comm booth until a gust of wind swung a snapped tree branch against it. The hollow *clink* ripped him from his funk. The booth had been erected in open ground near the entrance to the cave, but the storm had uprooted several trees, one of which now lay across it. Vaughn wedged his way inside the mess of broken branches and bracken. He prised the metal lid off its hinges, smashed the Plexiglass seal inside and activated the emergency transmitter.

A very young woman's voice interrupted the *bip—bip—bip* with "November Outpost. Horrigan speaking. Give me your six-digit ID number and I'll arrange for a pick-up." When he mumbled his unintelligible reply – to be fair, it *was* the first time he'd spoken in almost a decade – she added "Or you can key it in on the keypad."

He untangled his tongue. "I'm sorry. I don't have a six-digit ID number. I've been … away … for some time. What year is this?"

Silence on the other end.

"Hello?" he said. "My name's Ferrix Vaughn. I'm an agent with the Omicron Bureau. It's a little hard to explain. I can give you my badge number if you like. I'd appreciate a pick-up. I've no food or water, and I'm running low on oxygen. You have my coordinates?"

"Yes, I have … But what do you mean, you have no ID? That's not possible."

"I know. Believe me, I'm as mystified as you are. Take all the precautions you want, call the ranger in charge."

"And you don't know what year it is?"

"No. What year is it?"

"Twenty-two seventy-five."

So, the old man was telling the truth after all.

"You're alone?" she asked.

"That's affirmative. Alone and lost in the woods."

"Uh, okay. I'm, uh, on my way, Agent …"

"Vaughn."

"You're really close to November Outpost. Give me, uh, let's say ten minutes."

He almost chortled with relief. "Best thing I've heard in years."

"Message acknowledged. Out."

The forest was thicker than he remembered. There were no carcasses hanging from the trees. That idea unnerved him a little. No deterrent. He drew his Kruger and sat cross-legged against the outside wall of the cave, waiting for good news, waiting for bad news, waiting for what happened next. Away for less than a week, he somehow had a lifetime to catch up on.

Horrigan flew them northeast over the Keys, past two separate White Water tour boats full of passengers. These vessels were bigger than Jan's *Alcyone* had been, more like ferries. The safari industry had expanded in his absence, covering several new locations and more than tripling its tourist turnover. But it was still fairly low key, Horrigan assured him; its impact on the natural world was minimal and carefully monitored.

"I've subbed a few times on the White Water sail," she said. "You have a script to read. The rest is fielding questions and babysitting tourists."

"Do you like it?"

"Not really my thing, if I'm being honest. I like the teaching part. The rest goes with the assignment, I guess, but I'm really here for the plant life. I'm a xenobotanist."

Vaughn suppressed a knowing smile. This girl wasn't much over twenty, had only been here a little over a year, and already she sounded like a veteran ranger on the Hesp – enamored and jaded in equal measure. Chestnut hair in a bob cut, freckles, wiry physique, not unattractive: Horrigan was unselfconscious and more than willing to get her hands dirty, to pull her weight; and the fact that she'd given up a plum internship as a crop terraforming engineer in one of the top Core research laboratories to be here, dozens of light-years from her friends and family, told Vaughn she had the right stuff. More than that, she had Jan's essence, that unmistakable drive and passion that coursed through all true pioneers. She belonged here.

But did he?

Seeing Jan's island home as a busy tourist compound, with apartments and an information center and a large boathouse, ghosted him as they flew over. A feeling that he shouldn't be here, that Hesperidia didn't give a damn about him or Jan, what they'd had here, what they'd lost. This place had forgotten him completely. The time disparity trailed him wherever he went, snagging on stray memories, dragging *his* past behind him like a net of cobwebs through a refurbished home with brand new tenants.

The shrink-wrapped meals were much improved, at least. He devoured three nuked slices of pepperoni pizza and a packet of potato wedges with a barbecue sauce dip. After Threlfall's fruit salads and protein-rich snack bags Kincaid had dubbed "nuts 'n' revolts", it was a perfect homecoming meal. Pity about the low-sugar energy drink that tasted like detergent.

"You've really never heard of Doctor Juanita Corbija?" he asked. "She got the White Water tour up and running almost singlehandedly. She pretty much resurrected the whole Alien Safari enterprise."

"I've heard the name mentioned. Honestly, we don't mingle much. We're just too *busy*. You do hear rumors about the old days: the poachers and all that. Your Doctor Corbija sounds like quite a woman."

"She is."

"Like I said, if anyone can help you find her, the people at Miramar can. They liaise with ISPA regularly. They're great at keeping us in touch with our families; that's been one of the best surprises about this assignment. You're independent, but you never feel cut-off. My dad messages me every week, even when he's nothing new to say. Sweet, really. The Deputy Governor at Miramar took my induction, a guy called Nabakov. He's been here longer than practically anyone, as far as I know. Tons of Omega-grade qualifications. He's bound to know what happened to your Doctor Corbija."

During the ninety-minute flight to the Governor's headquarters on the eastern side of one of the long 'claw marks' islands cutting across the main continent, Vaughn resolved to leaving Hesperidia as soon as possible. More than that, he vowed to never return. It was just too painful. The one place since his family home that he'd ever imagined settling down in, now belonged to someone else. To a new generation of dreamers. He'd done his bit to protect it, to keep the bad elements away, and now he must move on.

Miramar was a reasonably fortified thirty-acre settlement in a grassy clearing surrounded by hundreds of square miles of mangrove-like jungle. A naturalist's paradise. The main building doubled as an administrative and communications hub and a hotel for arriving guests. It was ringed by several large hangars full of new-and-improved vicars, stork shuttles, and multi-purpose vehicles he'd never seen before. A communal water tower and a recycling plant stood apart from the compound, connected by pipe to a river flowing at the western edge of the fenced enclosure. Various residences, probably for permanent staff, were dotted around, closer in. The biggest, though by no means the best-kept of these, was situated the farthest away from the central hub, on the U-turn of the river as it wound back into the jungle.

"Ah, there's Nabakov now," she said, pointing down to a bearded, silver-haired man wearing sandals, shorts and a smart, short-sleeved cotton shirt. He stood on the edge of the lawn outside the HQ, shielding his visor from the sun's glare. Horrigan performed a rather ragged landing on the LZ, then said to Vaughn, "Do you want me to come in with you?"

"I wouldn't want to inconvenience you."

"Then it's settled. I'm tagging along. I can't wait to see their eyes bug out when you tell them what you've told me."

"Deal. And in case I don't get a chance later, I want to say thank you, Horrigan. I mean it. You saved my life."

She blushed. "Just doing my job."

"Exactly what I used to say. But just so you know, I won't forget it. What's your first name?"

"Joyce. You can call me Joy."

"I'm Ferrix." He held out his hand; she took it with as gentle a grip as he'd known in a long time. It made him like her even more.

The temperature had cooled a little since Threlfall's island, but the air was heavier here, muggier. If they had ice cold beer inside, he was going to buy a round for everyone in situ, and at least three for himself.

Nabakov gaped as he approached, then smiled and shook his head in disbelief. He clearly knew who Vaughn was, had heard of his mysterious disappearance. No doubt it had passed into folklore among the long-serving rangers. No doubt there'd been a top-level investigation into the vanishing of Core congressmen and Omicron agents and millionaire sisters with far-reaching influence. So why had Threlfall's device not been touched?

He halted at the distant sound of a dog's bark. It came from somewhere off to his left, across the acres of grassland, near the U-turn of the river.

"Who lives there?"

"Uh, that's Jane Hopper's place," answered Horrigan. "We met once. Kind of keeps herself to herself. Her mum used to be Governor here."

"Jane Hopper, huh?"

The dog was a fair distance away, but it seemed to be running in Vaughn's direction. Added to that, its bark intrigued him. He started toward it. The figure of a young woman rose into view on the river bank, drying herself off. She wore a black two-piece swimsuit that was more yoga pants and sports bra than bikini. As she flung her long yellow hair back behind her shoulders, the water droplets and her visor caught the sun simultaneously. Seeing the dog had run away, she called something Vaughn couldn't quite make out. The dog ignored her, kept barking and sprinting in his direction.

It certainly *looked* like Stopper. Same breed, similar height and proportions. And he was damned if its overall coloring and markings weren't comparable. The woman, too, moved a lot like Jan, that inelegant, low center of gravity gait that got her to where she wanted to go but would never win her a part in *Swan Lake*. She was slimmer than Jan, more toned. Younger than Jan had been when he'd left her. And the closer she got, the more she reminded him of the woman of his dreams.

There was no doubt: she had to be Jan's daughter.

The dog pranced and bounded around him, its stubby excuse for a tail wagging like mad. "Hey, boy. Come here, you big softy. You know what? You're just like another big softy I used to know. Uh-huh, aren't you a friendly dev—"

It reared up and jumped as high as it could, planting its forepaws on his shoulders and bowling him backward off his feet like a tenpin. Then it proceeded to slobber over every inch of him, paying particular attention to his ears, neck, and visor.

"Now you *have* to be related to that big old mud-lovin', mug-lickin' furball. What's your name, eh? What's your name, you big dosser?"

It tried to pin him flat when he made a move to get up, but Vaughn had had plenty of practice slipping that maneuver. He used his momentum to roll the dog onto its back, where he gave it a thorough belly rub, to its exceeding delight.

The woman halted prematurely. Her slick hair still dripped a steady stream. He noticed the yellow strands were only highlights; the roots were darker. She was crying.

"I think I knew your mother," he called out. "She was Jan, right?"

She flashed him a look of pure wonder.

Vaughn took a couple of steps. "You know who I am? She told you about me, right?"

She burst into sobs, quickly shielded her visor.

314

"I'm so sorry. When did she …?" But he couldn't finish his question. A prick of grief deep inside flooded him with bitter truth. Denial was no longer possible. What remained was … alienation.

"She never gave up hope," the woman managed between sobs. "She knew you'd come back."

"I was too late."

"She used to say you were never on time for a rendezvous in your life."

"She was right. About everything."

"Really? Can I have that in writing?"

He slowly forced a smile to match hers – crooked, a corner of her lips upturned with cheeky irony. Then there was that exotic Spanish twist in the accent. And the irreverent sense of humor. He lost his head again, caught between two times, two realities. All the while, the dog gazed lovingly up at him, then at its mistress.

"This is too much," he said. "I'm having a hard time—"

She ran over and caught him on the wobble, steadied him. "It's okay, it's okay. It's a lot for me too. We're going to need some time. Nineteen years is no picnic."

"Who—who are you, Jane Hopper?"

"Vaughn, it's me! I know you recognize me. You recognized me before I knew it was you. You always were more observant. Well, when it came to profiling, at least. Comes with the badge, I guess."

He held her at arm's length, studying her intensely. The smooth, glistening, husky skin, puffy around the eyes. The dark, unquenchable passion *behind* the eyes. The dark hair roots. The strong athletic figure.

It was Jan, only … it couldn't be.

"You haven't aged," he said. "You're *younger* than Jan."

"I know. Well, not younger, just in better shape."

"But you're not nineteen years older. No way, no how are you in your fifties. It isn't possible."

"It's possible. Improbable, but possible all the same. I promise I'll explain everything."

He glanced down at the adoring canine. "This can't be …"

She clamped her teeth on her lower lip, nodded enthusiastically. "You bet your sweet Omicron buns it is. There was no mistaking *that* greeting. Am I right?"

Vaughn's breath hitched. He gazed at them in turn. Several times.

"Jan?"

"Vaughn."

"Is this a dream?"

"If it is, it's a good one. I'd hang on to it if I were you."

"How can I know for sure?"

She shrugged. "I guess … those words you used to see at the end of one of your recurring dreams. You told me once. I've never forgotten."

"What words?"

She let go of him and walked away. Then she stopped, smiled over her shoulder and, crooking her index finger, beckoned him to follow her to her cabin by the river. "This way, genius."

Feet up on her settee, an ice-cold beer in hand, Vaughn told his entire tale in a little over an hour. He was used to giving succinct yet detailed reports, but it proved difficult to describe his ordeal in his usual detached, clinical manner. Interjecting his own feelings seemed the only way to do it justice, to bring it fully to life for Jan, who hung on every word and didn't interrupt once unless invited to do so. The more subjectively he told it, the more vivid it all became, the more he couldn't help but re-experience the crushing sadness, the awe, the loneliness, the horror. Unlike his hectic cases and rock-hopping investigations – always mobile, always thinking around the problem – on Wetworld he'd been trapped, impotent, at the mercy of forces beyond his control. Gods and magic. And he knew he wouldn't be able to detach from that experience for a long time. He wouldn't be able to brush it off, compartmentalize it the old Omicron way. It was going to change him in ways he didn't know how to handle.

When he'd finished, Jan took her turn. She lasted all afternoon and most of the evening. It spilled out of her, everything from the war to politics to her governorship of Hesperidia – *fourteen years* of her calling the shots, answerable to no one except on matters of federal funding – and the changing face of Alien Safari. His old pal Kraczinski had taken early retirement a few years back; the big guy's heart had finally given out not long after, during his ninth honeymoon, and they'd buried him outside his hacienda in a lavish ceremony that Jan described as "a weird mix of traditional Omicron decorum and hippy-dippy fancy dress with incense."

"Crash always did things his own way, even as a cadet. I'll miss him."

"Me too," she said. "He proposed to me while you were away. The third or fourth year; I can't remember which."

"Really? What did you tell him?"

"That I was waiting for someone else. Always would be. Poor guy took it well, of course. I get the impression he propositioned at least half the women he ever met in his life."

"A conservative estimate."

"And he was one of the first to comment on my ... non-ageing. I was made Governor the year after you vanished. Congresswoman Schaeffer arranged it as a kind of thank you for bringing her daughter back alive, and because she knew I was the only one with the guts to safeguard this place. On the tenth anniversary of my inauguration, Kraczinski took a selfie with me. He compared it to one he'd taken a decade earlier. He'd gone gray in that time, wrinkled, receding hairline, the works; but I hadn't aged a day. He knew I wasn't one for enhancements or cosmetic surgery, so he asked what my secret was. We both knew he wasn't joking. Stops should have slowed down by then as well, but he was racing around like a pup. No gray hairs, no medical issues of any kind. So I gave us both blood tests, kept it quiet. Turns out the Fleece did far more than heal our injuries. It somehow re-coded our DNA, so that our cells now continually regenerate. They don't degrade; we don't age, at least not in the normal sense."

"Amazing," replied Vaughn. "I skip over two decades and millions of light-years, and you *still* age less than me."

"What can I say? I could make a fortune advertising anti-wrinkle cream, but they'd start asking questions."

"Hence the name change, the dyed hair. I get it now. You're Jane Hopper, daughter of Juanita Corbija, because you need to explain why you're still young. Every ten, fifteen years, you'll have to come up with a new identity, maybe move to a different part of the planet, change your appearance, your backstory, your credentials. But you'll need help, someone with influence who can doctor the records." He thought for a moment. "A congresswoman, say. A mother, whose little girl you went to extraordinary lengths to rescue. Am I right?"

"Not bad, lawman. I'm almost impressed."

"Almost?"

"You're right about the congresswoman part. But that little girl followed in her mother's footsteps. *She* now has a seat in Congress as well. And the two of them combined, well—"

"Stop! My head's swimming again. And it ain't the beer."

She grinned as she took his bottle away and snuggled up to him. "I'm sorry you thought I was gone. That storm must have hit the cave a few days ago, wrecked my set-up. I did leave instructions for you, comms equipment, food and drink. I used to fly back there once a month with fresh supplies, to make sure everything was ready for you. Then it became once every few months. The number's still good, though. I've never let the receiver out of my sight, not once in nineteen years." She stroked her digital wrist-band, then kissed the tip of his nose. "You could have called me direct, and this would have been a lot easier on you. But for the storm …"

"Yeah. Story of my life."

"Then start over."

"I intend to," he said. "Believe me, as soon as I legally exist again, there'll be no more looking back. I'm done looking back."

"Glad to hear it. And what are you seeing in the other direction?"

He closed his eyes and let his other senses take over. "A whole lot more."

* * *

FAO: Agent Ferrix Vaughn, 7-31HZ9

Core date: 14.09.2275

Dear Mr Vaughn,

After carefully reviewing your recent request for reinstatement to the Omicron Bureau, and based in no small part on your exemplary record as an IC/OC officer, it is our decision that you be invited to resume your full duties immediately upon completion of your mandatory readjustment program.

We currently have no floating field vacancies in the Sector you listed in your Preferred Assignments, but the presiding officer there has promised to notify you immediately should that change. In the meantime, THIRTY-NINE other sectors have expressed keen interest in retaining your services. Please find enclosed the full list and contact details for those respective presiding offices, and feel free to contact us should you require any additional support.

Your custom shuttle is currently en route to Herculean L-12. Tracking details can be found here.

On the matter of your recommendation for a posthumous Nisus Award for Agent Henrik Sondergaard, I am pleased to confirm that the Omicron Board of Overseers has voted unanimously to award it at the next scheduled press event, date and time to be confirmed.

Thank you for your dedicated service.

Sincerely,

Cmdr. Kallander Ngeve, Omicron Bureau Head Office

* * *

He hangs back when Vaughn calls him, dawdles when Jan blows her yellow whistle. This isn't what they promised him. No. All morning they've been mouthing the word "treat", getting him worked up and so excited for an extra-special outing, and now they're cutting his playtime short? They're really going to give him short shrift like this? One game of fetch. One pitiful swim in the river. It just isn't on, so he sulks and starts licking dew from the bankside fronds.

It's already a hot day: the sun is bright and there are no clouds. He'll need plenty of water time alongside his playtime. It's either that or doze in the shade until the sun dips, and that just isn't what "treat" means, not by a long stick.

He slyly watches Jan as she tries her disappearing trick around the back of Vaughn's new ship. Or is it a trick? No matter how many times she tries it, eventually he gives in and runs after her … just in case she's really vanished. Ever since they were reunited in the old man's cave after he'd left her to swim after the little girl, he's been by Jan's side constantly. Apart from the few times she's flown up to those islands in the sky – for one or two sunsets, at most – they've been inseparable. And when Vaughn returned a winter ago, Stopper's playtime doubled for the longest time, the happiest time of his life. His two favorite humans all to himself. He got sad when Vaughn left again, but at least he comes and goes like he used to, at fairly regular intervals. Whenever he lands, Jan lights up, which in turn drives Stopper crazy with happiness. He never likes all the attention she gives Vaughn at first; hates it sometimes – growling and sulking is all he can do, which for some strange reason makes them laugh. But it's never long before Jan shares her affection between them, him and Vaughn, and that's when he's at his most contented, because they're at theirs.

Treat, however, means treat.

He resists as long as he can stand the possibility of them deserting him, then, tail between his legs, he hurries after them. They're a fair way up the field by now. Good thing he didn't dawdle much longer. Maybe the treat is something else. He'll just have to bug Jan for some water time later, and if that doesn't work, well, Vaughn is a soft touch. *He* might even go for a dip, which puts Stopper on edge because Vaughn is not a great swimmer like Jan is, but water time is water time.

They stop a ball's throw away from the upper landing zone. Jan used to put him on his lead around landing zones, but he's long since learned to steer clear of them … unless the ball happens to bounce near one. He will never not chase a ball, no matter how much she screams at him. She must have learned that by now.

He sits between them, tail wagging, as they gaze up. The sun's way too bright. They have their dark goggles, he doesn't, so he lies down in their shade and leaves them to it. Humans do so many things that make no sense to him; as long as they're not upset or in danger, mostly he just trusts them.

A sky ship comes down to land. It's bigger than Jan's striped ship and Vaughn's new sky ship, and strangely quieter than either. A hatch in its side slowly hisses open. Steps fold out with a *clink-clink-clink* until they touch the ground. A tall human woman appears, walks elegantly down the steps. She's wearing blue jeans and a hoodie and boots a lot like Jan's. White hair tied into a pony tail. Two young children follow her down, a boy and a girl. They're more tentative in their colorful survival suits. The woman turns to them and says "It's okay, you don't need to be shy. These are our adventure guides I told you about. Zach, Bronwyn, I want you to say hello to Jane and Vaughn. And in the middle there is—"

"Stopper," the girl says, her eyes wide with wonder.

His tail starts to wag.

"That's right." The woman leads her children by the hand. Her perfume is a new one, not particularly strong but he's never liked that stuff humans spray on themselves. Jan rarely uses it unless Vaughn's around. Underneath this perfume is a natural scent he's encountered before, long ago, a long way away. It makes him spring to his feet in anticipation. He's never seen this woman before, but his tail is wagging so hard his entire rear half wags with it.

Memories of a chase over sand and rock, through hills and craters and uncrossable chasms … white water … deadly creatures …

"Hello, Sarge."

He knows that name! The voice has deepened but he can still hear the sound of the girl inside. Dorcas? Inside the unnatural perfume … is *her* scent. It *is* her scent. This woman *is* Dorcas! The last time he saw her she wasn't much bigger than the little girl whose hand she's holding. Now she's bigger than Jan. Even bigger than Vaughn.

The moment Dorcas bends to pet him, he launches into her, spilling her onto her back. She giggles the way he remembers. He licks her and nuzzles into her hugs as though no time has passed since their journey together.

He hopes their next adventure will not be as arduous. But even if it is, he will do what needs to be done.

324

About the Author

Robert Appleton is a British science fiction and adventure author wild about survival tales in far-flung locations. Many of his sci-fi books share the same universe as his popular Alien Safari series. His rebellious characters range from orphaned grifters on Mars to a lone woman gate-crashing the war in a fabled biotech suit. His sci-fi readers regularly earn enough frequent flyer miles to qualify for a cross-galaxy voyage of their choosing. His publishers include Harlequin Carina Press, and he also ghost-writes novels in other genres. In his free time he hikes, plays soccer, and kayaks whenever he can. The night sky is his inspiration.

He has won awards for both fiction and book cover design.

Website: https://robertappletonbooks.com
Twitter: https://twitter.com/robertappleton

Buckle up for the next thrilling adventure in the *Alien Safari* series..

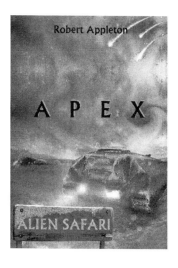

ALIEN SAFARI: APEX (Book 3)

New species. Old wounds. A fight for supremacy on the galaxy's wildest planet.

When Hesperidia's satellite defense system suffers a catastrophic failure, the meteor shower it was supposed to repel rains down over the terrified tourists on safari. Three large surface impacts trigger a crisis intervention from the colonial authorities. It results in the removal of the current governor, and auditions for a successor are soon underway. Jan, Alien Safari's pre-eminent ranger-scientist, finds herself in competition with a formidable new male colleague, who'll stop at nothing to win the top job.

Their assignment leads them to the frozen north, where the discovery of a deadly new species near one of the impact craters imperils not just the safari tours, but potentially all life on the continent as well. An expedition to capture the creature tests Jan's survival resources to their limits, and provides a shocking reminder that mankind, for all its technological prowess, can't hold a candle to the savage ingenuity of alien nature.

Meanwhile, Detective Vaughn, struggling to reintegrate after his absence, must face his tragic past head on when he learns that his niece has been targeted for assassination. To keep her safe, he brings her to an island haven on Hesperidia. But the timing of his return couldn't be worse. A perfect storm of incident, treachery and planet-shaking events endangers the very future of human existence on this miraculous alien world.

Available now in paperback and for all e-readers!

* * *

A selection of standalone sci-fi books set in the same universe as *Alien Safari,* also available as paperbacks or ebooks:

Sparks in Cosmic Dust

Pyro Canyon

Star Binder

Angel Six Echo

Printed in Great Britain
by Amazon